Acknowledgments

Abundant thanks to my agent, Evan Marshall; John Scognamiglio at Kensington Books; and Eileen Watkins, my New Jersey writing friend.

Chapter One

Pamela Paterson tried to keep her voice neutral, even pleasant. "Will Caralee be here tonight?" she asked her neighbor and best friend, Bettina Fraser.

Bettina turned from her cupboard and placed two pottery mugs on the pine table that dominated her pleasant kitchen. "I know she didn't make a very good impression last time," she said. "Margo warned me that her niece could be prickly. But Margo is a good friend and it's not like Caralee wants to become a permanent member. She just needs a little help with her knitting project. It's for a good cause, after all. The Arborville Players contribute a lot to the cultural life of our little town."

"That they do," Pamela said. "I'm looking forward to seeing their version of *A Tale of Two Cities*." She reached for the mugs and lined them up next to the others already arranged in a neat row. "One more," she said, "for Caralee."

"Two," Bettina said, reaching into the cupboard again. "Wilfred spent all afternoon working on that pie. I'm sure he'll want a piece."

An apple pie reposed on a colorful mat in the center of the table. Flaky golden-brown pastry formed an intricate lattice top, and syrupy apple slices dusted with cinnamon peeked out between the interlocking strips.

"I didn't really mind Caralee," Pamela said. "I thought she made some good points about small-minded people in small-minded towns. But I wish somebody had tipped her off that Roland is a lawyer before she got started on the legal profession."

"It was touching that Nell defended him," Bettina said. "Considering they almost never see eye to eye about anything."

"Knit and Nibble has been going for a long time now," Pamela said. "We're like a family—and people in families love each other even if they don't always get along." Knit and Nibble was the nickname of the Arborville knitting club, and Pamela was its founder and mainstay. She surveyed the table. "I think we're all set here. Eight mugs for the coffee or tea, eight dessert plates, eight spoons and eight forks, eight napkins."

"I bought some of that new coffee they've been getting at the Co-Op," Bettina said. "From Guatemala. We tried it this morning and it's very good. And I've got tea bags for Nell and Karen—not very elegant but I don't think they'll mind." She added a sugar bowl and a cream pitcher to the arrangement, smooth sage-green pottery like the mugs and plates.

They were interrupted by the cheerful *ding-dong* of Bettina's doorbell. Woofus the shelter dog—timorous despite his imposing size—tore in from the living room and took refuge under the table, nearly knocking Bettina over. She reached the front door with Pamela close behind and pulled it open to reveal Karen Dowling and Holly Perkins standing on the porch.

"Are we early?" Karen said nervously. She was a slight blonde woman, still in her twenties, and as shy as her friend Holly was outgoing.

"Of course not!" Bettina opened her arms in a welcoming gesture that turned into a hug. "Come in!"

Bettina's living room was as welcoming as Bettina herself. A comfy sofa stretched along the windows that looked out on the street and two equally comfy armchairs faced it across the long coffee table. Cushions covered in bright hand-woven fabrics provided extra seating on the hearth and enlivened the sage-green and tan color scheme.

The door was still open and Karen and Holly barely settled on the sofa when a cheery voice called, "Hello! Shall I come in?" Nell Bascomb entered the living room, her step lively despite her advanced years and the fact that she'd walked half a mile from her house, which was partway up Arborville's steepest hill. "Roland is just parking," she said. "Is Caralee coming?"

"As far as I know," Bettina said. "She told me they're not rehearsing her scenes tonight and she needs to make lots of progress on the knitting in time for the dress rehearsal." Bettina motioned toward one of the comfy armchairs. "Please," she said. "Have a seat. And leave the door open for Roland."

But instead of Roland, the next person to step through the door was a woman. Her height and slenderness would have made her striking enough, without the perfectly straight jet-black hair that skimmed her bony shoulders and bisected her high forehead with precision-cut bangs. She wore an austere long-sleeved black sweater despite the warm mid-September evening.

"Am I late?" she asked, looking around. Her voice was deep and musical.

"Not at all." Bettina was the only person smiling.

Pamela rallied to her friend's side. "Not at all," she echoed, commanding her lips to form a welcoming smile. Pamela herself was tall. She found looking up to meet another woman's gaze an odd experience, but that was the case now.

Caralee Lorimer stood uncertainly at the edge of the carpet. "Where do you want me to sit?" she asked.

"Anywhere. Of course." Bettina waved a hand toward the unoccupied armchair, then toward the hearth. "Pamela, you sit down too. Please."

"There's room here." Holly spoke up from the sofa. "Room for two more even." She moved closer to Karen, who had already taken yarn and needles from her knitting bag. Thus it was that Pamela found herself sitting next to Caralee Lorimer, who pulled her knitting from her bag and started in without another word.

"And here's Roland!" Bettina clasped her hands and gave a welcoming nod as Roland stepped through the door. He scanned the room, then turned and closed the door carefully behind him.

"I see I'm the last to arrive," he said. Carrying the briefcase that he used instead of a knitting bag, he threaded his way past the coffee table toward the hearth. "No, no," he said, waving off Bettina's attempt to point him to the remaining armchair, "I'll be fine on a cushion. You take the chair."

Pamela reached into her knitting bag and pulled

out a partial skein of yarn in a dramatic shade of ruby red and a pair of needles with the beginnings of a sleeve. She'd started the project the previous June, a departure from the conservative designs she'd favored in the past. It was to be a sleek high-necked tunic with cutouts that revealed bare shoulders. The woman at the yarn store had suggested it would be perfect for après-ski, a fashion need Pamela could not foresee having, but she had allowed herself to be talked into the extravagant project.

Next to her Caralee unfurled her project. The yarn was a nondescript shade of gray, and bulky, befitting the project's destiny. Caralee's role in *A Tale of Two Cities* was that of Madame Defarge, married to one of the revolutionaries—a wine-shop proprietor—and characterized by her constant knitting. The gray rectangle hanging from her needles was to be her prop.

"I like that color," Caralee said with a hesitant smile, nodding toward the skein of ruby-red yarn resting between her and Pamela on the sofa. "I didn't get a chance to say anything last time. You were sitting way across the room."

"Thank you," Pamela said. "It looks like you're making progress." Caralee's project had indeed grown longer since the previous week, but left to her own devices she seemed to have forgotten the principles Pamela and Bettina had tried to impart when she first requested their help in preparing for her role. The swath of knitting that dangled from her needles was lumpy and puckered, as if stitches had been dropped and not picked up, and knitting and purling had been interchanged at will. But Pamela supposed Caralee didn't really care, since the point

was just to create something that looked realistic
from a distance and gain enough skill to handle needles and yarn convincingly.

Caralee was silent then, and Pamela focused on her
own work, occasionally glancing around the room but
soothed by the quiet hum of conversation. Nell's busy
hands were shaping the beginnings of a toy elephant.
At present it was merely a fuzzy lavender oval, but
during the time she'd been a member of Knit and
Nibble Nell had turned out whole herds of elephants
in a rainbow of colors. The elephants, destined for
the children at the women's shelter in nearby Haversack, were only one of Nell's many do-good projects.

In the armchair flanking Nell's, Bettina was making
an elephant of her own, a gift intended for her new
granddaughter. As Pamela watched, Bettina leaned toward Nell and pointed to the oval taking form on her
needles. Nell studied it for a moment and then nodded, eliciting a smile from Bettina.

"New project, Roland?" Bettina asked, leaning in
the other direction, toward where Roland was perched
on the hearth, casting on from a skein of pink angora
yarn. Roland frowned, waved a silencing hand, and
began to count out loud, "Twenty-seven, twenty-
eight, twenty-nine, thirty—"

"I'm sorry," Bettina whispered. "I didn't mean to
throw you off."

Roland nodded and continued counting, more
quietly. Watching him, Pamela reflected that it would
be hard to conjure up a more incongruous sight. In
his well-cut suit, aggressively starched shirt, and expensive but understated tie, Roland DeCamp was
every inch the corporate lawyer, his lean face as intent on his knitting as if he was studying a particu-

larly opaque legal brief. "There," he said, looking up. "Now what were you saying?"

"Are you starting a new project?" Bettina repeated.

"Well, *duh*," Holly piped up from her end of the sofa. "He *is* casting on." But she smiled one of her dimply smiles and followed it with a laugh. Bettina was always ready to join in any sort of merriment and she laughed too.

"It's going to be a sweater for Melanie," Roland said. "She liked the one I made for Ramona so much I decided to make her one too. I'm getting a head start so I can give it to her for Christmas." Melanie was Roland's chic wife, and Ramona was the De-Camps' dachshund. Pamela had her doubts about whether Melanie would find a way to integrate a pink angora sweater into her wardrobe, but Roland's doctor had recommended knitting to calm him down and lower his blood pressure, and she knew Melanie had noticed an improvement.

"Christmas will be here before we know it," Nell observed with a sigh. "Time certainly flies."

Next to Pamela on the sofa Caralee twitched. "Original thought," she murmured under her breath.

"Not too soon, I hope," Holly said, addressing Nell. "I love this time of year—the leaves starting to change, and Halloween—"

"And children making a mess all over town with Silly String and eggs and toilet paper"—Roland shifted his intense gaze from his knitting to the assembled group—"and whose tax dollars go to pay for the cleanup?"

"I do enjoy the parade," Nell said. "The children have so much fun dressing up."

"Extra police on duty." Roland scowled. "And I forgot to mention pumpkins rotting on people's porches for weeks afterward."

"It *is* a shame that people insist on carving them," Nell said. "So much nourishment going to waste. Harold and I leave our pumpkin whole and then eat it when Halloween is over."

"You do?" Holly leaned forward. Pamela couldn't see her face, but her voice combined admiration and amazement. "Do you just bake it? Or . . . ?"

"Pies usually," Nell said. "Not too sweet though. A little sugar goes a long way. And I dry the seeds to put out for the birds and squirrels."

"I'd love to learn to make pumpkin pie," Holly said. "Will you teach me? I'll keep my pumpkin whole this year."

"It's a deal," Nell said. "I usually steam the pumpkin flesh and mash it, and I freeze it till Thanksgiving. Bring yours over and I'll steam it too. Then at Thanksgiving we'll work on pies."

"That would just be wonderful!" Holly wiggled with glee and the sofa trembled. She turned to Karen and said, "You save yours too and we'll all make pies together."

"Okay," Karen said in her small voice. Karen and Holly began to talk about a new home-improvement project Holly and her husband had embarked upon. Like the Dowlings, they were young marrieds engaged in restoring a fixer-upper house.

"Bourgeois topics," Caralee murmured, in a voice so low Pamela suspected she alone had heard the comment.

Holly was scarcely the image of a suburban matron however. She and her husband owned a hair salon and tonight she sported green streaks in her luxuriant dark hair, with matching green nail polish on fingers and toes.

In the armchairs that faced the sofa, Nell and Bettina worked industriously on their elephants, chatting quietly. The occasional word that reached Pamela's ears suggested they were discussing the exhibit of work by local artists that had recently gone up at the town library. Bettina had written an article on it for Arborville's weekly paper, the *Advocate*.

After several minutes passed, Pamela began to smell coffee. No one else seemed to notice it, or if they did they didn't comment, and Bettina continued knitting, occasionally nodding in response to a comment from Nell. But Roland was becoming restless on his hearth cushion. He set his knitting down and pushed back his flawless shirt cuff to expose his elegant watch. Frowning, he studied its face, then he surveyed the group.

"It's eight o'clock," he announced. "Don't we usually take a break at eight o'clock?"

"Oh, my!" Bettina jumped from her chair. "Time certainly does fly"—a strangled groan reached Pamela's ears from the direction of Caralee—"and here Nell and I were just chattering away."

Pamela looked up to see Wilfred Fraser standing in the arch between the dining room and the living room, a genial smile on his ruddy face and an apron tied over the bib overalls he'd adopted as a uniform after he retired. "I took the liberty of making the coffee, dear lady," he said as Bettina joined him. "And water is aboil for the tea drinkers."

"I'll help," Pamela said, rising from the sofa and hurrying across the room. Her words were echoed by Holly, who hopped to her feet.

"No, no!" Bettina waved her hands at Holly. "Three people is plenty."

"Too many cooks spoil the broth," Wilfred added.

"Wilfred made apple pie," Bettina said, pausing on the edge of the dining room as Pamela and Wilfred proceeded to the kitchen. "And there's ice cream to go on top. Just sit tight."

The kitchen was fragrant with the bitter spiciness of the coffee, which waited in a large carafe on the stove. Wilfred began to cut the pie and ease slices onto Bettina's pottery dessert plates.

"Caralee seems to be on her best behavior tonight," Bettina observed as she stepped into the kitchen.

"She *has* been quieter at least," Pamela said. She took a carton of cream from the refrigerator and filled the cream pitcher.

"Margo is such good friend of mine, and an *old* friend," Bettina said. "I'm sure she's got her hands full with Caralee as a permanent house guest now. But family is family." She sighed and handed Pamela a small wooden tray for the cream and sugar. "Too bad about the divorce. I'm sure Caralee felt much more at home in the city."

"How many for ice cream?" Wilfred asked as he laid the knife and server inside the empty pie plate and transferred the pie plate to the counter.

"I'll deliver the cream and sugar," Pamela said, picking up the wooden tray, "and take orders for à la mode."

She was back in a few minutes. Six steaming mugs of coffee were ready to be served and two teas were steeping alongside them. Bettina arranged four mugs on a larger wooden tray, along with forks, spoons, and napkins—the latter a homespun gray-and-green stripe from the craft shop. As Bettina headed for the living room, Pamela relayed the ice cream orders to Wilfred: "Seven with, but Nell and Roland just want a little bit, and Caralee doesn't want any at all and not a huge piece of pie."

"One pie for eight people," Wilfred said. "None of the pieces are huge."

"They're just right," Pamela assured him as he deposited a glistening scoop of vanilla ice cream on the flaky lattice surface of a pie wedge.

Bettina delivered the remaining mugs and Pamela delivered pie. When Wilfred entered carrying the last two slices, Holly followed his every motion as he handed Bettina her plate and then lowered himself next to Roland on the hearth.

"You are just awesome," she said. "And this pie looks amazing."

"Eat up, eat up!" Wilfred said jovially.

A companionable silence descended on the group, punctuated only by occasional moans of enjoyment. When the plates were nearly empty and people had reached the coffee-sipping stage, Nell spoke up. "How are your rehearsals coming, dear?" she asked, directing her kindly gaze at Caralee.

Caralee twitched on the sofa, as if surprised to be spoken to. "They're good," she said. "They're fine." She reached forward to set her empty plate on the coffee table.

"Such a powerful story," Nell said. "I love the movie, the old one, with Ronald Colman as Sydney Carton. And the actress who played Madame Defarge—such a dramatic role. You'll be perfect." Caralee grunted noncommittally and focused on her coffee.

"Oh, I love that movie too." Bettina's fork, laden with a bite of pie, paused halfway to her mouth. "And I remember reading the novel in English class so long ago."

When all that remained on the plates were pastry flakes and trails of melted ice cream, and all the mugs had been drained, Wilfred began to gather things up. Holly insisted on helping and hopped up to lend a hand. On the hearth, Roland was methodically thrusting needles and looping yarn, oblivious to the cheerful hubbub around him. Karen was blushing as Nell inquired how she was faring in her early stages of pregnancy—in June she'd announced that she and her husband were expecting their first child. Holly was congratulating Wilfred on his pie and interrupting herself to compliment Bettina on the design of her pottery mugs. And Bettina was assuring Nell that a little sugar had never hurt anyone, especially when combined with something as healthful as apples.

Pamela remained on the sofa, not quite ready to pick up her knitting again. Next to her, Caralee squirmed as she murmured, "Quite warm in here," and began to push up the sleeves of her black sweater.

Normally Pamela was not a nosy person, and Caralee certainly wasn't a close friend—hardly really a friend at all, though Pamela felt a certain sympathy for her. Perhaps, like many creative people, Caralee had never been willing to renounce uncompromising honesty in order to win social acceptance, and she seemed shy as well. Pamela herself was shy. When meeting new people, she sometimes had to remind herself that what she called her "social smile" was in order.

So not being a nosy person, Pamela wouldn't have made any comment at all as the sleeve on the arm closest to her slid up above Caralee's elbow—and she saw what was revealed. But she didn't think fast enough to suppress the horrified gasp she suddenly realized was her own.

Chapter Two

"Yes, it's quite a bruise, isn't it?" Caralee said dryly. Nearly half of Caralee's forearm was covered by a dark blotch that shaded from blue-gray to olive green. Down the center a scab like the stroke of a pen marked a long scratch.

"What on earth happened?" Pamela found herself whispering, despite the fact that Wilfred, Holly, and Karen had disappeared into the kitchen, Roland was intent on his pink angora, and Bettina and Nell were on the other side of the room and deep in conversation.

"Last week a pile of stuff fell on me in the storage room where the Players keep their scenery. It knocked me down and almost knocked me out. I still have a cut on my head too." She shrugged. "Perils of acting, I guess. I usually get to rehearsal before everybody else, so I was rummaging around for some chairs to set up. Some fool had jammed them in so tight I had to struggle to get them out. Then it all came down."

"Did you see a doctor?" Pamela asked, reaching out to touch Caralee's hand but then pulling back.

She studied Caralee's face. It was quite emotionless. Apparently she saved her emotions for the stage.

Caralee shrugged again. "I was basically okay," she said, "and the show must go on, though I didn't realize how bad it was till the next day. The odd thing is, that night I told a couple of the guys what had happened and we rearranged the storage room to make sure nothing else could fall. But the same thing happened again, just last night. Luckily I jumped out of the way in time."

Caralee was silent then and returned to her knitting. Pamela watched for a minute, but the project taking shape on Caralee's needles was almost as disturbing a sight as the bruise on her arm. The yarn was coarse, the shade of gray reminded Pamela of her basement floor, and the stitches were a jumble of knitting and purling with no apparent logic.

At the other end of the sofa, Holly and Karen were back from the kitchen and had returned to the topic of home improvements, conferring about paint colors and wallpaper patterns suitable for a baby's room. Bettina joined the conversation, lamenting that the "Boston children," as she called her Boston-based son and his wife, had forbidden any gender-specific décor, clothing, or toys for their baby daughter.

"I was so looking forward to dolls, and doll clothes," she said. Her other two grandchildren, offspring of the "Arborville children," were boys.

"I wouldn't mind a doll for my little . . . when she comes . . ." Karen's shy voice trailed off.

"I would love to give her a doll," Bettina said. "I just don't see the point in being so . . . *rigid*. Girls will be girls." Bettina tossed her head and her earrings bobbed. They were jade pendants, set off by her bright red hair, and they matched her gauzy jade-colored shirt and wide-legged pants. "Why, look at Roland here, with his pink angora sweater for Melanie, and I'm sure she'll be thrilled."

"Did Ramona like her pink doggy sweater?" Holly leaned past Caralee and Pamela toward where Roland sat on the hearth.

Roland looked up, as startled as if he'd been asked an unexpected question in a corporate meeting room.

"The pink sweater you made for Ramona," Nell said. "Holly is wondering if Ramona liked it."

"I'm . . . I'm not sure she noticed it was different from her old one." Roland licked his lips. "Dogs . . . I don't think they see colors the way we do." He frowned for a minute and then added, "In fact, I'm quite sure they don't."

"I love those programs on the nature channel," Bettina said. "Such things you learn."

"Yes," Nell agreed, and she launched into a description of a recent series on rhinoceros conservation. Pamela felt awkward carrying on conversations that required nearly shouting to be heard across a room, but Caralee hadn't proven to be a very forthcoming conversational partner. Nevertheless Pamela felt awkward too sitting next to a fellow knitter in complete silence. So she was just as happy when Roland once again consulted his impressive watch to announce that it was nine o'clock and time for him to say goodnight.

Caralee reached under the coffee table and pulled out the attractive carry-all she stored her knitting in, and Holly and Karen began to pack up, chatting now about window treatments that could serve as a baby turned into a little girl and then even a teenager.

From across the room, Bettina caught Pamela's eye. "Don't leave yet," she mouthed, as Roland and Nell stood up.

People made their way toward the door, Holly taking Nell's arm and insisting she accept a ride back up the hill since Holly and Karen were going almost that far anyway. Pamela and Bettina watched as the three of them headed toward the street and Roland followed toward where his Porsche waited at the curb. As Caralee paused under the porch light, from across the street came a male voice. Pamela couldn't make out the words, but Caralee turned and raised an arm. The gesture was either a wave or a motion like one would make to shoo a fly away. Pamela wasn't sure which.

Caralee crossed the street, then Bettina nodded toward the house next to Pamela's. "Well," she said, "he'll be back in a few days."

"Who?" Pamela said.

"Richard Larkin, of course. I know you've been looking after things for him."

A slight line appeared between Pamela's brows and she tightened her lips. "I told him I'd pick up stray mail and make sure newspapers didn't pile up in his driveway. That's all. It's what any neighbor would do."

Richard Larkin was a recently unattached man who had bought the house next to Pamela's the previous year. "You know he's interested in you," Bettina said, controlling a giggle. Sweet-natured as she was, she occasionally enjoyed teasing her more serious friend.

"I don't know that at all." Pamela stepped off the porch onto the path that bisected Bettina's carefully groomed lawn.

"You're barely forty," Bettina added, "and he's an attractive, eligible man."

"Thank you for hosting the group," Pamela said somewhat stiffly, "and thank Wilfred again for the pie."

Bettina reached out and gave her a hug. "See you tomorrow," she said. "I've got to cover a morning event at the senior center but I'll drop by after. I'll bring some Co-Op crumb cake."

"I'm really not interested in him," Pamela said, a little less stiffly. Bettina meant well. "See you tomorrow." She set off down the walk.

A minute later, she was stepping over the curb on her side of the street. She paused to let a few people go by—apparently the Players' rehearsal in the auditorium next door was just breaking up—then paused again on her own front walk. A tall and thick hedge separated her yard from the grounds of the church, but just now she could hear voices as clearly as if the voices' owners were standing on her own lawn.

"This is the last time I'm going to discuss this with you," said an angry woman's voice. It was a familiar voice, and Pamela suddenly realized it was Caralee's. "So don't talk like that again. Just don't. Because it's not doing you any good and I don't want to hear it."

"You don't understand," said a male voice, more sorrowful than angry, but equally loud. "I can't help how I feel—" The voice broke and Pamela heard a gulp. Despite the gulp, the voice went on, gasping for air between words. "Don't be so mean. I'm just asking you to listen."

"I don't want you to mention this ever again," Caralee said. "Goodnight. You're pathetic!"

Pamela was still staring at the hedge when Caralee

spoke from the sidewalk. "You heard that?" she said, still sounding irritated. "Sydney Carton, aka my fellow actor Craig Belknap and my colleague at Hyler's Luncheonette. He's the one who goes to the guillotine at the end."

She strode past Pamela and hurried up the street.

Chapter Three

Pamela was not alone in her house, despite the fact that her architect husband had been killed six years earlier in a construction-site accident and her only daughter, Penny, had returned to her college in Massachusetts at the beginning of September. She climbed her front steps, traversed the wide porch that had attracted her and her husband to their hundred-year-old house so long ago, unlocked the heavy oak door with its oval window, and peered cautiously inside. But nothing stirred. The lamp in the corner of the entry illuminated the aged parquet floor, the worn but lovely Persian rug, the small wing chair where she sat to read her mail.

She made her way cautiously to the kitchen and then along the hallway that led to the laundry room, tiptoeing as she got closer to her destination. Trusting the hall light to reveal all she needed to know, she slowly pushed the laundry room door open. From the floor two eyes, glowing amber, met hers. The rest of the cat, a sleek swath of jet-black fur, blended into the shadows. But a few sleeping kittens—

the ginger ones that took after their dashing father—
were just visible, clustered around their mother in
the comfortable bed Pamela had arranged for their
mother's confinement.

"Goodnight," she whispered, backing away and
tiptoeing back to the kitchen.

Upstairs, she stopped in her office and brought
her computer to life, waiting through the attendant
chirps and hums. No new messages had arrived from
her boss at *Fiber Craft*, though she was sure there
would be a work assignment in the morning—her
boss was an early riser. But Penny had sent a note to
say she'd gotten an A on the test she'd been so worried about.

Back downstairs, in pajamas and robe, she applied
herself once again to the ruby-red yarn and the in-
progress sleeve, while a mystery with a plot as genteel
as the actors' British accents unfolded on the screen
before her.

Pamela stood at her counter grinding coffee beans
while Bettina set out portions of crumb cake on
dessert plates from Pamela's wedding china. The
grinder growled and whirred in spasmodic bursts,
making conversation momentarily impossible. On
the floor, a black kitten and a ginger one tussled near
Bettina's sandaled foot, stopping their play to investigate her toes.

"They already have sharp little claws, and this ginger one is a tough character," Bettina said.

"All the girls are," Pamela said. "They take after
their mom." Catrina had been adopted as a stray the
previous fall after surviving many frosty November
nights outside.

The kettle's whistle summoned Pamela to the stove, and a minute later she was pouring boiling water through the fragrant, fresh-ground coffee she'd spooned into the filter cone. As the coffee dripped into the carafe, she set out two cups and saucers from her wedding china. Pamela saw no point in saving her pretty things for some imagined future time. And anyway, aside from her wedding china, most of her pretty things were tag-sale finds valuable to no one but her, like the cut-glass cream and sugar set that waited on the kitchen table.

"I do know who Craig Belknap is," Bettina said, returning to an earlier topic of conversation after they were settled on either side of the table with their coffee and crumb cake, "but I don't know why she would have been arguing with him. If anything, she owes him a favor."

"The job at Hyler's?" Pamela asked, teasing a forkful from the golden crumble-topped sponge cake in front of her. "He's got an in with the management?"

"He works there," Bettina said, "but you never see him because he's back in the kitchen."

Pamela finished chewing and swallowed. "What was Caralee doing when she lived in Manhattan?" she asked.

"Same thing," Bettina said, "but a grander place than Hyler's Luncheonette, I'm sure—and the tips for a tuna melt with fries probably don't match what a server gets from somebody who's just dined on a dozen raw oysters and a filet."

They sipped their coffee and finished off their crumb cake, chatting about Bettina's grandchildren and Penny's reports from college. When the last crumbs had been forked up from the wedding plates and the last drops of coffee had been drained from the wedding cups, Bettina climbed to her feet, careful not to step on the tussling kittens, whose number had grown to five.

"I'm off to the mall," she said. "Feel like taking a break from work today?"

"Too much to do," Pamela said. "I've got four articles to edit for the next issue, and my boss wants them back today. Besides, you know . . . I'm not really . . ." She looked down, taking in the none-too-new jeans and simple cotton blouse she'd put on earlier that morning.

"You could dress up more," Bettina said. "I certainly would, if I was tall like you and had your figure."

"You *do* dress up," Pamela said, smiling fondly at her friend. Bettina had an extensive wardrobe, and she dressed for her life in Arborville with as much flair as a Manhattan fashionista. For her visit to the town's senior center to cover an event for the *Arborville Advocate*, she'd chosen a silky wrap dress in a swirling print of navy, bright pink, and turquoise. She'd accessorized it with turquoise wedge-heeled sandals that revealed bright pink toenails, and she'd accented her hazel eyes with turquoise shadow.

After Bettina left, Pamela inventoried her cupboards. She certainly wasn't hungry after a mid-morning snack of crumb cake, but the previous night's dinner had consisted of a baked sweet potato, one chicken thigh remaining from a chicken she had roasted on Saturday, and a homegrown tomato. The grocery list fastened to the refrigerator door with a tiny magnetized mitten reminded her that she needed a loaf of the Co-Op's special whole-grain bread, as well as butter and cat and kitten food. Catrina was eating several times a day to keep up with the demands of the six kittens she was nursing, and the kittens themselves were starting to sample solid food. As far as provisioning herself for the next few days' meals went, she'd wait to see what looked good at the Co-Op.

After retrieving several canvas bags from the closet in the entry—her canvas bag supply was an homage to Nell, who spoke frequently about the virtues of renouncing paper and plastic—she stepped onto the porch to collect the day's mail. It consisted of a utility bill, a card offering one month of free lawn service, and a catalog featuring just the type of jewelry she would have worn if she was a jewelry person: stones that were pretty rather than precious and designs that evoked exotic lands.

Scanning her own mail reminded her that she'd promised Richard Larkin to make sure no mail accumulated in his box while he was gone—the mail carrier could be a bit forgetful about whose mail was to be held and whose delivered. She darted around the hedge that separated her yard from his and peered toward the metal box fastened to his house's shingled façade. Nothing was sticking out, and anyway he'd be back tomorrow.

She wasn't sure how she felt about that, but she wished Bettina would stop trying to play matchmaker. Yes, she'd once let slip that with Penny off to college and on her way to being independent, she might consider dating. But Richard Larkin, attractive as he was, might not be the right person. The shaggy hair that had originally marked him in her eyes as too bohemian had proven to be the effect of a temporarily demanding work schedule that left no time for a visit to the barber. But still, she wasn't sure. Or

maybe she just wasn't really ready yet, despite the fact
that even Penny had urged her to remedy her soli-
tary state.

Her own mail deposited on the mail table in her
entry, she was on her way. Arborville's walkability had
attracted Pamela and her husband long ago when
they were shopping for a house, and Pamela still did
most of her errands on foot. Arborville's tiny commercial district, with the Co-Op Grocery and an unpreten-
tious collection of narrow storefronts, including Hyler's
Luncheonette, was only five blocks distant and the
route was a pleasant one—up tree-lined Orchard
Street and then left at the stately brick apartment
building that faced Arborville Avenue. Pamela often
detoured through the parking lot behind the apartment building, where a discreet wooden fence hid
trash cans and whatever else the building's inhabitants
had recently discarded. One person's trash truly was
another's treasure, and she had recently rescued an
ornate picture frame that exactly suited an antique
sampler she had found at a thrift shop.

Today was a perfect mid-September day. Yards were
still green, trees were still leafy, but the sun's angle was
no longer the direct blaze of midsummer, and the
sidewalks were littered with acorns. Pamela took her
time, and when she reached the Co-Op she dallied
outside for a few more minutes. Besides supplying
the inhabitants of Arborville with food, the Co-Op
also supplied information. The large bulletin board
next to the automatic door had only recently been
supplemented by AccessArborville, the town's listserv, and people still consulted the bulletin board for
news about town events. Moreover, the bulletin
board welcomed postings from anyone with anything
to publicize.

Pamela's heart sank to discover that more than one person was offering kittens to good homes. Soon it would be time to find homes for Catrina's lively brood, but how many kittens could a tiny town like Arborville absorb at once?

Inside the market, Pamela selected a cart from the small collection waiting near the entrance and wheeled it toward the bakery counter, where a tempting assortment of loaves in various shapes and hues beckoned. She chose her favorite whole-grain, a gleaming oblong the color of toasted wheat, waited while it was sliced and bagged, and moved on to the cheese counter. There she hesitated between Gouda and cheddar, and finally came away with half a pound of each.

She maneuvered the cart into the produce section, where a row of bins piled high with greens of every sort faced bins of squash and root vegetables across a narrow wood-floored aisle. She added a head of romaine to her cart and moved on to collect a bundle of carrots and a bunch of celery. A special display at the end of the aisle featured sweet corn, still in its husks, and billed as "New Jersey's Own." Pamela couldn't resist, and piled six ears into her cart. A display of local apples occupied the corresponding spot across the way. She picked out four, rusty red with golden streaks.

Farther down the fruit aisle, neighboring bins offered peaches, plums, and apricots. September was the last chance for good peaches, local peaches that tasted the way peaches were supposed to taste. Pamela pushed her cart a few yards farther and cupped a peach in her hand. It was pale gold, velvety, with a rosy blush. It wasn't soft yet, but she knew peaches were happy to ripen off the tree. A bowl of peaches on the kitchen counter could perfume a kitchen for a few days and then turn into a pie—or a cobbler. In fact peach cobbler was exactly what she planned to make the following Tuesday when Knit and Nibble met at her house. She'd wait a few days to buy the peaches though.

The question of dinner for the next few nights still needed to be addressed, and she couldn't forget the cat and kitten food and butter. A quick detour through the canned goods section allowed her to cross the first two items off her list, and she picked up a pound of butter on her way through the dairy aisle. At the meat counter she studied the offerings. The Co-Op had good meat, much of it from local farms, but it was hard to be inspired when cooking for one.

A package of smoked ham hocks caught her eye—not the most exciting perhaps, compared to the marbled steaks, dainty lamb chops, and racks of baby back ribs, but Pamela loved making bean soup. And she liked her meals to reflect the seasons. A salad was the perfect dinner at the end of a long summer day, but by mid-September a steaming bowl of soup, ladled from a pot that had simmered on the stove all afternoon, would be most welcome. And she could cook today and have a week's worth of meals. She added the ham hocks to her cart.

Pamela was happy to set down the two canvas bags, laden with groceries and heavier than she'd expected them to be, when she stepped up onto her porch. Inside the house, she was greeted by six hungry kittens and their equally hungry mother. She freshened their communal water dish and spooned cat food into a bowl for Catrina and kitten food into the large bowl the kittens shared—though their first ventures with solid food had involved climbing into the bowl.

When the groceries were stowed away, she toasted a slice of the fresh whole-grain bread and ate it with a few slices of Gouda, finishing the meal off with an apple. It was only one p.m. She'd work her way through two of the articles that waited upstairs on her computer, then take a break and get the soup started.

At four p.m. Pamela was back in the kitchen, studying the dried beans in the jars she had lined up on the counter. The beans ranged in color from white to deepest maroon, with a jar of speckled pinto beans at the end. She poured from this jar and that until she'd filled a two-cup measure. In a large heavy pot on the stove, chopped onion, carrots, and celery were already softening in a few tablespoons of olive oil, and sprigs of parsley and thyme from the herb pots on the back porch waited on the counter. When the beans, water, and a ham hock had been added to the pot and all was on its way to a low simmer, she returned to her office and article number three, "Victorian Needlework in the Victoria and Albert Museum."

Pamela worked until six-thirty, when the tempting aroma of bean soup summoned her down to the kitchen. The ham hock had simmered among the beans and other vegetables as she edited her way through the Victorian needlework article and "The Role of Weaving in Modern Mayan Culture." It was time to extract it from the pot and trim off the now-tender bits of ham. She scooped it out onto a cutting board and set to work with her favorite paring knife.

But after a few minutes she paused in her task, letting her knife rest. It was unusual to hear sirens on this block of Orchard Street, or any block of Orchard

Street in fact. Emergency vehicles sometimes sped along Arborville's main artery, Arborville Avenue, at the top of the hill, or busy County Road, at the bottom. But this siren was close and drawing closer. She set the knife down and quickly washed her greasy fingers at the sink.

Outside it was still daylight, but the sky behind the church steeple was reddening. A man and a woman were standing on the sidewalk in front of the church. They were looking eagerly up the street, but the expressions on their faces suggested that whatever they were waiting for wasn't connected with a happy event. The siren had become so loud now that when Pamela turned to look in the direction they were looking she wasn't surprised to see a police car only a few houses away and bearing down on them. Pamela blinked as the lights on its roof flashed in sequence, left to right and back again, like so many flashbulbs.

The police car swerved toward the curb as it neared Pamela's house and then coasted to a stop in front of the church. The doors swung open and two officers leapt out as if jointly responding to an internal command of "Ready, set, go!"

"This way," the woman called from the sidewalk. She motioned the officers to follow and she headed toward the driveway that led to the church parking lot. The man who had been waiting with her joined the procession, and the four—the officers in their dark-blue uniforms with the heavy leather gun belts and stiff visored caps, and the man and woman in jeans and T-shirts—disappeared around the side of the church.

Pamela stood uncertainly in her yard. She was tempted to follow the procession toward the parking lot and whatever it was that had seemed serious enough to summon the police. But she knew that the sensible choice would be to go back inside, finish cutting off the ham bits, and add them to the nearly ready bean soup. Then a third alternative presented itself.

She was just turning toward her house where the sensible choice in the form of the ham hock and the bean soup awaited, when from across the street came Bettina's voice. She turned back to see Bettina scurrying toward her, with Wilfred several paces behind. Bettina was still wearing the chic wrap dress she had started the day in. Wilfred, judging from his apron, was evidently in charge of the evening meal.

"What could be happening?" Bettina panted. "We heard the siren but we couldn't imagine it was on its way to Orchard Street."

Wilfred joined them. "Most unusual," he said. "The church, of all places."

"Rehearsal," Bettina observed. "The Players are here tonight. I saw Caralee arriving when I opened the door for a UPS delivery a little while ago."

"Uh-oh!" Wilfred held up a finger and closed his eyes. He frowned as if straining to make out a sound. "More sirens." He opened his eyes. Pamela heard them too. This time they were coming from both directions.

At nearly the same moment, another police car appeared at the top of the hill, and an ambulance swung around the corner from County Road. The competing sirens intertwined in a discordant competition of wails and howls, growing so loud that the sound was almost a physical presence. With a few last resentful growls, both vehicles nudged into spots at the curb and were silent.

EMTs in dark pants and white shirts hurried from the ambulance toward the church parking lot, followed by another police officer and a man in a sports jacket and slacks.

"There's Detective Clayborn," Bettina said. "Whatever's going on, I'll be getting the details from him for the *Advocate*."

"This doesn't look good," Wilfred said. Concern had banished the genial expression he usually wore and he seemed almost a stranger. Bettina reached for his arm and he tugged her to his side.

Chapter Four

Now a small group of people appeared in the church driveway, herded along by two of the uniformed officers until they reached the sidewalk. "Here come the Players," Bettina said, nodding toward an older woman in a colorful long skirt, a man in jeans, and several younger women. "But I wonder who those guys are." A second group, walking a few yards behind the Players, consisted of four older men sporting summery business-casual ensembles of khaki pants and polo shirts.

"Those are some of the Arborville Arborists," Wilfred said. "It's a volunteer group that looks after the town's shade trees. I guess they use one of the church's meeting rooms. They've been after me to join since I retired, but I'd rather hang out with the historical society."

Brief interviews were apparently on the agenda, the officers pulling out notebooks and each taking one person aside. Pamela made out a few words from the nearest pair, a woman officer and the older woman in the colorful long skirt. "Nothing helpful,

I'm sure," the older woman was saying, ". . . in the auditorium . . . heard screaming . . . didn't see anything,
either before or after."

After a few minutes, she was dismissed and, after
waving to a few of the people waiting to be interviewed, started up the sidewalk, her skirt swaying
around her legs.

Bettina detached herself from Wilfred and inter-
cepted the woman, Pamela following along. "What
on earth has happened?" Bettina asked. Then, as if
to explain her interest, she gestured toward her
house across the street and added, "We're neighbors."

"A terrible thing," the woman announced as dramatically as if she was reading from a script. "A beautiful young woman has been crushed in a freakish
accident."

"A pile of furniture in the storage room?" Pamela
whispered, barely breathing.

The woman shifted her gaze to Pamela. "Why,
yes," she said, "exactly that."

"Caralee Lorimer?" Pamela whispered, holding
her breath this time.

The woman's eyes grew large and she drew in a
long breath. She regarded Pamela as if she wasn't
sure whether to be impressed or alarmed. "How did
you know?" she said at last.

"I just—" Pamela shrugged uncomfortably. "I just . . .
had a feeling. I knew she was at the rehearsal. She is . . .
was . . . in our knitting group. You said 'a beautiful . . .' "
Pamela waved her hand, hoping the gesture would sub-
stitute for finishing the thought. She had been gradually backing up and realized that she was now standing
on the grass. Bettina and Wilfred were staring at her

too but they seemed very far away. Or was it just that dusk had begun to fall as the sun sank lower and everything was becoming indistinct?

She felt a bit light-headed and willed herself to breathe deeply. Suddenly Bettina was at her side. "You were starting to sway," Bettina whispered, looking a bit shaky herself. She slipped an arm around Pamela's waist. "Let's go inside."

"Goodnight, I guess," the woman from the Arborville Players said, now just looking puzzled. She continued on her way up the sidewalk, and Wilfred followed Pamela and Bettina into Pamela's house.

"You just sit right down," Bettina said as they entered Pamela's kitchen, where the ham hock, ham bits, and knife still waited on the counter. Pamela obeyed, taking a seat at her kitchen table. "And you drink some water." Bettina filled a glass at the sink and slipped it into Pamela's waiting hand. She took a long swallow. "And now," Bettina said, perching on another chair, "you tell me how you knew it was Caralee."

As Pamela described the conversation she'd had with Caralee the previous night, Bettina tightened her lips and shook her head sadly. "We'll see what the police have to say when I talk to Clayborn—I'm sure there's time to get an article in this week's *Advocate*." She shook her head again and her eyes looked mournful. "Margo will be devastated," she said. "She was like a second mother to Caralee. I suppose the police will notify her—maybe they already have."

Wilfred had wandered from the kitchen, dodging kittens on the way, as soon as Pamela finished describing why she had suspected the victim of the furniture collapse was Caralee. Now he returned.

"A big van is out there," he said. "It's from the

county. And the ambulance is still at the curb."

"That's the crime-scene unit," Bettina said, familiar with details of police work from her job with the *Advocate*. "Arborville is too small to have its own. And they probably want to get photographs of all the details before they . . . they . . . take the body away." Her voice broke, and the final words came out as a muffled wail.

"Dear, dear wife." Wilfred stepped behind her and squeezed her shoulders. She raised her hands to his.

Husbands could be such a comfort, Pamela reflected. The initial shock she'd felt was giving way to a tight throat and moist eyelids. She blinked a few times and a tear overflowed onto her cheek. Friends were a comfort too, she told herself, gazing across the table at Wilfred and Bettina.

"We must eat something," Wilfred declared. "There's nothing we can do to help anyone right now, and we'll all feel better with some food in our stomachs." He stepped to the stove, where he lifted the lid of the heavy pot where the bean soup had simmered. "This looks like bean soup," he said, and lit the burner under the pot. "And the rest of this ham needs to be chopped up and added to it. But first—" And more quickly than one would think a portly man in his mid-sixties could move, he darted through the door. From the entry, they heard his gentle voice say, "Out of the way, kittens. Mind my feet." The front door opened and closed.

"I don't know what he's up to," Bettina said, rising and wiping her eyes with her fingers. "But I see a loaf of Co-Op bread on your counter."

"There's cheese in the refrigerator," Pamela said. "I bought two kinds."

Bettina set to work slicing bread and cheese and

arranging the result on Pamela's wooden cheese board. As she worked, she talked—half to herself. "I'll call Margo tomorrow," she murmured. "There will be a funeral. Maybe she'll need help arranging. Such a tragic thing to happen in our little town."

The front door opened and once again they heard Wilfred advising the kittens to be careful of his feet. Then he was lifting three frosty bottles of beer from a canvas bag. "To go with the soup," he said. Pamela started to rise, but both waved her back into her chair.

"She had that argument with Craig Belknap," Pamela said suddenly.

"We'll let the police figure things out," Bettina said. "They'll talk to all the Players."

At the counter, Wilfred busied himself cutting the rest of the ham bits from the hock. Bettina found a few of Pamela's homegrown tomatoes in the wooden bowl on the counter, and soon they were gathered around the dining room table eating and feeling a bit more cheerful.

Pamela insisted that she would be okay in the house alone. If she accepted Wilfred and Bettina's invitation to spend the night across the street, Catrina and the kittens would feel deserted, especially if their breakfast wasn't forthcoming first thing in the morning. By the time Wilfred and Bettina left, no vehicles of any kind remained at the curb and all the lights were off next door.

An insistent meow distracted Pamela from an urgent quest: She had been invited to speak on new frontiers for old crafts at a conference sponsored by *Fiber Craft*, but no room numbers were posted outside the meeting rooms in the conference facility. She hurried from one room to another, desperately asking the assembled conference-goers what topic they were waiting to learn about. But in every room there was that curious meowing. What would cats be doing at a *Fiber Craft* conference?

She rolled onto her back and opened her eyes. She was not roaming the halls of the Hilton Garden Inn. She was at home, in her bedroom. She'd slept later and more soundly than she'd expected after the drama of the previous night. Usually, this time of year the sun brightened her white eyelet curtains early enough that no alarm clock was needed. According to the glowing numerals on her bedside clock, it was already nine a.m., but the curtains hung in shadowy folds, suggesting that the sky behind them was gray.

"Okay, okay," she murmured, rising and pulling on her robe. Catrina stopped meowing as the bedroom door swung open, but she tipped her face up and gazed at Pamela. Her expression suggested that she was as worried about Pamela's well-being as about her own empty stomach.

Downstairs, kittens were tumbling around the kitchen, chasing and tackling one another with tiny squeaks meant to be ferocious, and batting the tightly wound ball of yarn she'd given them to play with when they'd first begun to venture from their communal bed. Pamela spooned cat food and kitten food into fresh bowls and set them in the corner of the kitchen where mother and children had learned to expect their meals. The sky did look gloomy, she noted as she stood at the counter settling a paper filter into its plastic cone and adding three scoops of coffee.

After she got water started in the kettle, she hur-

ried outside to collect the *Register*. She doubted that
Caralee's death would be front-page news, but she
knew the *Register*'s reporters could be quite persistent in covering local stories, not to mention the people from the local TV channel. Their truck had
probably shown up while she and Bettina and Wilfred were eating their bean soup.

Pamela ate a slice of whole-grain toast, drank her
coffee, and paged through the *Register*. As she folded
the first section and set it aside, a headline on the
front page of "Local" caught her eye. It read AR-
BORVILLE ACTRESS DIES IN FREAK ACCIDENT. Freak accident? Was that official?

According to the article, a member of the Players
came upon Caralee's body after entering the storage
room in search of chairs shortly before rehearsal was
to start at seven p.m. Police were summoned, an ambulance was called—though Caralee was clearly dead—
and the sheriff's crime-scene unit responded as well.

Could reporters have stayed around long enough
and been persistent enough to get a statement con-
firming that the death was an accident? Detective
Clayborn had been on the scene right away, but didn't
it take time and deliberation to decide whether an
event that killed someone was an accident? Perhaps
Bettina would have more to report.

Most days Pamela's work happened in her upstairs
office, but she'd never been one to lounge about in
pajamas and robe. Though she'd slept late and it was
nearly ten a.m., the workday could still be salvaged,
and work would take her mind off the thought of
poor Caralee meeting a fate that had been so curiously foreshadowed. Teeth brushed, hair tidied, and
dressed in her warm-weather uniform of jeans and a
cotton blouse, she settled down at her desk. She was

staring at her computer screen as a progress bar
tracked the slow arrival of an email, undoubtedly
from her boss and undoubtedly attachment-laden.

As she waited, her mind returned to the dream
from which Catrina's meows had delivered her.
She'd had the dream, and others like it, before—
often when a challenge loomed. In the dream she
always persisted, opening doors and asking questions,
but in the way of dreams there was seldom a satisfying
denouement. Cats meowed, the sun came through the
curtains, or the landscapers started up next door, and
she awoke.

At the same moment that the email finally popped
up in her inbox, the doorbell rang. Halfway down
the stairs, she already knew it was Bettina. Through
the lace that curtained the oval window in her front
door, she could make out a splash of bright orange.
She opened the door to discover that Bettina's face
reflected anything but the cheer that would have
suited her fetching outfit. In fact Bettina had been
crying.

"Oh, Pamela!" she exclaimed, reaching out to be
hugged, which Pamela obliged. "I just couldn't help
it," she added, stepping back and wiping her eyes. "I
sobbed all the way here in my car. Margo is heart-
broken, and talking to her I just kept thinking, what
if I lost one of my own children?"

"Come in here." Pamela led her to the kitchen, settled her at the table, and took the facing chair. "There's
some coffee left," she said, popping up again.

Bettina waved her hand. "I've had plenty," she
said. "I just want to talk."

"I guess . . ." Pamela hesitated. She didn't want the
words to come out wrong, but she was curious. "I
guess . . . Caralee showed a different side of herself

to her aunt? Of course, no one would be happy if a niece died, but to be so devastated . . . there must have been a special bond."

"There was," Bettina said. "Caralee's father was Margo's brother, her favorite brother. He died when Caralee was in college. His marriage to Caralee's mother wasn't a happy one, and she wasn't a happy mother, at least where Caralee was concerned. Parents don't have favorites, they say, but everybody knows they do. Caralee's mother left Arborville after her husband died, so Margo took over that role. Caralee would come back here on her college breaks and they stayed very close."

Pamela nodded sympathetically. "And Margo's own children?" she asked.

"A son, grown up and living in Europe. They're close too, and he keeps in touch—he didn't move there to escape from Mom or anything. And she has a married daughter in Timberley. But she loved Caralee and she'd gotten so used to having her in the house."

"You saw the *Register*?" Pamela asked. She'd left the paper on the table when she went upstairs to work and she patted it now.

"I know what you're wondering," Bettina said. "Do they really think it was an accident?"

"Well, do they?" Pamela leaned across the table.

"No reason to think otherwise—according to Clayborn." Bettina shrugged. "I spent fifteen minutes with him before I went to Margo's."

"Did you tell him last night wasn't the first time furniture in the storage room had come crashing down on Caralee?"

"I did." Bettina's grim expression was at odds with

the cheery orange tint of her lipstick. "He said they interviewed everyone in the Players and no one had any reason to want Caralee dead. He also said that it would be very hard to prove in court that falling furniture had been used as a murder weapon."

"But what about Craig Belknap?" Pamela asked.

"Clayborn told me that I pay my taxes so I don't have to trouble myself with work better left to the police. He seemed a little grouchy this morning."

"Probably hadn't had enough coffee yet," Pamela said. "Speaking of which, are you ready now? I could do with another cup."

There was just enough left in the carafe for a scant cup each. Pamela set her cut-glass sugar bowl on the table and, dispensing with formality, served Bettina her cream in its grocery-store carton.

"The funeral is tomorrow," Bettina said after a fortifying sip of coffee. "At St. Willibrod's."

"What time?" Pamela asked.

"Do you want to go?" Bettina looked mildly surprised.

"Of course," Pamela said. "She was in our group, if only briefly, and you're Margo's friend and you're going."

"It's at ten," Bettina said. "I know you'll want to walk, but I'll be wearing my good shoes and I plan to drive."

"I'll take a ride." It was true that some shoes were more suited for walks around town than others, not that any of Pamela's were very fancy.

"I'll ring your bell at a quarter to." Bettina stood up. "And I'll let the other knitters know the details. Margo is hosting a reception at her house afterward. I told her I'd help—maybe it will be catering though.

I'm not much good when it comes to food." Bettina
had a repertoire of seven meals, one for each day of
the week.

After Bettina left, Pamela rinsed the cups at the sink
and returned to her computer. The slow-to-arrive
email had brought with it ten attachments, each a sub-
mission to *Fiber Craft*. The message itself asked Pamela
to read the ten articles and advise for or against pub-
lication. While she'd been downstairs with Bettina,
an email had arrived from Penny too. The note
started out enthusing about a visit to the Isabella
Stewart Gardner Museum with her art history class,
but then the mood changed. "Mom," Penny wrote, "I
just got a message from one of my friends back in Arborville telling me to look at the *Register*'s website,
and I looked. I hope you're not going to get involved
in this!"

On the surface, pleasant little Arborville did not
seem the kind of town where people got murdered,
and Pamela certainly did not seem the kind of person to set to work sleuthing and make connections
overlooked by the police. Yet both had happened,
and more than once.

"Of course not," Pamela responded. "It was a
tragic accident, just like the *Register* says."

It was tragic, and at the thought her throat grew
tight. She swallowed hard. Margo had loved Caralee,
prickly as she was, just the way most mothers loved
their daughters. Penny wasn't prickly in the least.
Pamela had already lost a husband. She couldn't
bear to think how she'd feel if she was in Margo's
place.

The report on the ten articles was due back the

next day, a day whose morning and part of whose afternoon would be taken up with the funeral and reception. Pamela ate a quick lunch, fed Catrina and the kittens and freshened their water, and climbed the stairs to her office, happy for the distraction of work.

She spent the next few hours immersed in the worlds of modern silkworm husbandry, wool carding, jacquard paisley, rigid heddle looms, and ancient Icelandic spindles. When she stopped to take a break, she was halfway downstairs before the events of the previous evening came back to her. And as she lowered her foot from the bottom step to the parquet of her entry floor, another recollection surfaced as well.

A cardboard box for Richard Larkin waited under the mail table. It contained a few issues of the *Register* (now sadly out of date), a month's worth of the *Advocate* (four in all), several catalogs, a small batch of letters (mostly junk mail), and an issue of *Urban Architect*. (Like the husband she still missed, Pamela's neighbor was an architect.) Today he would be back. There was no rush to deliver the box though. He'd probably arrive tonight. A drive from Maine could take many hours.

She warmed up a bowl of the bean soup from the previous night and considered eating it on the porch, since it didn't look like she'd fit in a walk today. But the gray sky that had been responsible for her oversleeping that morning hadn't lightened, and sitting outside didn't seem that cheery a prospect. Instead, she sat at her kitchen table and watched a tussle between two of the kittens, a ginger female who was rapidly becoming the most assertive of the litter and a male brave enough to challenge his sister. Catrina had given birth to three males and three females, a large brood—and unplanned. The males were all black, which had surprised Pamela—since their father was a raffish ginger tom who prowled the neighborhood as confidently as if all he surveyed was his to command.

Pamela's afternoon was spent in front of the computer too, and at six p.m. she hit SEND and dispatched her evaluations of the ten articles back to her boss at *Fiber Craft*. She was too weary to cook, and another bowl of bean soup made a welcome, if repetitious meal. Her eyes were so tired from staring at the computer screen that instead of working on the in-progress sleeve, she dozed on the sofa half-listening to a PBS program about glaciers.

It was Friday morning. The frantic whistle of the kettle greeted Pamela as she stepped back inside after retrieving the *Register* and that week's *Advocate*, which had lodged in the hedge between her yard and Richard Larkin's. Her toast had popped up and was growing cold in the toaster. Catrina and the kittens had eaten what they wanted from their respective bowls and retreated en masse to their lair in the laundry room.

Pamela had stayed outside longer than she'd intended. After collecting the newspapers, she'd remained standing on the sidewalk, staring at Richard Larkin's empty driveway. He'd been expected back the previous evening—or perhaps night, she'd decided, as eight p.m. came and went, and then nine and ten. At ten-thirty, she'd roused herself from the dozing state she'd been lulled into by the nature channel, checked his driveway one more time, and gone to bed.

A slight change of plans. That was the most likely explanation. Why come back on a Thursday? Why not stretch the trip over the weekend? There was no reason to worry about him, she decided. No real reason to even think about him.

She spread butter on her cold toast and poured a cup of coffee. The *Advocate* would reveal nothing about Caralee's death that she hadn't already learned firsthand from Bettina, and she could check the garage sale listings later. But she unfolded the daily paper and quickly skimmed the "Local" section to discover that the *Register* apparently considered its initial coverage of Caralee's death sufficient. There was no follow-up article.

Breakfast complete, Pamela climbed the stairs to check her email and then crossed the hall to ponder the contents of her closet. Her few jackets were all wool, too warm for what was shaping up to be a summery mid-September day. She fingered her only dress, a pale green sheath. But she'd bought it long ago for a wedding, and in her mind it was linked with celebration rather than mourning. She pushed aside a few hangers that held jeans and pulled out a pair of navy cotton slacks. A crisp white shirt and navy pants would certainly be suitable, with low pumps.

In the bathroom, she brushed her dark hair, which usually hung loose to her shoulders, and gathered it into a clip at her neck. She added a bit of lipstick and her silver button earrings, and she was just turning away from the mirror when the doorbell chimed.

"I won't say anything," Bettina said, surveying the

outfit. "The point is to pay our respects and I know it's not a fashion show." But Bettina herself looked smart in a black linen skirt suit accessorized with pearls. "Shall we be on our way?" she added. Pamela followed her down the steps. Wilfred's ancient Mercedes waited at the curb. Wilfred, in one of the well-cut suits he'd worn in his working life, was at the wheel.

Chapter Five

The mourners that were scattered here and there in St. Willibrod's pews made up a varied congregation. Saints gazed down from the richly colored stained-glass windows on Manhattanites—even people with tattoos!—and people whose unremarkable grooming choices identified them as Arborville through and through. A simple wooden coffin was positioned at the top of the aisle, adorned with a dramatic cluster of huge white chrysanthemums accented with glossy dark-green leaves.

"Margo had to arrange everything," Bettina whispered as they slipped into a pew. "It was like Caralee's mother couldn't even be bothered."

From the choir loft, low organ notes throbbed, shaping a melody that Pamela recognized though she couldn't name. Echoing the somber mood, from the altar a dignified woman wearing a white robe trimmed with green spoke out: "In the midst of life we are in death, but there is life eternal for those who trust in the Lord. Today we commemorate the earthly life of our sister Caralee Lorimer."

Suddenly people were on their feet. Pamela consulted the program she'd been handed as she and Bettina entered the church. She rose and began to recite the "Our Father" as overlapping voices echoed around her. Next to her, Bettina dabbed at her eyes with a tissue.

As the prayer ended, a young woman with Caralee's dark straight hair, but chubby and considerably shorter, joined the minister in the altar area. Staring fixedly at a sheet of paper that fluttered in her trembling hands, she read the words, "Remember me when I am gone away," in an uncertain voice. She looked up, seemed to catch the eye of someone in a pew near the front, smiled hesitantly, and returned to her task, speaking more confidently. As the poem drew to a close with the reflection that it would be better for the person being addressed to forget the loved one rather than remembering and being sad, Bettina leaned toward Pamela and whispered, "That's her cousin, Margo's daughter, Megan."

The young woman made her way back to her pew, and the minister took over again, announcing Psalm 46 and intoning "God is our refuge and strength, an ever present help in trouble." The comforting words flowed over one another in a cadence that was itself comforting, and when the rhythmical language of the psalm ceased, the minister evoked in more prosaic terms Caralee's youth in Arborville and her return to the arms of her community and her beloved aunt. "May she rest in peace," the minister concluded, lifting her eyes toward the choir loft.

A woman's voice rang out, and "Swing low, sweet chariot" filled the high-ceilinged space. The delivery was so confident as to suggest the voice's owner was used to filling large spaces with her voice, perhaps more at home on a Broadway stage than St. Willibrod's choir loft.

When the song ended, the organ music resumed and pallbearers took their places on either side of the coffin. They proceeded down the aisle, bearing the coffin between them, and the congregation followed.

"Nell came," Bettina whispered to Pamela, as Nell, dressed in a somber suit that looked as if it had seen decades' worth of funerals, eased her way out of a pew closer to the front and joined the procession.

They caught up with her on the church's wide slate porch, where she was talking to Caralee's aunt. Nell was holding one of Margo's hands in both her own and murmuring condolences, the look in her kind eyes as comforting as her words. Both turned to greet the newcomers, and Bettina introduced Pamela. It was the first time Pamela had laid eyes on Margo, but she barely needed Bettina's introduction to realize who this tall, thin woman had to be. She looked like Caralee twenty years hence, or even like Caralee made up for the role of a striking woman in her late fifties who had let her naturally jet-black hair turn attractively gray.

"I'm so sorry for your loss," Pamela said as Bettina hugged her friend. Margo nodded and swallowed hard.

"I have to go," Nell said. "I volunteer at the women's shelter in Haversack Friday mornings and they'll be wondering where I am." With a final squeeze of Margo's hand, she was off.

As Nell made her way down the slate steps toward the street, she passed a man in a dark suit heading up. His face wore an expression of deferential sorrow. "Shall we leave for the cemetery now?" he asked after greeting Margo.

The hearse, gleaming black with tasteful touches of chrome, was parked at the curb. The double doors at the back were ajar and the coffin, still adorned with the dramatic arrangement of chrysanthemums, waited nearby on a dolly.

The man touched Margo's back lightly to direct her toward the steps. She nodded, but paused to speak. "I hope you'll come to my house," she said to Pamela. "There's to be a small reception, starting at noon."

"Of course," Pamela said.

"Are you driving up to the cemetery?" said a voice behind Pamela.

Looking momentarily puzzled, Bettina nevertheless responded cordially. "Yes, we are," she said. "Do you want a ride?"

"I'd love one. I walked here," the same voice replied.

Pamela turned to see a small curly-haired woman whose round face seemed unused to looking unhappy.

"I'm Caralee's friend Beth Dalton," the woman said. "I recognize you—you're Margo's friend, the person who was teaching Caralee to knit."

"And this is another of the knitters," Bettina said with a gesture in Pamela's direction. "Pamela Paterson."

"Are you an actress too?" Pamela asked.

"Oh, nothing like that," Beth said. She laughed a small laugh that was more like a sigh and twisted her mouth into a half smile. "I never even left Arborville. Caralee was the adventurous one—even in second grade I could see that she was destined for an exciting life." She shook her head sadly. "I didn't think she'd end up like this though. What a tragic thing!"

They descended the church steps and walked toward the slate path that led around the side of the church to the parking lot. Many people were claiming their cars and lining up to leave the lot through the one exit. By the time they made it out of the lot and around the corner to the front of the church, the hearse had disappeared, and the Mercedes was last in the mournful procession heading along Arborville Avenue.

The cemetery was nearby, and old. Long ago, when Arborville wasn't even Arborville yet, but just a collection of orchards and farms, a cemetery had been established at the crest of the hill that formed the backside of the palisades, lofty cliffs overlooking the Hudson River. Wilfred guided the Mercedes up that steep hill, through the section of Arborville people called the Palisades, and followed the procession veering left at the crest. The iron gates that hung from the ancient stone gateposts were open now, and they brought up the rear of the last few cars making their slow way over the gravel road.

They parked and followed a few other stragglers to where the coffin waited near the deep rectangular hole that had been carved to receive it. Margo stood at the head of the grave, next to the minister who had conducted the funeral service. At Margo's other side was the woman who had read the poem, Margo's daughter Megan, Bettina had said. About twenty other people were standing about, the Manhattanites clustered on one side of the grave and the Arborville people on the other.

"That chrysanthemum arrangement on the coffin

really is striking," Pamela whispered. "It almost seems a shame to bury it too."

"It was from Craig Belknap," Bettina whispered back. "That's him over there. I met him yesterday afternoon." She nodded toward a nondescript man, not tall or short, or fat or thin, or dark or fair. But his face looked pleasant and friendly if, at that moment, extremely sad.

"Feeling guilty about arguing with her the night I overheard them, and then the very next night she's dead? I wonder if they made up before . . . it happened." Pamela said it half to herself.

Beth Dalton had stuck close, perhaps feeling more kinship with them than with Caralee's sophisticated Manhattan friends. Now she spoke up. "They argued all the time," she said. "Ever since they met when she joined the Players. They even had an argument Wednesday night. I stopped by Hyler's for a bite after work and I could hear voices coming from the kitchen, their voices. Then he came storming out, still wearing his apron, and tore out the front door. It was a little after five. I got the impression from the server that he was supposed to work until seven."

The minister had begun speaking. Beth made a guilty face and put her hand over her mouth, and Pamela once again yielded to the soothing cadences of the prayer.

"These sandwiches look just like the ones at Hyler's." Pamela surveyed the platters of sandwiches arranged on the crisp linen cloth spread over Margo's dining room table. Some were ham and cheese on rye, some tuna salad, some roast beef—and some were thick club sandwiches on toast. All were cut into dainty quarters speared with frilled toothpicks. The platters were garnished with pickle slices, cherry tomatoes, and radishes cut into rosettes.

"They *are* just like the ones at Hyler's," Bettina said. "Craig Belknap made them. He bought all the ingredients and Hyler's let him use their kitchen. He was here yesterday afternoon working things out with Margo."

At one end of the table, a tray held cans of soft drinks, with straws nearby. At the other end was an assortment of pies, including a lemon meringue, topped with a pouf of egg white beaten with sugar and lightly browned.

"He got the desserts from the same bakery that supplies Hyler's," Bettina added.

Some people had already helped themselves to food and arranged themselves in clusters that grouped like with like. Margo's Arborville friends and neighbors had taken seats in the living room, perching along the edge of her long sofa, on her armchairs, and even on her hassocks. Pamela overheard references to the community gardens, the middle school, and the town listserv as they leaned their graying heads toward one another. But Margo herself stood in the dining room with Megan and a woman who Bettina identified as Caralee's mother.

The Manhattanites, with their eye-catching hair colors and styles and their sleek ensembles, stood in the dining room too, juggling sandwich plates and cans of soda and talking of agents, auditions, and contracts. At the center of the group was a lanky man with close-cropped hair and an exotic cast to his handsome features that would have made him ideal for a role as a Russian czar. He was the only one in the group wearing a suit, albeit a very fashionable suit, with narrow pants and a jacket that just skimmed his narrow torso. Craig Belknap stood uncertainly at the fringes of the group, talking to no one. After what Beth had said about what happened at Hyler's Wednesday evening, Pamela hoped she'd have a chance to talk to him during the reception. Caralee's death raised questions—at least in Pamela's mind, even if Detective Clayborn was happy to call it an accident.

"I should have a word with Caralee's mother before I get started on the food," Pamela said.

"Her name is Caroline," Bettina murmured.

Caroline Lorimer was a small prim-looking woman with brown hair arranged in a prim style. She had dressed for her daughter's funeral in an unremarkable brown pantsuit.

Pamela summoned up her social smile, muted in keeping with the occasion, and turned away from the table toward where Margo stood with Megan and Caroline.

"It's a lovely event," Pamela said. Margo nodded sadly. "I'm Pamela Paterson, a longtime Arborville resident," she added, addressing herself to Caroline. "I'm so sorry about your daughter."

"She had a way of finding trouble," Caroline announced, sounding more annoyed than sorrowful, "and now it found her." She scrutinized Pamela. "I don't think I knew you when we lived here," she said. "What street do you live on?"

"Orchard . . ." Pamela wasn't sure whether to add "next to the church," but Caroline supplied the words herself. Apparently someone had told Caroline that Bettina and Pamela had been among the first people to learn of Caralee's death.

Megan spoke up, her voice more confident than when she had read the poem during the service. "Caroline is considering a lawsuit," she said.

The pained expression that came over Margo's elegant features made her opinion of the idea—or at least the announcement of it at that moment—clear.

The sound of the front door opening and the slight commotion that ensued drew their attention to the living room. A tall thin man had entered, with patrician features and smooth gray hair swept back dramatically from a high forehead. It was Anthony Wadsworth. Pamela had never met him personally, but she'd seen his photo numerous times in the *Advocate*, often in connection with articles written by Bettina. He was the Arborville Players' head and the director of all its productions.

"Wouldn't you know he'd have to make an entrance," Bettina sighed. "And couldn't even be bothered to go to the funeral."

Margo excused herself and headed toward him, trailed by Caroline and Megan.

"So sorry," he boomed in a British-accented voice. "Such a busy morning. Theater business, you know. Quite a scramble to recast Madame Defarge, but the understudy turned out to be the best choice. Hidden in plain sight, you might say."

"The mousy creature at his elbow is his wife, Rue," Bettina whispered.

As if the music had just started up again in a game of musical chairs, everyone was suddenly on the move. The Manhattanites, perhaps sensing that Anthony Wadsworth would be a useful person for an aspiring actor to get to know, began to migrate toward the living room. The Arborville folks, on the other hand, seemed to decide en masse that their plates needed to be refilled with dainty sandwich quarters speared with frilled toothpicks.

Bettina had darted toward the refreshment table when Margo and the others left the dining room to greet Anthony Wadsworth. Pamela had tried to follow her but was jostled in one direction by a svelte woman with a stiff crest of light pink hair and in another by a portly gray-haired man in a baggy sports jacket. Now she found herself standing face-to-face with the lanky man in the suit, who had been abandoned by his confreres.

Their eyes met and it seemed rude to dart around him without a word. Besides, the expression on his handsome face was so bereft that without even thinking she suddenly heard herself say, "You must have cared very much for her."

"I adored her," he said, his voice unsteady. "She was my wife."

"But, I thought . . ." Pamela paused. She didn't want to sound like a busybody.

"She left me."

Pamela didn't know what to say. Of course, looks aren't everything in a marriage—or even very much, considering all that goes into living together day by day. But this man was so *very* handsome, with his finely modeled cheekbones and dark, deep-set eyes and expressive lips. And now that she was talking to him, he seemed so gentle. She asked herself what could have made Caralee decide she'd rather move back to Arborville than remain married to him.

"I was hoping I could win her back," he added. "But now . . . obviously . . ." He lifted his hands in a despairing gesture. They were handsome too. "I'm not sure I even want to stay alive."

They were interrupted by one of the Manhattanites. A well-toned woman dressed in a perfectly fitting sleeveless sheath seized the lanky man's arm.
She looked at Pamela and then at him. "Come and
listen to Anthony," she said. "He's been everywhere
and done everything—not like somebody you'd expect to meet in a town like this." She looked at
Pamela again. This time she let her eyes travel down
to the low-heeled pumps Pamela had resurrected
from the recesses of her closet that morning. They
lingered there a moment and then traveled back up,
past the many-years-old navy slacks and the utilitar-
ian white shirt. When they reached Pamela's face,
the woman smiled a triumphant smile.

Pamela watched the woman lead her quarry back
into the living room, pondering what had just happened. It was almost as if the woman had seen Pamela as a rival for the affections of the lanky man, free
to love again—at least in the woman's mind—now
that his ex-wife was truly out of the picture. It had
been years since she had viewed herself as anyone's
potential romantic partner.

From the living room came the voice of Anthony
Wadsworth, assuring his audience that community
theater was not to be spurned as a venue in which to
hone one's craft. "That's how I got my start," he went
on, "Stratford-on-Avon." He paused for a laugh that
sounded as calculated as his accent. "Not exactly
community theater, you might say, but it wasn't London. Of course that came later."

"What are your plans for future Arborville productions?" Pamela recognized the voice as that of the
woman who had carried the lanky man away.

"Plans!" Anthony Wadsworth said. Pamela was watching him now. He thrust his chin up, closed his eyes

dramatically, and flung a hand to his forehead. "So many masterworks for the stage, so little time. But surely another Shakespeare—we did *Romeo and Juliet* last year—*King Lear*, perhaps. I haven't trod the boards for years, but that's a role I can see myself in. And then for a change, something comic, perhaps . . ."

He was still talking but Pamela was suddenly very hungry, and the crowd at the refreshment table had thinned. She continued in the direction she'd been going before she encountered the lanky man. Despite the great interest in the sandwiches, especially on the part of the Arborville contingent, piles of them remained. Apparently Craig Belknap had been replenishing the platters. As she took a plate and arranged one sandwich quarter of each kind on it, she made a mental note to check for him in the kitchen if she didn't encounter him as she circulated among the guests.

Bettina was standing at the far end of the dining room, near the window that looked out on Margo's backyard. Next to her was the mousy woman Bettina had identified as Rue Wadsworth. Each was holding a plate with a slice of lemon meringue pie on it.

"Delicious pie," Bettina said as she carved off a forkful of the quivering lemony custard topped with a glistening dollop of meringue. "Have you met Rue Wadsworth?" She turned to Rue. "Pamela Paterson is another member of the knitting group."

Pamela nodded and smiled as best she could with her mouth full of tuna salad. Rue Wadsworth nodded and smiled back. She was a slight woman in her sixties with large eyes and a pointed chin, a pixyish look enhanced by her fine, short hair. Pamela was searching her mind for a sociable thing to say and wondering when she was going to have a chance to concentrate on her food, when a fourth woman joined their group, a genial grandmotherly type.

"Rue Wadsworth!" the woman exclaimed. "How long has it been?" Pamela recognized the newcomer as someone she had seen around town, someone who conversed animatedly with other residents of Arborville as she studied the bulletin board outside the Co-Op, picked up children in front of the grammar school (undoubtedly grandchildren, in her case), or grabbed a bite at Hyler's.

"Hello." Rue's voice was as soft as her husband's was loud.

"Of course, I always know what Anthony is up to," the grandmotherly woman said. "I love those Christmas letters you write. Such detail—everything he's done in the whole past year. He just lives for the Players, doesn't he? Arborville is so lucky to have him." She paused for a large bite of roast beef sandwich, then went on. "You're probably already working on this year's letter. Christmas will be here before we know it."

"I *am* working on it," Rue said. "There will be lots to report on this year, the Players' season of course, and Anthony was honored by the Chamber of Commerce, and he gave a talk on Elizabethan theater at the Timberley Library. So well received. And I'll have to mention the . . . tragedy, but I'm not sure yet how I'll handle it—I'll figure something out. Then there's the move to California next summer, a tiny town. I'll have him all to myself." She glanced around. "So many people here. Such a nice tribute to the Players. It shows how highly people value Anthony's contribution to making Arborville the kind of town it is."

Pamela caught Bettina's eyes and stifled a laugh. They concentrated on their food for a few minutes, watching as more people discovered that the pies had been cut into serving pieces and forks and fresh plates supplied. From the kitchen came the smell of coffee being brewed. Megan came by carrying a stack of used plates, collected Bettina's and Rue's, and moved off toward the kitchen. Rue leaned down to retrieve a large canvas satchel.

"I brought something," she said hesitantly, un-snapping the top of the satchel. "I thought Caralee's mother might want it, but she doesn't. And Margo doesn't want it either. She said she would mourn Caralee all over again every time she looked at it." She lowered a hand into the satchel's depths. "But one of you might want it because you're in that knitting group and you were teaching her." She tugged.

Up came a fuzzy gray mass. Pamela stared at it, hoping her face didn't give away her momentary puzzlement. But as Rue continued to tug, a pair of knitting needles came into view, threaded through loops that edged one of the object's fuzzy gray borders.

"Madame Defarge's knitting!" Pamela and Bettina exclaimed in chorus. "Won't you need it for the production?" Bettina added.

"No, we most definitely won't," Rue said. "And this is—wouldn't you say—sort of *cursed*." She thrust it at Pamela, who extended a tentative hand and then found herself holding the piece of knitting, which was still tethered to Rue's satchel by a strand of yarn that disappeared into the satchel's depths.

"And here's the rest of the yarn." Rue rummaged in the satchel and came up with a partial skein of the coarse gray yarn whose color had reminded Pamela of her basement floor. Pamela reached out her other hand.

"Margo probably has a bag for that somewhere," Bettina said, and headed for the kitchen.

She was gone several minutes. Pamela listened, holding the skein of yarn in one hand and Caralee's homely knitting project in the other and wondering what could have happened to Bettina, as Rue regaled her and the grandmotherly woman with a description of an article Anthony was writing for an online directors' forum. At last Bettina reemerged from the kitchen, but instead of a bag she was carrying a tray of cups.

"Pressed into service," she said with a laugh. "Margo is finding you a bag."

Megan had been making trips back and forth to the kitchen, clearing away the platters, now mostly empty, and the plates that people had abandoned here and there when they'd had their fill of sandwiches. Now she followed Bettina, carrying a second tray of cups.

"Coffee on its way," announced a male voice, and Craig Belknap stepped through the kitchen door bearing a huge coffee urn, spigot and all, just like the ones Hyler's used. It probably *was* one of the ones Hyler's used, Pamela reflected, borrowed for the occasion. Apparently lured by the prospect of coffee, Anthony Wadsworth strolled in from the living room, trailed by the flock of Manhattanites. The well-toned woman in the sheath dress still clung to the arm of the handsome, lanky man. Craig set the urn in the middle of the table, seized the electric cord, glanced around to find an outlet, and stooped to plug it in. Megan scurried to the kitchen and returned with a bowl of sugar in little packets.

Still carrying the knitting project and the skein of

yarn, Pamela followed Craig when he returned to the kitchen. "Margo was looking for a bag for me to put this in," she said, "but she seems to have gotten distracted."

"That's Caralee's." He stared at it, and she stared at him. His looks had initially struck Pamela as nondescript, but now she reflected that nondescript looks could be an advantage for an actor. Besides, there seemed few emotions his face was incapable of expressing. As she watched, his expression changed from curiosity to recognition to sadness to anger. "I know who you are," he said at last. "You're in that knitting club."

"She wanted to learn to knit," Pamela said with a shrug. "So she could be a convincing Madame Defarge."

"You were standing behind the hedge eavesdropping last Tuesday night." His eyes were definitely not nondescript. They were a piercing shade of blue. And at the moment, the few days' growth of auburn stubble that he sported lent his face a rakish charm.

"I was on my way home," Pamela said. "I was standing in my own front yard. And I wasn't even standing. I only stopped for a minute because you were both talking so loud. It was hard to ignore."

"*I* wasn't mad at *her*," he said, giving Pamela the full effect of his amazing eyes.

Suddenly she heard herself say, "Caralee said some awfully hurtful things to you. If somebody said things like that to me, I might want to hurt them back. "

He took a step forward, his expression suddenly threatening. "What?" he bellowed. Pamela glanced toward the dining room to see a few curious faces turned toward the kitchen. "So you think—what?—I killed her? You're crazy." He gestured around at the piles of dirty plates and the platters still holding a few forlorn sandwiches and wilted radish rosettes. "And I'm doing this—why?" His voice mellowed slightly. "Because I feel guilty? Or so people won't figure out that I'm—" He paused and his mobile face assumed a look of comic malevolence. He lifted both arms and wiggled his fingers as if flourishing an impressive set of claws. "*The mad killer of Orchard Street.*" He laughed a ghoulish laugh, and then his face sagged. "In fact, I cared a lot for her," he murmured sadly. "And I didn't even go to the rehearsal Wednesday night, if you must know. I wasn't anywhere near the church. Besides, the police think it was an accident."

"If you weren't at the rehearsal Wednesday night, where were you?" Pamela asked, though she was touched by his evident grief.

"They weren't working on my scenes," he said. He stooped toward a messy stack of miscellaneous bags on the counter and handed her one with the Co-Op logo on it, adding, "This should be big enough for the knitting."

Pamela took the bag and slid the lumpy knitting project and the partial skein of yarn into it. But she wasn't ready to leave. She stepped toward the kitchen door and turned to block the entrance to the dining room. "Were you at home Wednesday night?" she asked in a voice that she tried to make conversational.

"No, I wasn't," Craig said forthrightly. "And it's none of your business where I was."

"Beth Dalton said you left Hyler's before your shift ended." Pamela hated to sound like a gossip, but if somebody had rearranged the furniture in the storage room so it would fall on Caralee that night, the rearrangement would have had to happen before she got there around six-forty-five.

"That's none of her business," he said, "and now, if you don't mind . . ." He turned toward the sink and the rest of his words were lost as he twisted the tap and water gushed from the faucet.

"Richard Larkin didn't waste any time getting back to work," Bettina said as they pulled up in front of Pamela's house.

"He's home?" Pamela was startled to hear the eager edge to her voice. "I mean," she said, trying to sound calmer, "when did you talk to him?"

"I didn't," Bettina said, "but he was due back yesterday and I see his car's not here now—so he must have been up and out and back to the office this morning without even one day of rest. Such a dedicated, hard-working man, a man any woman—"

"Please just stop!" Pamela turned to face her friend. Bettina blinked a few times and looked suitably chastened. "He didn't come back yesterday," Pamela said in a small voice. "His car wasn't there last night, even late, and it wasn't there first thing this morning."

"Why come back on a Thursday?" Bettina said, twitching one black linen-clad shoulder in a shrug. "He probably just decided to stay away through the weekend. He'll probably drive back on Sunday."

"Yes," Pamela said, looking down at her hands, which for some reason were twisting nervously. "I was thinking that too. He probably will."

Bettina consulted her watch, a pretty gold bracelet with a delicate oval face. "We've got to run," she said.

"Maxie is delivering the Arborville grandchildren at two, and I can't chase them around the yard in this suit." Pamela reached for the door handle, but before she could slide out of the car, Bettina grabbed her hand. "I heard you talking to Craig Belknap in the kitchen and it sounded juicy. You have to tell me everything in the morning. I'll be over at nine."

Chapter Six

Inside the house, a few kittens scattered as Pamela stepped into the kitchen. One of them, the bold ginger female, made her way to the communal kitten-food bowl, now empty, and turned to give Pamela a meaningful look.

"I guess it *is* past lunchtime," Pamela said. She put several scoops of something its label described as "hearty chicken" in a fresh bowl and set the used bowl to soak in the sink, filled with hot water and a squirt of dish soap. The aroma of "hearty chicken" was evidently quite alluring, even intermingled with the aroma of "lavender spring" dish soap. Soon all six kittens were clustered around the large bowl, the three ginger females and the three black males, their wispy tails momentarily still as they focused on their meal. Catrina sat off to the side, guarding her brood as attentively as if the venue wasn't Pamela's unimpeachably secure kitchen but the chilly streets of Arborville where she had lived out the first few months of her life.

Upstairs, after Pamela had changed her clothes and checked her email, she consulted the Internet to learn that kittens could be ready for adoption as young as eight weeks, generally at twelve weeks or older. They were now a little over a month old. Perusing the bulletin board in front of the Co-Op a few days earlier had made it clear that Arborville was not lacking in kittens, free to good homes. But she resolved to embark on her quest to place her kittens very soon. It would be easier to line up commitments for adoptions while they were still too adorable to resist.

Pamela opened her eyes, and in the morning brightness the last fragments of a dream slipped away. She could remember no details of the plot, but a phrase remained lodged in her brain. *The police think it was an accident.* That was what Craig Belknap had said about Caralee's death. Why had her brain refused to let go of those words as the rest of the dream faded? It certainly wasn't a sentence that a copy editor would pounce on, not like the tortured locutions people writing about the expressive possibilities of macramé or postmodern quilt designs sometimes seized upon.

But—she rolled over onto her back and stared at the pale blankness of the ceiling—there was that word "think." A person could *think* something that wasn't true. She imagined the sentence being uttered with a dismissive laugh, not that Craig Belknap had uttered it that way. The police *think* it was an accident, meaning . . . it wasn't. Certainly he hadn't meant to announce his guilt—if he *was* guilty—but people sometimes gave away things they didn't mean to give away. Maybe the sadness was just an act. After all, he was an actor.

Bettina was coming at nine. There would be a lot to talk about.

Six hungry kittens prowled the kitchen, investigating corners, raising themselves on their hind legs and pawing the cupboard fronts as if they imagined they could scale forbidding walls to reach the heights from which they knew their food descended. Pamela stepped carefully among them, pausing as one of the ginger females identified her slippered foot as a perfect target for a practice lunge.

As Pamela stooped to deliver a fresh bowl of kitten food, Catrina made her languorous way down the hall from the bed in the laundry room, where she'd been enjoying a brief respite from her energetic brood. Pamela served her breakfast and was rewarded with the soft sweep of Catrina's sleek flank against her ankle.

Those chores taken care of, Pamela headed out to retrieve the newspaper. On the front walk, she glanced toward Richard Larkin's driveway, feeling a sudden pang at the absence of his car. But of course, why would it be there? Surely Bettina was right—he'd tacked a few extra days onto his volunteer stint and he'd be back Sunday night. Pamela would welcome him home, hand over the mail and newspapers she'd collected, and they'd resume their neighborly coexistence.

Back inside, she ground twice as many coffee beans as usual, scooped them into the filter nestled in the plastic cone atop her carafe, and set four cups of water boiling on the stove. And since Bettina liked a sweet treat with her coffee, she decided to make cinnamon toast when her friend arrived. In preparation, she took the jar of cinnamon from her spice rack, set it on the counter next to the sugar bowl, and added a fresh supply of butter to her cut-glass butter dish.

Most of the kittens had scattered after they finished their breakfast, but a few lingered in the kitchen. As the kettle began to hoot, they raised their tiny faces in surprise, then went back to a game that involved paw to paw combat.

Pamela was still in her robe and pajamas when Bettina arrived, already dressed for the day in crisp lime-green pants and a green-and-white-striped shirt that set off her vivid red hair. "I know I'm early," she said, as she stepped over the threshold, her green ballet flat narrowly missing a kitten, "but I'm dying to know what Craig Belknap had to say for himself yesterday. And before I forget, Wilfred is grilling ribs tonight. You'll come, I hope."

"Ribs? Of course," Pamela said. "And on the subject of food, coffee is just dripping, and I'm going to make cinnamon toast. Can I interest you in a slice?"

"Two?" Bettina said, twisting her face into a comically hopeful expression. Silver earrings set with large green stones dangled from her ears and she'd accented her hazel eyes with a hint of green shadow. Her voice grew serious as she followed Pamela into the kitchen. "I can't stop thinking about poor Margo," she said. "I know she saw her brother in Caralee, and she lost him long ago, and her marriage wasn't very happy. She doesn't get too much comfort from her own daughter, so now she's really—"

The coffee had finished dripping and the dark, spicy aroma was so inviting that without completing the thought Bettina hurried to the cupboard where Pamela kept her wedding china and reached down two cups and saucers. Pamela moved the cut-glass sugar bowl from the counter to the table, set the cut-glass cream pitcher next to it, and filled the pitcher with heavy cream from the refrigerator.

"Does Margo believe Caralee's death was an accident?" she asked after her first sip of coffee.

"She knows Caralee argued with Craig a lot," Bettina said. "But she doesn't know what about. Caralee wasn't the type to confide . . . in anyone."

"I could sense that," Pamela said. "She was a bit . . . reserved. I guess that's why she liked the acting—she could emote, but as another person."

"So what *did* Craig Belknap have to say for himself?" Bettina added a final dollop of cream to her cup, stirred the contents to an even shade of rich tan, and took a sip.

"He said, 'The police think it was an accident.'"

"Well?" Bettina looked puzzled. "They do."

"But," Pamela said, "that doesn't mean it *was* an accident. It only means the police think it was." Pamela had often lectured her daughter, Penny, on the importance of critical thinking. Now she hoped Bettina didn't feel she was being lectured.

Bettina nodded. "He could have said that almost as a kind of self-congratulation—meaning, I got away with it."

"Caralee thought somebody was rearranging that furniture on purpose," Pamela said. "We know that. And according to Beth Dalton, Craig went dashing out of Hyler's before his shift ended on Wednesday—and after an argument with Caralee."

Bettina nodded again. "So he rushes to the storage room, determined to get it right this time, and when Caralee arrives everything is in place, ready to topple over, and he's long gone."

"And he won't say where he was after he left Hyler's Wednesday evening." Pamela stood up and reached for the sugar bowl. "If we're going to have cinnamon toast, I should get busy," she said, and stepped over to the counter.

There she set out three slices of whole-grain bread on a small cookie sheet and spread them with plenty of butter. In a small bowl she mixed two tablespoons of sugar and a teaspoon of cinnamon. She sprinkled the fragrant mixture over the buttered bread and slid the cookie sheet into the oven on the very top shelf, the one right under the broiler.

"I wonder if he was in love with her," Bettina said as Pamela twisted the oven knob all the way to the broiler position. With a whoosh the broiler came on.

"I have to pay attention to this," Pamela said, "or we'll have burnt cinnamon toast." She reached for an oven mitt on the hook near the spice rack and slipped it over her hand.

"He got her that job," Bettina commented. "Maybe he thought she should show her appreciation by falling in love with him."

"In that argument I overheard on my front lawn, he said he couldn't help how he felt," Pamela said. "That could be a classic lover's plea." She stooped to look through the glass window in the oven door. The tantalizing smell of melting sugar, infused with cinnamon, was beginning to fill the kitchen. "Then," Pamela went on, "he begged her not to be so mean and said he was just asking her to listen. She told him not to ever mention whatever it was again, said goodnight, and told him he was pathetic. Then she stalked off."

"Wow!" Bettina shuddered and drew in her breath. Her earrings quivered. "That could be crushing."

"I liked him though. There just was something about him," Pamela said. "And he seemed so genuinely sad about her death." She opened the oven door and peeked inside, releasing a drift of warm, sugary air. "They're getting very close," she murmured as she straightened up. "But, back to the topic at hand, what we have to do is find out who has a key to that storage room and whether it's generally locked or unlocked. If nobody can get in there until right before the rehearsals start, when other cast members are already milling around in the auditorium, Craig Belknap wouldn't have been able to set up the collapsing pile of furniture no matter how early he left Hyler's." She bent down to peer through the window in the oven door again. "Let's go over to the church and see what we can find out."

"The church custodian might know something," Bettina said. "Wilfred chats with him sometimes— they both like old cars. His name is Ben and he was out there working when I crossed the street. But first things first!" She joined Pamela near the stove and bent toward the window in the oven door. "I'm sure they're ready."

Bettina watched as Pamela twisted the oven knob to OFF and transferred the cookie sheet from the oven to the stove top. She knew her way around Pamela's kitchen as well as Pamela did herself, so she opened a drawer, pulled out a spatula, and transferred the three slices of cinnamon toast to the cutting board that Pamela held out. The edges of the bread were just the right shade of golden brown and the topping and butter had fused to form a sugary crust speckled with cinnamon flecks.

Pamela sliced each piece in half, transferred the halves to a serving plate, and triumphantly placed it in the middle of the table. Bettina greeted the sight with a moan of pleasure and set about refilling the coffee cups. A pair of napkins completed preparations for the feast.

"It's perfect," Bettina exclaimed after sampling a slice. "I haven't had cinnamon toast for years."

"I make it for Penny sometimes," Pamela said. "She still asks for it when she's at home." She bit into her own slice, savoring the butter-infused toast and the slight crunch of the sugary crust. She followed the bite with a sip of coffee—Pamela preferred hers black, and its bitterness was all the more appealing for the contrast with the sweet treat.

"Will she be back before Thanksgiving?"

"I don't think so, and I do miss her. Early September to late November is a long stretch. Last year was even harder, since it was my first year having her away." Pamela took another bite.

"They do grow up." As if to comfort herself, Bettina reached for a second slice of cinnamon toast. "Speaking of which . . ." A high-pitched meow drew their attention. The bold ginger female had wandered in from the back hallway and was gazing at them, her dark eyes large in her tiny heart-shaped face.

"Catrina is a good mother. They'll be ready to adopt in a month," Pamela said. "There are two flyers on the Co-Op bulletin board right now offering kittens free to good homes and I'm going to have to get busy."

"We'll take them," Bettina said. "I offered when it . . . happened, and I meant it. It's the least we can do. Wilfred still feels terrible." She looked down and smiled as the kitten investigated her stylish green shoe.

Catrina had been adopted the previous November, a tiny shivering stray. Pamela had planned of course to do the responsible thing, but she had scarcely imagined mating would be on the little creature's mind for a very long while. Biology had taken its course, however, and the attractive ginger tom had come around in the spring. One day when Wilfred stood on the porch delivering a gift of heirloom tomatoes, Catrina had bolted out the front door and six kittens had been the result.

"What would you even do with them?" Pamela said. "And what about Woofus?"

"He's afraid of his own shadow," Bettina said with a laugh. "He won't be a problem."

"Well," Pamela said, "maybe one. But I can't let you take them all." She studied the ginger female. "Maybe I'll keep one." She smiled. "They *are* awfully cute."

"That's the thing," Bettina said. "Let them come out when Knit and Nibble meets here on Tuesday. I can just see Roland. He won't be able to resist." They both laughed at the thought of the buttoned-up corporate lawyer succumbing to the charms of a kitten.

Chapter Seven

When the last crumb of cinnamon toast had been eaten and the last drop of coffee drained from the cups, Pamela hurried upstairs to dress. She pulled on yesterday's jeans and studied the small collection of tops that her closet offered, wishing briefly that clothes held as much interest for her as they did for her fashionable friend. But she quickly decided on a chambray work shirt, slipping her arms into it and buttoning it up without a moment's further thought.

An alarmed squirrel bolted off the porch as they stepped out the front door, leaving behind a half-eaten nut. Squirrels had been busy in the yard too. Pamela's lawn was still the rich green of late summer, but dark pockmarks marred its surface, where busy paws had exposed the soil underneath.

"Wouldn't it make more sense for them to bury nuts under the bushes?" Bettina said. "It must be tough to dig through grass roots."

"It's difficult to know what they think," Pamela said, "but there's certainly plenty of food around for them this time of year." Indeed, acorns littered the ground, golden brown and some still wearing their tiny darker caps. The acorns crunched underfoot as she and Bettina made their way down the front walk.

Ben was hard at work, sweeping the slate path that led from the church steps to the sidewalk. Bettina greeted him with a cheerful "Hello."

He looked up with a start, collected himself, and replied, "Morning, ladies." He was a shaggy, bearded man dressed in dark-green pants and a matching shirt.

Pamela was racking her brain for a way to introduce the topic they'd come to inquire about, wishing she and Bettina had worked out a strategy before leaving her kitchen. She hated nosiness, and bringing up the recent tragedy by asking pointed questions about the storage room that had been its setting seemed the very definition of that trait. But as soon as Bettina started to speak, she realized that her own presence was scarcely necessary.

"You look busy," Bettina said, accompanying the comment with an encouraging smile. "Lots to do around here, I'll bet."

"You're right about that," Ben said, thrusting his shoulders back as if trying to work out a kink. "I gotta finish the cleanup out here, then go in and vacuum the church, put the hymn books where they're supposed to be, and scrub up the kitchen so it's nice for the fellowship ladies to make the coffee after the service tomorrow morning."

"Things are back to normal then? After the . . . accident."

"Normal as they ever get."

"Wilfred and I knew something was going on Wednesday night, of course, with all the police and the ambulance . . ." Bettina opened her eyes wide.

"Were you here? When it happened?" Her voice conveyed a mixture of awe and flattery.

"Nope," Ben said. "And I didn't have nothin' to tell the cops or that reporter lady from the *Register*. Wish I had, but I'm outta here by five every night."

"Somebody else must lock up then," Bettina said. "Nights when the Players rehearse or people use the meeting rooms. Or maybe it doesn't matter, except for the main doors that go out to the parking lot."

"They keep that storage room locked," Ben said, "the room where they keep all the scenery and junk."

"But that's where that young woman . . ." Bettina raised her fingers to her lips as if to silence herself.

"I unlock it." Ben pushed a few acorns off the path with the toe of his shoe. "I unlock it at five and then I go home. It locks again if you set the lock and pull it closed. So they can do whatever they want after I leave. The main doors are unlocked all day because people are coming and going. The last people out at night—the Players or whoever's using one of the meeting rooms are supposed to set the lock on those doors too."

He grasped the broom handle with both hands and swooshed a few dead leaves into a small pile. "The storage room's open now though," he said. "Rue Wadsworth's been here on and off, going through stuff to use for that show they're doing, *Tales from a City* or whatever it's called. And they dragged a lot of their junk out into the auditorium. Guess they don't want to take any more chances having it squash people."

"Quite the mess, isn't it? I can see that's what you're thinking." Rue Wadsworth began speaking as soon as Pamela and Bettina stepped through the door of the auditorium, a spacious room with a high, beamed ceiling and a well-waxed floor of blond wood. At the far end was the stage, its red-velvet curtain drawn closed.

Rue was holding a man's coat that looked like something George Washington would have worn, but she dropped it in her lap to wave toward the jumble of furniture and scenery piled at random around the room. Hangers crowded tightly together on a long clothes rack held colorful dresses, most with long, full skirts and elaborate sleeves. More clothing spilled out of an open trunk. Additional trunks and clothes racks were lined up along the wall.

In fact, it *was* quite a mess. Pamela marveled that the painted backdrops, chairs, tables, dressers, bedsteads, and even pots and pans—not to mention the clothes racks and the trunks—had all come out of the storage room. She wondered for a moment whether, with so much jammed into so little space, the collapse that killed Caralee might truly have been an accident. But no, there were Caralee's words to contradict that idea. She had said that after the first furniture collapse she and some of the other Players had made sure the piles of furniture were stable.

As Pamela ruminated, Rue had been talking, rambling on in her soft voice about costumes for the upcoming production. Bettina was listening attentively, or at least making a good show of it, and Pamela tuned back in to hear ". . . *Carousel*. We did it the season before last. Not the right era, of course, but at least the dresses are long." Rue tugged at the dress closest to her on the rack. "Not the right color either—I see the downtrodden masses mostly in gray, but what can you do? Limited budget, and Mr. W. gets such ambitious ideas. He's a dear man, though, and so talented . . . and anyway, where was I? Maybe I can dye them."

She picked up the coat lying in her lap and sighed. "Hopeless. Not the right collar at all. I'm going to have to make the noblemen's costumes from scratch . . . sewing and sewing. That's my life these days." She tossed the coat on the floor and leaned over to tug a garment loose from the tangled mass hanging over the rim of the open trunk. "What do you think?" She held up a shapeless blouse the color and texture of burlap. "Madame Defarge?" She squinted at the blouse. "The *new* Madame Defarge, of course. Such a pretty girl, much prettier than Caralee, and she'll be much better in the role. Not that Madame Defarge is supposed to be pretty . . . just *drab* . . . really, and this blouse could work." She stood up and reached toward one of the other clothes racks for a hanger. "I've never seen anybody as thrilled about anything as when Mr. W. told her she was the new Madame Defarge." Rue maneuvered the blouse onto the hanger and stepped back toward the clothes rack. "Blast, blast, blast," she muttered as she struggled to free up space for the blouse among the profusion of dresses.

The clothes racks seemed homemade creations, built from lengths of sturdy pipe like one would find in a plumbing supply shop. Perhaps the Players numbered a plumber among their members. In each rack, four long pieces of pipe formed a sturdy square. A short piece set crosswise at each of the lower corners formed the rack's base. The pipes were connected to

one another with fittings that also seemed to have
come from a plumbing supply shop, and wheels fastened to the ends of the short pieces of pipe made
the racks moveable.

At last Rue gave up and draped the blouse, hanger
and all, over the top of the rack. In the sudden silence, Pamela glanced at Bettina, willing her friend
to jump in with something—anything—that might
steer the conversation in some useful direction. But
Rue was off again. "I think I really will dye them," she
said. She reached for the dress at the end of the rack,
tugged its hanger off the crossbar, and held the dress
up. It was bright yellow, with a flouncy skirt, a narrow
bodice, and long tight sleeves with puffs at the shoulders.

"If it was dark gray . . ." Rue said. "And I'll perform surgery on the sleeves—get rid of those puffs
and then add a shawl in some dark color. Quite the
Tale of Two Cities look, wouldn't you say?" Pamela and
Bettina both murmured agreement. "So that solves
that problem," Rue went on, "but there's no rest for
the wicked."

Rue turned away and struggled briefly to fit the
dress back in among the others that crowded the
rack, before giving up and draping it next to the blouse
destined for Madame Defarge. "No rest for the wicked
indeed," she repeated, and Pamela and Bettina exchanged despairing looks. But then, without prompt-
ing, Rue segued into the very topic they were longing
to discuss.

"First day I've been able to get back to this," she
said. Her gesture, which began with a finger pointed
at the open trunk and then swept along the clothes
rack with the colorful dresses, suggested she meant
the costume project. "After . . . you know. Such a to-

do, the police and all. No thought of canceling the production for Mr. W. though. The show must go on. But Mr. W. insisted everything be cleared out of the storage room before anybody set foot in there again. So thoughtful. 'And I don't want *you* going in there, Mrs. W.'—that's what he said to me, dear man. But I don't know what will happen if the church wants to use the auditorium for something besides the Players before we get things organized."

"You were here during the day last Wednesday then? Before it happened?" Bettina cut in.

"No rest for the wicked," Rue said. "Going through those trunks." She pointed at the trunks lined up along the wall. "All this stuff was still in the storage room then, of course. And what a wasted afternoon— all modern clothes. Nothing usable at all. Then I went home, a little after six like I always do, to get dinner for Mr. W. Hamburgers it was. He's easy to cook for. His mind is on his art. But when we came back for rehearsal—and learned what had just happened. I can tell you, I shuddered when I realized I was in and out of that room all afternoon, with that pile of furniture just *waiting* . . . But don't I sound selfish! Poor Cara-lee, of course, that's the tragedy."

"Did you lock the storage room when you went home for dinner?" Pamela asked, though she already knew the answer.

"Oh, no. Can't do that." She tightened her lips and shook her head decisively. "We wouldn't get back in till Ben opened it the next day. No, the room was open, just waiting for Caralee to come and get the chairs out, like she always does." She paused, with a short intake of breath. "Like she always *did*, I should say."

"So somebody could have gone into the storage

room between the time you left and Caralee came . . ."
Pamela didn't mean to sound accusing, but she was
excited about what she and Bettina were learning.

Rue looked up, alarmed. Her huge eyes were open
so wide Pamela could see white around the irises,
making her seem almost cartoonlike, with her pointed
chin and pixyish hairstyle. "You don't think somebody did that on purpose, do you?" she said, jumping
to her feet. "Made sure the furniture would fall when
Caralee pulled out the chairs?" She seemed almost
comical in her blustering. "I can assure you—no one
in this group would ever do anything like that—we
all . . . we all . . . love each other."

The pretense of casual conversation had clearly
been abandoned. Might as well be hanged for a
sheep as for a lamb, Pamela said to herself. Then she
said, to Rue, "Caralee and Craig Belknap had a huge
argument the night before the . . . accident," struggling mightily to avoid giving ironic emphasis to the
final word.

"Oh, really?" Rue twisted her lips in a parody of a
smile. "Well, I wouldn't know because I have better
things to do with my time than eavesdrop." She went
on, "And anyway, the night the accident happened, I
was here till after six. I didn't see hide nor hair of
Craig Belknap, and why would he show up at all? We
weren't working on his scenes."

"We learned something," Pamela said as she and
Bettina headed down the church driveway toward
the sidewalk. Ben was still outside, trimming dead
branches out of the unruly shrubbery that bordered
the slate path. He waved and they waved back.

"It was useful," Bettina agreed. "I wonder what she thinks of us though."

"Nosy busybodies, probably. I hope she doesn't tell Craig Belknap about this conversation. It would only reinforce the impression he got when I was quizzing him at the reception."

"Do we still suspect him?" Bettina asked, pausing.

"He went tearing out of Hyler's well before his shift ended," Pamela said, grabbing the pinkie of her left hand with the thumb and forefinger of her right. She counted through the remaining fingers as she spoke. "He won't say where he was going. Rue went home a little after six, leaving the storage room unlocked. Caralee showed up a bit before seven, pulled out the chairs, and was crushed. Therefore"—she held up her thumb—"we have a brief window when *somebody*, maybe Craig, could have done whatever he wanted to do to make sure that pile of stuff would tumble over on top of Caralee."

"They weren't rehearsing his scenes that night," Bettina said.

"That doesn't mean he couldn't have been at the church earlier." Pamela shook her head sadly. "That would be why he went dashing out of Hyler's. Except why would he have to leave Hyler's so early? Beth said it was five. He couldn't do what he wanted to do while Rue was there, and she said she always goes home after six to cook. And arguing with somebody doesn't mean that you want to kill them. Especially if you're in love with them."

"True," Bettina agreed. "But why is he being so secretive about where he was Wednesday night?"

"I don't know."

Bettina's eyes strayed toward her own house. "Now

where is he going?" she said. Wilfred was climbing into his ancient Mercedes carrying Caralee's knitting project. She shrugged. "See you tonight at six?" She stepped toward the curb. "Wilfred wants to squeeze in at least one more barbecue before fall is really upon us. And I'm going up to the Co-Op right now to buy a quart of that good deli potato salad."

"I have corn!" Pamela said suddenly. "I bought it last Wednesday and haven't done anything with it yet. I'll bring that, and my own tomatoes. It's the tail end of the crop but I've still got a few. And what about dessert?"

"Brownies from the Co-Op. I'm glad you reminded me." And Bettina was off, a flash of lime green and stripes, hurrying across the street.

Pamela continued along the sidewalk to her own house, unable to help noticing that Richard Larkin's driveway was still empty. But Bettina was probably right. Richard must have decided to prolong his stay in Maine by a few days and come back in time to start the work week fresh on Monday morning—not that she cared, she insisted to herself. She climbed the steps to her porch, collected her mail from the box, and stepped inside.

In the entry, the bold ginger female was wrestling with one of her glossy black brothers as Catrina rested contentedly in a patch of sunlight that made the colors in the worn Persian carpet—a thrift store find—glow.

Saturday was a work day—not *Fiber Craft* work, unless a pressing deadline loomed, but laundry and housework. No rest for the wicked, Pamela murmured to herself, then laughed at the recollection of Rue Wadsworth's monologue. Upstairs, she opened her bedroom windows. As a fresh breeze rippled the white eyelet curtains, she stripped her bed and made it up again with lavender-scented sheets from the linen closet, lining up the vintage lace pillows against the brass headboard. She added the dirty sheets to the straw hamper in the hall, along with the towels from the bathroom, and carried the hamper down to the laundry room where she set a batch of whites to washing.

The afternoon passed quickly as she scrubbed the bathrooms, vacuumed, and finally dusted, upstairs and down. Dressers, shelves, cabinets, tables, and chairs needed attention, as well as the thrift store treasures and tag-sale collectibles that decorated so many surfaces. Midway through, she paused for a bite of lunch and fed Catrina and her brood. Then she transferred the first load of wash from washer to dryer and launched another, darks this time.

At last everything was clean, the wash folded and put away, and towels replaced in the bathrooms. It was almost time to cross the street for Bettina and Wilfred's barbecue, with the tomatoes and corn that would be her contribution. The ears of corn sat on her kitchen counter, still sheathed in their coarse green husks, with tufts of corn silk, now dried to a pale brown, emerging from the ends. Next to the corn were three tomatoes, glowing red, the size of fists and just about as curiously shaped, their irregularity and nose-tickling acidity marking them as homegrown.

Wilfred looked up from the grill he was tending, rising heat waves making him seem to shimmer. He wasn't cooking yet, just monitoring the progress of the charcoal fire, but he'd already tied his apron over his bib overalls.

"The boss is in the kitchen," he said as Pamela stepped onto the patio. She carried a canvas bag laden with the sweet corn and tomatoes.

"Where were you taking Caralee's knitting this morning?" Pamela asked, regarding him from across the grill. Caught up in the satisfying routines of house-cleaning and laundry, she'd forgotten until just now the curious sight of Wilfred climbing into his ancient Mercedes with the swath of lumpy gray wool draped over his arm.

"I wanted to show it to my cousin John. He was a radioman in the Navy." Wilfred rearranged a few pieces of smoldering charcoal with a poker.

"And now he's a knitting enthusiast?" Pamela recalled from an article in *Fiber Craft* that sailors, in the old days at least, had whiled away long days at sea plaiting rope into charming designs. But she couldn't imagine what interest Caralee's inept creation could hold for a sailor—or anyone, really.

"Morse code." Wilfred tapped the side of his forehead and gave her a smug smile. "I got to looking at that thing and all of a sudden I was seeing patterns: a bump and a smooth spot and three bumps and a hole, then a bump and a smooth spot and a bump and a hole, and like that."

"Why would Caralee—or anybody—use Morse code in a knitting project?" Pamela asked, aware that she was squinting and hoping her face wasn't telegraphing too much of the skepticism she felt.

"You got me," Wilfred said with a laugh, "but the first name John decoded was Anthony Wadsworth."

Chapter Eight

From the door that connected the kitchen with the patio came Bettina's voice. "Is he telling you about the knitting?" she called.

Pamela turned. "Anthony Wadsworth?"

"There are other names too—or at least other words." Bettina had changed from her morning outfit of lime-green pants and striped blouse into a flowing wide-legged jumpsuit patterned with huge blooms in shades of orange and gold. "Let's get busy shucking that corn," she added.

Wilfred spoke up from his position at the grill. "The coals are ready, dear wife," he said. "It's time to launch the ribs."

Inside, Pamela added the sweet corn and the tomatoes to the dinner ingredients arranged on Bettina's well-scrubbed pine table. They joined three racks of baby ribs waiting on a tray with a bowl of barbecue marinade—Wilfred's own recipe, Pamela knew—and a basting brush, as well as a bowl of Co-Op deli potato salad and a plate of brownies.

Pamela glanced around. "Where's Caralee's knit-

ting now?" she asked. "I'm longing to know what else
it says."

"And you shall, but no rest for the wicked"—Wilfred had entered the kitchen and now reached for
the tray of ribs—"the coals cannot wait." And he was
out the door. "No rest for the wicked," Bettina
mouthed, and laughed.

Wilfred had been gone barely a minute before the
sweet, spicy aroma of sizzling barbecue sauce began
to waft in from the patio. Bettina, meanwhile, had
picked up an ear of corn. She was tugging away the
layers of husk, exposing the creamy golden kernels
in their perfect rows.

"He was out all day," she said, "at John's and then
doing something for the historical society, and he
barely had time to stop at the farmers market in Newfield for the ribs. I don't know any more about what
message Caralee hid in that piece of knitting than
you do." Bettina deposited a handful of corn husks
on the counter and delicately picked a few bits of
corn silk from the freshly peeled ear. "He brought
back peaches too," she added. "It's still peach season
and there are some for you too, if you'll take them.
He got more than we can eat." A rustic pottery bowl
on the counter was heaped with peaches, and next to
it sat a shopping bag labeled "For Pamela."

"They're just ripe," Pamela said. "They smell so
sweet. I was going to make peach cobbler for Knit
and Nibble Tuesday. I'll use these." She reached for
an ear of corn and began peeling back the layers of
husk. Meanwhile Bettina had stepped over to the
sink and was filling a giant pot with water.

"This should be ready for the corn just about
when the ribs are done." She set the pot on the stove
and added a cover. The burner ignited with a whis-

pery whoosh, and she returned to the corn-husking project. When all six ears had been peeled and deployed on the counter next to the stove to wait for their water to boil, Bettina fingered one of the tomatoes. "These are beautiful," she said. "What shall we do with them?"

"Slice them and arrange them on one of your platters from the craft shop," Pamela said. "All they need is a little salt and some olive oil and pepper."

Bettina reached an oval platter in a pretty shade of sage green down from a cupboard and set it on the pine table next to the tomatoes. Next to it she placed a cruet of olive oil, a tall wooden pepper grinder, and a jar of sea salt. "Do you want to do the honors?" she asked, handing Pamela a knife and a cutting board.

Through the glass door that slid open to make Bettina's patio an extension of her kitchen they could see Wilfred, wreathed in smoke as he bent over the grill. He was dipping his basting brush in his bowl of marinade and applying it to the sizzling ribs with the delicate touch of an artist. Bettina slid the door aside and the cool September breeze brought with it the seductive aroma of fat and barbecue sauce meeting hot coals.

"How are they coming?" Bettina called.

"Getting close," Wilfred answered. "How's the corn?"

Pamela turned away from her tomato slicing to check the corn water. She lifted the cover. Small bubbles were beginning to rise from the depths of the pot. "A few more minutes," she reported. "Then we can put them in." She finished slicing the tomatoes and laid them out in three parallel rows on the oval platter, adding a tiny sprinkling of sea salt. She had read once that to bring out the essence of a tomato, one should salt it and let it sit for five minutes before doing anything else to it. Now she let the tomatoes rest while she carried the potato salad to the dining room.

Bettina's dining room table was set for three. Dinner plates in the same sage green as the tomato platter were centered on round placemats woven of raffia in shades of gold, russet, and brown. Carved wooden napkin rings held russet napkins. Sleek stainless steel flatware was tucked alongside the plates. Bettina had arranged chrysanthemums in a low bowl between her candleholders, which echoed the flatware with their muted silvery glow and modern lines.

Back in the kitchen, Pamela carefully dribbled olive oil over the tomatoes, then added several twists of pepper from the grinder, enjoying the contrast of the sage-green platter and the rich red of the tomatoes, with their speckles of coarse-ground pepper. Meanwhile Bettina was lowering the ears of corn one by one into the deep pot of boiling water.

"It's boiling again," she said after a minute or two. "Now cover back on and let them sit with the heat off." She looked around. "Butter!" she said suddenly. "We have to have butter on the table, and salt and pepper of course. And Wilfred put some beer in to chill this morning."

Wilfred had appeared in the doorway, carrying the three racks of ribs, now back on their tray and still sizzling from the grill. "I'll slice them apart in here—but quick, quick, quick so they don't get cold." Bettina fetched another platter from her cupboard as Pamela hurried to unwrap a stick of butter and set it on the butter dish that matched Bettina's sage-green dishes. She delivered butter and salt and pepper to the dining room, and returned to watch

Wilfred wielding Bettina's sharpest knife as he expertly sliced three racks of baby back ribs into a pile ready for eager fingers.

"We'll need extra napkins," Wilfred observed. "Eating ribs is messy work—not to mention the corn."

"You're right," Bettina said. "We'll have to dispense with formality." She opened a cupboard and pulled out a package of paper napkins. "Can you do the corn?" she added to Pamela. "There's another platter up there." She nodded toward the cupboard the other platters had come from.

After a bit of last-minute bustle, they were all seated at the dining room table with a tall glass of beer at each place. Wilfred served the ribs, glistening with ruddy barbecue sauce and speckled with black where the sauce had charred, and Bettina set an ear of corn on each plate. "Just to start," she said. "There's plenty more." The potato salad made its way around the table, but there was scarcely space left on the plates for more than a few spoonfuls. The tomatoes would have to wait.

They ate in silence for a few minutes. Then Wilfred deposited a rib bone on his plate and looked over at Pamela. "Did Rick call you?" he said, using Richard Larkin's nickname.

"What?" Startled, Pamela stared at him over the ear of corn she was about to bite into. Her heart thumped once. "Have you talked to him?" she blurted out, and then prayed neither Wilfred nor Bettina had sensed how eager she sounded.

"No," Wilfred said. "That's why I asked if you had. He was supposed to be coming back around this time. I wondered if he'd gotten in touch to say his plans had changed."

Bettina had been chewing. Now she swallowed

and joined the conversation. "Wilfred is going to build a dollhouse," she said. "For the children who come to the women's shelter with their mothers. Nell asked him to do it, and he's anxious to show Richard the plans he's drawn up."

"Well, I haven't heard anything from him," Pamela said, grateful that her heart had calmed down after that initial thump. "I don't know why he'd call *me* particularly . . . if he decided to come back later."

Bettina touched Wilfred's arm. "Richard probably just decided to stay up there through the weekend," she said. "He'll be back Monday and I'm sure he'll be very interested in your plans for the dollhouse."

They—mostly Wilfred and Bettina—chatted about town doings, and then Wilfred asked Pamela how Penny was getting on at college. Pamela answered distractedly, asking herself why she'd gotten so excited when he mentioned Richard. Crumpled paper napkins accumulated as the platter of ribs was transformed into three piles of bones, and ears of corn dripping with butter turned into denuded cobs. Wilfred collected the bones and cobs and carried them to the kitchen, making space on the plates for tomatoes and more potato salad.

"I am stuffed!" Bettina set down her fork and leaned back in her chair. "What do you say we wait a bit for brownies and coffee?"

"I vote yes," Pamela said, mirroring her friend's actions.

"So then"—Wilfred stood up—"how about a little decoding?"

Caralee's knitting project waited on the coffee table in the living room, a fuzzy gray sprawl. The three of them sat along the edge of the sofa, bending toward it. To Pamela the stitches still seemed a random assortment of knit, purl, and dropped stitches, with no clear pattern evident, but as she looked closer she realized that the holes weren't dropped stitches at all, but rather had been carefully worked, like tiny buttonholes.

Wilfred pointed to the spot near the bottom where, after a stretch of smooth stockinette stitch, chaos seemed to set in. "'A,'" he said, pointing to a spot where, after a hole, a purl was followed by a knit and then three purls in a row. "And then come 'n . . . t . . . h . . . o'"—he inched his finger along—"'n . . . y'—Anthony. And next we have 'W . . . a . . . d . . . s . . . worth.'" He flashed a triumphant smile and Bettina clapped her hands.

"And there are several more words." Pamela shook her head. "This is amazing, Wilfred."

"Hardly rocket surgery, dear ladies," Wilfred said. "Here's my handy code-breaker." From the pocket in the bib of his overalls he pulled a small card and placed it on the coffee table. In two parallel columns, it showed the alphabet and the Morse code symbol that represented each letter. "So," he said, "the way Caralee translated it into knitting, a single purl is a dot and three in a row are a dash. The knits separate the dots from the dashes and the holes mark off the separate letters."

Pamela focused on another row where the decision of whether to knit or purl seemed happenstance, forming strings of random bumps interspersed by holes. She consulted the card and read off "T . . . h . . . o . . . m . . ." Her finger hurried ahead and she cried out "Thomas!" A few seconds later, she added, "Swinton?" She wrinkled her nose. "Is that someone we've ever heard of?"

"I have!" Bettina clapped her hands again. "I inter-

viewed him for the *Advocate* last year—he's 'one of
Arborville's intellectual treasures.'" She laughed.
"Not my words—I never know what headlines they're
going to stick on top of my articles."

"Is he that writer?" Wilfred asked. "The one who
wrote that novel with the scenes set in the Mittendorf
House? A couple of the guys in the historical society
read it." The Mittendorf House dated from the Revolutionary Era. It had been owned by a Tory sympa-
thizer but was confiscated by Washington and
presented to one of his generals.

"I wonder what led Caralee to code his name into
Madame Defarge's knitting." Bettina shook her head
in puzzlement.

"Here's a familiar name," Wilfred said, running
his finger over another patch where purls and holes
interrupted a smooth stretch of knitting. "Kent Varnish. He's the president of Hands Across Arborville."

"I think Nell knows him," Bettina murmured.
"She knows all the do-gooder people in town."

"And it looks like there's one more, up here, right
before Caralee left off." Pamela pointed to a spot just
a few rows below where the swath of knitting dangled
from the needle. "Some name that starts with"—she
consulted the card—"'M.'"

Bettina leaned forward. "'Merrrrr . . . *ick*.' I'm
getting the hang of it. And it's Merrick Timmons,
I'm sure. How many people in Arborville are named
Merrick?"

"*None* that I know of," Pamela said with a laugh.
"You really do have your finger on the pulse of our
little town."

"The *Advocate*." Bettina winked. "I get around."
She settled back onto the comfortable sofa and

crossed her arms. "He moved here last year with his wife, Rachelle—a trophy wife, no question. She's half his age, if that. They bought that huge house up in the Palisades that went unsold for so long because nobody wanted the expense of the upkeep."

"*Well!*" Pamela leaned back too. "This is an interesting development. But why . . . ?"

Suddenly Bettina sat bolt upright. "It all has to do with *A Tale of Two Cities,* of course. Like Holly would say, *duh!* Madame Defarge uses her knitting to encode the names of aristocrats destined for execution."

Pamela laughed with delight. "Caralee was really trying to immerse herself in her role . . ."

Bettina finished the thought. "By imagining that the play's director was destined for the guillotine."

"Artistic differences?" Pamela shrugged. "But what about these other people. There must have been something about all of them that Caralee didn't like."

Bettina turned to Pamela, suddenly excited. "Could that be a reason for one of them to kill her? That she knew things about them?"

"Maybe," Pamela said.

"So maybe Craig Belknap isn't the killer." Bettina raised a shoulder and her lips shaped a half smile. "You do like him. And Sydney Carton is such a sympathetic character in *A Tale of Two Cities,* trading places with his friend to save him from the guillotine. And why would Craig leave Hyler's at five if Rue usually hung around the auditorium till after six? He couldn't do anything to the furniture till she wasn't there to see what he was up to and it's only a few blocks from Hyler's to the church." The smile be-

came broader and she added, "This calls for brownies."

Wilfred jumped up. "At your service, dear wife.
And who wants coffee?"

An hour later, the three of them stepped out onto
the porch. Pamela carried a bag of peaches. A huge
golden moon hung over her house.

"Harvest moon," Wilfred sighed contentedly.
"And fall is in the air."

"I'll call Margo first thing tomorrow," Bettina said.
"We know what the connection between Caralee and
Anthony Wadsworth was, but maybe Margo knows
what was going on with Swinton, Varnish, and Timmons."

Back at home, Pamela set the peaches—already
making the kitchen fragrant with their fruity sweetness—on the kitchen counter. No cats, large or
small, were in sight. She tiptoed down the hallway
and peeked in the laundry room door. In the dim
light that reached from the kitchen, she could see
the six kittens lined up along their mother's side,
hungrily nursing.

Chapter Nine

"I wore my walking shoes," Bettina announced as Pamela swung the door back. "I knew you'd insist on walking." Bettina was standing on the porch, her navy polka-dot shirtdress accessorized with a pair of festive red sneakers. Behind her, the sidewalk was crowded with Sunday morning churchgoers hurrying through the bright September morning.

"I'm always up for a walk," Pamela answered. "But where are we walking to?"

Bettina started to step through the door but lingered on the porch and turned away to scan Richard Larkin's driveway. "Not back yet, I see," she commented as Pamela stood back to let her enter.

"You said he wouldn't be back till tomorrow," Pamela said. She'd been pleased that she herself had avoided checking his driveway as she retrieved the *Register* a few hours earlier, and worked now to banish the thought of him from her mind.

"I called Margo this morning." Bettina veered off course to avoid a kitten. "I asked her what Caralee's connection with Swinton, Varnish, and Timmons might be, and she didn't have a clue. Caralee was very private."

They had reached the kitchen. Sections of the *Register* were still spread out on the table, but toast crumbs and an empty coffee cup showed that breakfast was over. "Do you want some coffee?" Pamela asked. "I can make more."

"Let's wait till later." Bettina raised both hands as if to fend off the idea of coffee—at least right away. "We might have things to talk about. We're going to visit Beth Dalton."

"Caralee's childhood friend?"

Bettina nodded. "Margo said they'd renewed their friendship when Caralee moved back to Arborville— and if Caralee told her secrets to anybody, it would be to somebody she'd known since first grade."

The walk to Beth Dalton's took them along County Road, past the nature preserve that separated Arborville from the next town to the west. The trees were still lush with summer foliage, no red or yellow leaves yet to hint that soon there would be no leaves at all. They continued past the intersection where County Road met the street that led up to the library and the police station, and a few blocks later they reached the small complex of garden apartments where Beth Dalton lived.

One-story brick buildings formed a U-shape around a patch of bright green lawn, which in turn surrounded a bed of marigolds and chrysanthemums in vivid shades of gold and maroon. A wreath twisted from hobby store vines and berries adorned Beth's door, which opened before Bettina had even removed her finger from the bell.

"I was expecting you," Beth said. Were the words a greeting or a warning? At first Pamela wasn't sure. Beth's face hadn't been designed to look serious. Framed by short, bouncy curls, it was round, with chubby cheeks and a wide mouth. But she wasn't smiling, and her eyes were dull. "Margo told me you were coming," she added.

Bettina produced a sympathetic smile. "If you don't feel like talking . . ." she began, and Pamela held her breath. Who else might be able to explain the names Caralee had coded into the piece of knitting?

"I'll talk." Beth pulled the door open and Pamela exhaled. Seated on a pretty velvet love seat, with Beth facing them in a matching armchair, they listened as she described her long friendship with Caralee.

"She did the things I wasn't brave enough to do," Beth said. "Going away to college while I lived at home and went to Wendelstaff, moving to the city and becoming an actress—and here I am teaching English at Arborville High. And getting married, to an actor—" She had grown excited as she talked, as if just listing Caralee's adventures was a thrill. Now her voice dropped. "And then divorced. That was sad. But I don't think *he* killed her."

Pamela and Bettina looked at each other. This was a possibility they hadn't discussed.

"Somebody was after her though." Beth frowned and shook her head, setting her curls bouncing. "Somebody made sure that pile of stuff in the storage room was unbalanced enough that when she pulled out a chair it all came down." Beth leaned forward. "It had happened before, you see. Twice before. Then the third time was . . ."

Pamela nodded. "She told me about the other

times too—and the first time was a close call. She fell and hit her head, and she got that awful bruise on her arm."

"But what can anybody do?" Beth asked plaintively. "The police just think it was an accident."

"Bettina is a reporter," Pamela said. (Maybe it wasn't necessary to specify that the paper Bettina reported for was the weekly throwaway.) "She works closely with the police." Beth looked impressed. "Bettina has been known to drop a word here and there, when there's a crime—point out details they might have overlooked."

Bettina nodded enthusiastically. "In fact," she said, holding up her index finger and crossing her middle finger over it, "Detective Clayborn and I are like this."

"Caralee could have had enemies," Beth said. "Margo told me about the names coded into that piece of knitting. Clever, and typical of her—so serious about her acting, getting into character by doing just what Madame Defarge does."

"And picturing their heads falling into a basket as the guillotine comes down." Bettina shuddered. "But why those names?"

"I don't know," Beth said, "except Wadsworth is the Arborville Players guy, of course. Maybe she thought he was a bad director. But Swinton, Varnish, and Timmons?" She shrugged. "Swinton is that writer. Varnish volunteers for everything in town. I've never heard of Timmons—but she hated people who were fake, not what they pretended to be. She hadn't said anything about those four people on her blog though."

"Her blog?" Pamela had been lounging against

the love seat back. Now she felt her back stiffen. "She had a blog?"

Beth suppressed the beginnings of a smile. "You'll find it if you search for 'Back in the Burbs . . . and Remembering Why I Left.' She started it when she moved back to Arborville."

"She had a blog," Bettina commented as she and Pamela set out along County Road.

"But she didn't talk about any of those four people specifically on the blog," Pamela said musingly. "I can't wait to take a look at it though. You don't have to be anywhere in the next hour or so, do you?"

Pamela and Bettina paused for a red light at the big intersection. Long ago, County Road had been little more than a dirt trail used by stagecoaches, people on horseback, and carts. An inn built of pink sandstone had served the needs of travelers at that intersection. Now it was a restaurant well known to gourmets from neighboring towns and featuring its own kitchen garden.

"No plans at all," Bettina said. "We'll make some fresh coffee and look at 'Back in the Burbs.'"

"'And Remembering Why I Left,'" Pamela supplied. She herself had lived in Manhattan early in her marriage, but she'd never felt that Arborville was an alien place. She and her husband had loved restoring their old house and putting down roots. Now, with him gone, she still felt his presence when she walked in the front door.

"Caralee might not have talked about those men on the blog *yet*," Bettina said, "but she could have scolded them in person."

"And hinted that they might soon see their ugliest secrets revealed to all and sundry on 'Back in the Burbs,'" Pamela added. "We know she had no trouble speaking her mind."

Bettina laughed. "She sure let Roland know what she thought of lawyers."

"So let's suppose she knew something about Anthony Wadsworth . . . something that would have ruined his career . . . or his image—if it came out." A landscaper's truck rumbled by and Pamela raised her voice.

"He certainly had access to the storage room," Bettina agreed, raising her voice as well.

"But only when it was unlocked," Pamela said, "and he wouldn't have been able to rearrange things after Tuesday's rehearsal without calling attention to himself. The rearranging—whoever did it—had to happen Wednesday."

"The storage room was open all Wednesday afternoon because Rue was working on the costumes—"

Pamela interrupted. "Wouldn't she have noticed though? And asked him what he was doing? And then told the police after it turned out that Caralee had been killed?"

"She's his biggest fan," Bettina said. "Apparently those Christmas letters she sends are one long celebration of Anthony Wadsworth. And besides, any woman would want to protect her husband. I certainly would."

Pamela smiled at the notion of Wilfred as a criminal, then she furrowed her brow. "Whatever Caralee knew about Anthony Wadsworth would have had to be terrible for him to be that desperate to silence her—and to kill her like that, especially. The publicity from this incident certainly can't be good for the Arborville Players."

Catrina had taken refuge upstairs from the demands of her brood. She was lounging on Pamela's computer keyboard and looked up lazily as Pamela and Bettina entered the room.

"Down you go," Pamela said as she gently transferred Catrina to the floor. Bettina pulled an extra chair up to Pamela's desk, welcomed Catrina onto her lap, and gave her a welcome head scratch as Pamela summoned her computer to life.

Soon they were contemplating photographs of their own pleasant suburb—except the photographs had been selected and manipulated to rob it of its pleasantness. Not only had the scenes been chosen to support the idea that a person of culture and intelligence would not want to live in Arborville, but the photographs themselves had been drained of color and subtly distorted to create the effect of a reflection in a funhouse mirror.

The first blog entry was dated July 15—not long after Caralee had left her husband and her life in Manhattan and moved in with her aunt. A few words explained her change of residence, and a photograph showed a stretch of Arborville Avenue, including the façade of the Co-Op Grocery. But in the foreground of the shot was a Co-Op customer, a chubby woman in a pair of unflattering shorts. From a shopping cart heaped high with Co-Op bags, she was loading groceries into the back of a giant SUV.

"Oh, dear," Bettina sighed. "I think that's Marlene Pepper, though it's hard to tell with whatever Caralee did to make everything look so *ugly*." She sighed again. "It's true that people buy more food than they should be eating and drive cars that are bigger than they need to be . . . but we all have our faults. And Marlene Pepper is really a very nice person." She studied the image and added, "I would never wear those shorts."

"Caralee could be mean," Pamela said, "but we knew that." She scrolled down to the next entry, dated July 31. The text simply read "No comment needed." Below the text was a photograph.

"That looks like St. Willibrod's parking lot," Bettina said, leaning forward. "I never realized so many of St. Willibrod's parishioners drove luxury cars." Caralee had angled the shot to capture a row of cars that included two Audis, three BMWs, a Mercedes, and a Lexus, as well as the week's sermon topic. The marquee that occupied a neighboring patch of grass read BLESSED ARE THE POOR.

A subsequent post included a photo that captured a group of students loitering in front of Arborville High. All were transfixed by their mobile devices except for the girl who was putting on lipstick. A sign read WELCOME BACK, SCHOLARS!

As the next entry scrolled into place on the screen, Bettina asked, "Did she post this one after she met Roland?" Caralee had photographed one of the oversize houses in the development Arborvillians still referred to as "The Farm." Twenty years earlier the Van Ripers had sold their ancestral farmland to a developer. The developer had divided it into lots and erected houses more noteworthy for their square footage than their aesthetic appeal. Roland DeCamp and his wife, Melanie, had bought a house there when they moved to Arborville.

"I *do* like my hundred-year-old house better," Pamela said. "Not everybody who lives in Arborville has bad taste."

Bettina shrugged. "She was looking for things to disapprove of. So what did she disapprove of about those four men?"

"There's one more," Pamela said. "September seventh—just a week before Caralee was killed." She scrolled down. There was no picture this time, just a few words: "All that glitters is not really an intellectual treasure. Stay tuned for details."

Pamela heard a sharp intake of breath. "Thomas Swinton," Bettina said. " 'One of Arborville's Intellectual Treasures.' That was the headline the *Advocate* used for my interview with him last year."

"She won't be supplying any details now." Pamela clicked to close the blog. "But I wonder what she was going to say. And did he kill her to keep her from saying it?"

"I'll interview him again," Bettina said. "It shouldn't be too hard to find out if he knew Caralee—and where he was last Wednesday night between six and seven. The last time I interviewed him he seemed more interested in talking about himself than about the book. And he's so vain I'm sure he'll be happy to do a repeat."

"What's his book like?"

"Weird." Bettina stood up. "Some of the characters have been alive for centuries. I didn't read the whole thing, but I've got it at home. Come on over and I'll dig it out."

Catrina had wandered away when Bettina became more interested in studying the computer screen than in scratching her head. But as they stepped into the hall she met them. She twined her lithe body around Pamela's ankle, then looked up and showed her teeth as a demanding meow escaped from her throat.

"Six children to feed, and they're getting bigger by the day," Pamela said. "No wonder she's hungry."

"My offer still stands—when they're ready to be adopted." Bettina smiled down at the cat. "It's been a long time since we've had a little furry thing at home."

"We-e-ell." Pamela drew the word out. "Maybe one, if you think Woofus could deal with it. But I can't let you adopt all six, even if Wilfred *does* feel responsible for their very existence."

"Six kittens *would* be a handful, and then they'd grow up and we'd have six cats," Bettina said thoughtfully. "But how about my other idea? Bring them out when Knit and Nibble comes on Tuesday. Very few people can resist a kitten."

"We can ask them about the mystery men too," Pamela said. "Maybe somebody in Knit and Nibble knows more about Thomas Swinton and the rest than we do."

"I doubt if Holly or Karen would be helpful," Bettina said, "and Nell is definitely not a gossip. Roland is in his own world. But no harm in trying."

Pamela studied the book's dust jacket. Superimposed over an indistinct image that suggested urban ruin, gigantic letters announced the title: *Time and Time Again*, and letters even more gigantic identified the author: Thomas Swinton. Smaller letters revealed that the book was "a sprawling novel set in a dystopian New Jersey."

"It starts in the future," Bettina said. "Then it goes back to when the Lenni Lenape lived here, before the Europeans came. A big part takes place during the Revolutionary War. That's as far as I got, but people keep being reborn."

They were standing in the cozy den Bettina had created for Wilfred from the bedroom that had been their oldest son's. Bookshelves filled one wall, and an antique oak desk and a comfy armchair with a matching footstool completed the furnishings. Old maps in frames that echoed their age hung here and there, with ornate script spelling out place names bestowed when New Jersey was still an English colony.

"Wilfred mentioned that some scenes take place in the Mittendorf House." Pamela opened to a spot about halfway through and found herself looking at page 276. Thomas Swinton had written a very long book.

"I'll call Swinton tomorrow morning and ask for another interview," Bettina said.

"Give me a few days to read this." Pamela leafed a bit farther on and skimmed a paragraph. A character was heading off to the Civil War. "My knitting will have to take a back seat for a while,"

"Does it look that good?" Bettina seemed surprised.

"I don't know yet," Pamela said. "But I'm coming with you when you talk to him again. You can say I'm a huge fan."

A delicious smell was drifting up the stairs. Then Wilfred entered the room, an apron tied over his bib overalls. "I found some of my homemade chili in the freezer," he announced. "Who's ready for lunch?" He glanced at the copy of *Time and Time Again*, which Pamela still held open in her hands. "Are you going to read that?"

"I'm thinking of it. Did you?"

Wilfred wrinkled his nose. "Some of the guys at the historical society said the Revolutionary War parts were very convincing, but the time travel thing put me off. I'd rather read real history anyway. He who does not study the past is condemned to repeat it."

They proceeded down the stairs. Woofus looked up in alarm when he saw Pamela and retreated from his perch on the sofa to take refuge behind it.

"Poor dog," Bettina said. "He has flashbacks to the days before he was rescued by the shelter."

In the kitchen, Pamela and Bettina took seats at the pine table, which Wilfred had set with three deep bowls from Bettina's set of craft-shop pottery. A basket of sliced sourdough bread from the Co-Op bakery waited in the middle of the table, along with a wooden cutting board that held a wedge of the well-aged Stilton that was Bettina's favorite.

Wilfred served the chili, basking in the compliments that followed the first few spoonfuls. They ate in silence for a bit, then chatted about this and that until Bettina looked at her watch and discovered she was due for babysitting duty with the Arborville grandchildren in five minutes.

"I'll let you know the details for our meeting with Swinton," she called to Pamela as she hurried out the door.

Pamela helped Wilfred with cleanup and then went back to her own house, Thomas Swinton's heavy book tucked under her arm.

Chapter Ten

Richard Larkin's car had not magically appeared in his driveway overnight. No car was in evidence when Pamela went out to fetch the *Register*, and it was only seven a.m. If he was back in Arborville, he wouldn't have left for work yet. In fact, Pamela had awakened even earlier than usual—despite having stayed up till nearly midnight reading *Time and Time Again*. The sun had made the curtains at her bedroom windows glow and she'd opened her eyes and that had been the end of sleep. But she was positive that waking up early had nothing to do with Richard Larkin's possible return.

Bettina had been sure he'd decided to stay away just a bit longer—through the weekend. But—*through the weekend*. The thought struck Pamela with such relief that she set down her coffee cup and closed her eyes to reflect on it. Maine was eight hours away, even more. If a person wanted to prolong their stay in Maine *through the weekend* they'd wait till Monday to drive back. That was certainly what he'd decided to do. Not that she cared, she assured herself as she opened her eyes and resumed drinking her coffee.

The kittens were clustered around their bowl in the corner, nibbling eagerly at a few tablespoonfuls of chicken-fish blend. Catrina had wandered off, perhaps to look for the patch of sun that appeared reliably on the entry carpet every morning.

Pamela finished her coffee and rinsed the cup at the sink. Upstairs, she traded her robe and pajamas for jeans and her chambray shirt, stepped across the hall to her office, and awakened her computer. After the customary beeps and whirrs that constituted its morning greeting, it set to work receiving its first email of the day—an email so slow to arrive that Pamela knew it could only be from her boss at *Fiber Craft*. Indeed, her premonition proved to be correct. Stylized paper clips spaced across the top of the message signaled the presence of three attachments, identified as "Lapland," "Surrealism," and "Raffia." The message itself summoned Pamela to an editorial meeting at the magazine's offices in Manhattan, to take place at the end of the month, and requested that she edit the attached articles and return them by six p.m. the next day.

A message from Pamela's alma mater announced that the current president was stepping down, after seventeen years of service, to devote herself to volunteer work in Honduras. Three other messages were quickly labeled junk and dispatched. Finally, smiling, Pamela opened a message from Penny reporting on her doings over the weekend: She'd discovered a thrift shop with fabulous vintage clothing within walking distance of the campus, and her dorm had sponsored a food drive for the town's food pantry.

Pamela returned to the message from her boss,

opened the first attachment, and set to work editing "The Vertical Looms of Lapland's Sami Culture." She was immersed in the world of the Sami people and their ingenious weaving techniques when the door-bell chimed. For a moment the sound didn't regis-ter—she was staring at a picture of a loom constructed of thick twigs lashed together with leather thongs. Then she remembered Bettina had promised to call Thomas Swinton that morning. Undoubtedly it was her, with something to report, and it was time for a break besides. Pamela commanded the computer to save her work and headed down the stairs.

Through the lace that curtained the oval window in the front door, Pamela could see Bettina's figure, dressed in a brilliant fuchsia that stood out against the greenery beyond. Bettina started to talk as soon as Pamela opened the door, and by the time she stepped over the threshold she'd reached the last words of her first sentence: "Richard Larkin." What-ever led up to those words had been indistinct.

"He's back?" Pamela felt her brows rise and her eyes grow wide.

"No." Bettina reached out to grasp her friend's hand. "I said, 'I guess it's going to be a bit longer be-fore we see Richard Larkin.' "

"Well . . . it's not . . . important." Pamela detached her hand from Bettina's and motioned as if to push away whatever conclusion Bettina might draw about her initial excitement. Then she reflected for a minute. "Did he call you?"

"No—but I haven't seen his car this morning."

"He could come tonight," Pamela said. "Maybe he wanted to stay through the whole weekend. Maine is probably really pretty this time of year."

"You've been thinking about him, haven't you?" Bettina tilted her head to study Pamela's face.

"I haven't," Pamela said firmly. "It's just—" She searched for words, then pointed to the cardboard box under the mail table, the box in which she had been collecting mail that strayed into Richard Larkin's mailbox and newspapers that strayed onto his driveway. "I want to get rid of that. What have you brought?" she added quickly before Bettina could pursue the Richard Larkin topic.

"Goodies from the Co-Op bakery counter, of course." Bettina put the white bakery box into Pamela's waiting hands. White string circled it and formed a bow on top. "What would you say to a chocolate croissant?"

Pamela laughed. "Definitely not 'no.' I've been editing all morning—vertical looms in Lapland— and I'm ready for a break."

"I've been busy too," Bettina said as she followed Pamela to the kitchen. Her fuchsia outfit had proved to be a close-fitting linen skirt and a matching jacket styled like a short kimono. The effect of the fuchsia with her bright red hair, which she herself described as a color not found in nature, was striking. "The mayor gave a talk on civic responsibility at the middle school this morning," she said. "Something more cheerful to write about for the *Advocate* than the sad Caralee business. And speaking of that," she continued as Pamela began spooning coffee beans into her coffee grinder, "Thomas Swinton is thrilled that I want to interview him again, and he can't wait to meet you—his biggest fan, as I described you. We're invited for lunch this Saturday."

Bettina set two dessert plates from Pamela's wedding china on the table. Untying the string on the bakery box and folding back the cover, she placed a chocolate croissant on each plate. Layers of flaky crust formed the pastries, like small pillows glazed golden brown. At each end a dark knob of chocolate marked where the filling had oozed and then congealed.

At the counter Pamela was busy with coffee preparations. She set the kettle boiling on the stove and slipped a filter into the plastic cone atop the carafe. Bettina sidled up next to her to fetch two forks from the silverware drawer. "You could call Laine or Sybil," Bettina began, but the sharp growl of the coffee grinder cut her off. Pamela lifted the grinder's cover to check on the state of the beans. Bettina tried again. "His daughters, I mean. They've been in touch with him, I'm sure."

"I know what you mean," Pamela said, and pushed down on the grinder's cover. The half-ground beans clattered and churned in the grinding chamber. She stole a glance at Bettina, who looked perturbed. "I just . . ." Pamela removed the grinder's cover and poured the beans, now finely ground, into the filter. "I don't . . ." From the stove, the kettle whistled. Glad of the distraction, Pamela completed the coffee-making process without another word.

"It wouldn't be like you were chasing him," Bettina said after they were settled at the table, coffee cups filled and Pamela's cut-glass cream pitcher and sugar bowl at the ready. "He's definitely interested."

"He may be." Pamela took a sip of coffee. "And he's very nice. And I agree with you that he's good-looking. But I like my life the way it is."

"It won't always be the way it is," Bettina said. "Penny is growing up. She'll graduate. She'll get a job and move into her own place. She'll meet someone."

Pamela stared into her coffee cup. "I wouldn't mind being married," she said, "like you and Wilfred, or Nell and Harold. Old. And comfortable together."

"Old?" Bettina said, pretending to be horrified. "I'll have you to know that I'm Wilfred's child bride. I was twenty-five and he was forty when we were married."

"You know what I mean though." Pamela studied Bettina's face, as if searching to see whether her friend really did know. "It's the getting to know each other, the settling in. I don't want to go through that again." She returned to contemplating her coffee. "I do find him attractive," she said. "I'm trying not to." She picked up her fork and probed the croissant, teasing off a morsel of pastry garnished with a dab of chocolate.

Half an hour later, the carafe was empty and all that remained on the dessert plates was a scattering of pastry crumbs and a few chocolaty smears. Thanks were exchanged, for the coffee and for the croissants, and Bettina went on her way. Pamela saw her to the door, then returned to the kitchen. She lifted one of the peaches, heavy in her hand, from the bowl where she'd placed them. It was pale gold in spots, rosy in others, its soft fuzz making it seem to glow. Its aroma was like a fruity perfume and its surface yielded just enough under her thumb to tell her that tomorrow's cobbler would be perfect. Upstairs, she returned to the article about the vertical looms of Lapland, then moved on to "The Influence of Surrealism on Modernist Textile Design."

Lunchtime came and went, and it wasn't until three p.m. that she realized she was hungry. The chocolate croissant hadn't been a nourishing meal, or a healthful one, but it had been quite filling. She'd edited all

three articles and returned them to her boss, so after
a quick bite of toasted whole-grain bread and some
of the Co-Op Gouda, she decided to take a walk. The
September day deserved to be enjoyed. Then she'd
spend the rest of the afternoon with *Time and Time
Again.* She'd been asking herself what Caralee could
have ferreted out that a best-selling author and Arborville's intellectual treasure could be desperate to
keep hidden. But she hadn't thought of anything yet.

That night an insistent sound, high-pitched but
gentle, roused Pamela from a dream in which she
was exploring the Mittendorf House. Reluctantly,
she abandoned the adventure just as she reached the
Mittendorf House kitchen, with its huge stone fireplace and bundles of dried herbs hanging from the
rafters. A glance at the glowing numerals on her bedside clock told her it was barely eleven-thirty. Her
dreaming mind had packed quite an adventure into
the half hour since she came up to bed.

The sound seemed to be coming from outside her
bedroom door. It wasn't the type of sound to cause
alarm, but it *was* insistent—and growing louder. She
sat up, casting off the last remnants of the dream.
The moon, which had been full just a few days ago,
was still bright enough that the familiar landscape of
her room was recognizable in pale shapes and shadowy outlines, and the sound resolved itself into one
she was familiar with. She stepped to the door and
eased it toward her. Through the six-inch opening
slipped a streak of black. It brushed past her bare
ankle like the flick of a soft wool scarf.

"Catrina?" she murmured as the cat—it *was* Catrina—scaled the few feet from floor to mattress top

with the aid of her claws and settled right where Pamela's back had previously reposed, a dark spot against sheets that the moonlight had turned silvery. "What about your babies?" Pamela added.

Catrina seemed unconcerned. She didn't complain as Pamela moved her aside to take up her own rightful place in the bed, but she snuggled against Pamela's side as soon as Pamela climbed in beside her and pulled the covers up.

In the morning, the kittens greeted their mother matter-of-factly, none the worse for their first night spent on their own. But they were obviously eager to nurse. They followed Catrina back to the bed in the laundry room as Pamela headed out to retrieve the *Register*—and insist to herself that it made no difference to her that Richard Larkin's car had not appeared overnight.

The kittens emerged sometime later, as Pamela was drinking her coffee, to investigate the contents of their food bowl. "Perhaps you're getting ready to be adopted," Pamela said to them as they jockeyed for position around the bowl's rim. Bettina's idea had been a good one. Knit and Nibble would be right there in Pamela's house that evening. What better advertisement for free kittens than to see them at play, stalking one another and tussling, playing with their ball of yarn, trying so hard to be fearsome, succeeding only in looking cute? And then to pick one up and hear its tiny purr as it squirmed this way and that to maximize a good rub.

She'd keep them a bit longer, until they weren't nursing anymore. But if she could line up some commitments . . . Holly might be a good prospect, and maybe Karen Dowling if she wasn't worried about a new cat and a new baby arriving at once. But Dave Dowling was allergic to wool, Pamela recalled. Would he also be allergic to cats? Nell might succumb to the kittens' charms. Nell had had cats, Pamela knew, cats that had grown old and died. Perhaps she'd like to start over, with a new cat. Roland was hopeless— Pamela laughed even to think of the staid corporate lawyer being seduced by a kitten. He'd probably be horrified at the thought of cat hair on his pinstripe suit. But Bettina would take one.

And Pamela would take one. She'd already decided which—the bold ginger female. The kitten hadn't inherited her mother's looks, but certainly the will to survive that had sustained Catrina in the months she'd lived on the streets had been passed on to this particular daughter.

A cobbler wasn't a pie. A pie, or its crust at any rate, required artful sifting, measuring, and kneading. Then the crust had to be carefully rolled out to a circle a bit larger than the pan that was to contain it, fitted delicately into the pan without tearing, and the edges precisely crimped. Making a pie was like following a complicated knitting pattern, perhaps a pattern for a delicate sweater in a lace or openwork stitch. Making a cobbler was like making a big slouchy shawl, with rustic yarn so forgiving that a dropped stitch here or there made no difference.

Pamela was a good pie maker, and she enjoyed the challenge. But when the weather began to suggest that fall wasn't far away, a cobbler still warm from the oven was the ultimate comfort food. Now she stood in her kitchen consulting her standard cobbler recipe, a yellowed newspaper clipping stapled to a large index card. The baking dish she'd use waited on the kitchen table, already buttered—a humble Pyrex rectangle that she'd had since the early days of her marriage.

The peaches Wilfred had brought back from the Newfield farmers market waited in their bowl. Four cups of fruit the recipe called for. The peaches would provide that much and more—so she'd use more. Cobblers were very forgiving. She picked up a peach and her favorite paring knife, ran the knife around the peach to make two matching halves, and picked out the dark, rough-textured pit. Already her hands were sticky with peach juice.

She cut each half into two quarters and peeled the first quarter, pulling the delicate fuzzy skin loose in one long strip. Then she sliced the quarter into a waiting bowl, bite-sized pieces. The peach flesh was a rich gold, much deeper than the color of the skin, and glistening with sweetness. This stage of cobbler-making, preparing the fruit, could be laborious—unless one started with blueberries. But the peaches peeled and sliced easily, and as she repeated the rhythmic motions again and again, Pamela felt herself slipping into the trance-like state that accompanied knitting—but with sticky fingers.

When the last peach had been turned into slices, Pamela scooped the contents of the bowl into the Pyrex baking dish. The peaches were already sweet, very sweet, but Pamela sprinkled a heaping table-spoon of sugar over them. And because a secret ingredient was always fun, she opened the cupboard above the stove where she kept things that came in tall bottles, like Worcestershire sauce and vinegar. Way at the back she found what she was looking for—a tall brown bottle with an ocean vista and a palm tree on the label. It was rum and it had been up there forever. The sudden whiff of alcohol as she poured a tablespoonful almost took her breath away, but the alcohol would disappear in baking and the rum would enhance the flavor of the peaches. She dribbled the tablespoon of rum here and there over the peaches and added another for good measure.

Now it was time to make the cobbler dough. She set butter to melting in a small saucepan while she sifted flour, baking powder, and salt into her favorite mixing bowl, the caramel-colored one with white stripes near the rim. She added a few tablespoons of sugar to the flour mixture, then poured in melted butter and stirred until some of the flour mixture formed buttery lumps. She continued stirring until the lumps were smaller and distributed evenly. Then she added a bit of heavy cream, and a bit more, until she'd created a soft, sticky dough. Now came the stage of cobbler-making that most definitely distinguished a cobbler from a pie. She picked up handfuls of the dough and deposited them here and there atop the peaches in the Pyrex baking dish. When all the dough had been transferred to the peaches, she began to pat the small mounds of dough, evening them out and making sure that no giant bare spots remained on the cobbler's surface. When she had finished, the peaches seemed covered with a pale, lumpy coverlet. A few threadbare spots allowed a glimpse of the golden fruit beneath.

Before baking, the cobbler had to be chilled, longer or shorter as one wished. Pamela wanted to take it out of the oven right before people arrived for Knit and Nibble, so it would still be warm when the time came

for refreshments. She covered the dish with plastic
wrap and slipped it into the refrigerator. It could
chill all afternoon with no harm done. And she
could handle the day's *Fiber Craft* chores, as well as
making sure the parts of the house that Knit and Nibble would see were tidy.

Chapter Eleven

At six p.m. Pamela stood in her kitchen again, wearing one of her hand-knit creations. She'd barely thought of sweaters, at least to wear, all summer, but when she'd stepped outside to sweep the porch and the front walk, the evening air had carried a hint of fall. So she'd taken from her closet shelf a light pullover knit from a cotton and linen blend in a pale amber shade, like autumn leaves. Back downstairs, she'd eaten the tail end of the bean and ham hock soup. Now she was waiting for the oven to heat and butter to melt in a small saucepan on the stovetop so she could put the finishing touches on the cobbler, which had been stripped of its plastic wrap and was sitting on the counter.

When the butter was ready, she used a pastry brush to dab it over the cobbler's doughy covering until the dough shone. Then she sprinkled sugar over the whole surface until it resembled a bare field dusted with snow. She slipped the cobbler into the oven and set about gathering cups, saucers, and dessert plates from the cupboard where she kept her wedding china.

Bettina was the first to arrive, just in time to sigh with anticipation as Pamela transferred the cobbler, now a fragrant, bubbling masterpiece, from the oven to a trivet on the table. The pastry crust had turned a tawny gold, embellished with glistening patches of sugar. The rich peach juice, now a dark syrup, had seeped through in the spots where the crust was thin and around the edges, where it clung to the sides of the Pyrex dish.

Bettina was dressed for the fall evening too, in a pants and jacket ensemble fashioned of soft jersey the color of an eggplant. With it she wore her jade pendant earrings and a dramatic jade necklace.

"I have ice cream to go on top," Pamela said. "And the cobbler will still be warm when I serve it."

"Heavenly!" Bettina sighed again. "I can't wait."

"I have plenty of heavy cream too." Pamela reached into the refrigerator and set a carton of cream on the table. "Some people might like that instead."

"They might," Bettina said, "but I'm in the ice cream camp."

Pamela busied herself grinding beans for the coffee while Bettina set the stack of six dessert plates near the cobbler and lined up the cups and saucers in two neat rows. She added forks, spoons, and six lacy vintage napkins to the arrangement, along with a fancy silver-plated serving spoon for the cobbler. The doorbell chimed just as she was filling the cut-glass cream pitcher.

"I'll get it," Pamela said. She surveyed the table before she headed for the entry. "The sugar bowl is low."

"I'm on it." Bettina opened a cupboard.

* * *

Nell Bascomb greeted Pamela with a quick hand squeeze and a smile. "I know my hands are chilly," she said. "It feels like fall out here." Indeed, it smelled like fall too. The gust of air that had come in when Pamela opened the door carried with it a trace of fireplace smoke. "Roland is just behind me," Nell added. "He's checking to make sure the side he parked on is legal today."

Roland's voice came from halfway down the front walk. "Do they ever actually sweep Orchard Street?" he asked. "Or do they just come around to ticket the cars on the wrong side?"

Pamela was saved answering by Holly, who scurried up beside Roland just as he began to climb the porch steps. "I knew you were here when I saw your amazing car at the curb," she said, and the porch light reached far enough to show that a dimple accompanied her wide smile. "It must be so much fun to drive."

Roland paused and turned toward her. "I didn't buy it for fun," he said, "I bought it because it's an excellent piece of engineering. Very dependable." He continued his climb. Undaunted, Holly followed him.

"It could still be fun though," she persisted, her smile undimmed.

Nell was lingering at the threshold. "Roland doesn't do fun," she said. Then, "How are you, dear? And where's your sweet friend? She's okay, I hope."

"She's fine and she's on her way." Pamela stepped back, and Nell, Holly, and Roland trooped inside. "I came right from the salon," Holly added. "My five o'clock was late. She's a good customer so I didn't want to rush her." She surveyed Pamela's living room. "I could spend hours in here," she said. "Just admiring all your amazing things." The streak in her dark hair was turquoise tonight and her nails glittered with matching polish.

Roland took his usual spot at one end of the sofa and pulled his knitting project out of the briefcase he used in place of a knitting bag.

"It's grown a lot!" Holly clapped her hands. "You'll be done in plenty of time and your wife is going to love it." The piece of knitting—apparently a sleeve, to judge by its shape—was considerably longer than it had been when Roland tucked his work back into his briefcase the previous week.

Roland looked up with a frown. "Of course it will be done. I calculated the total number of stitches in the finished garment and divided that number by the days remaining until December twenty-fifth. I knit for seventeen minutes every day to meet the daily quota. Extra on Tuesdays, of course."

Bettina had come out from the kitchen and settled on the sofa between Roland and Nell. Her own project, the elephant she was making for her new granddaughter, sat ready in her lap. But first she fingered the edge of the pink angora rectangle that hung from Roland's needles. "This ribbing looks pretty good," she said.

Roland clutched his needles tightly and jerked the piece of knitting out of Bettina's grasp. "Of course the ribbing looks good," he said. "Anyone who can read a knitting pattern and count to two can knit ribbing."

Holly had pulled the footstool up to the end of the sofa where Nell sat. She had finished her first Knit and Nibble project, a bulky white jacket fashioned from yarn nearly as thick as rope, and was making an

elephant for Nell to give the shelter children. She'd
chosen a multicolored ombré yarn that gave the elephant a particularly flamboyant air.

Pamela's knitting bag waited by the rummage sale
chair with the carved wooden back and needlepoint
seat, but she was still on her feet. She didn't want to
settle down until Karen arrived and everyone was
present and accounted for. After a few minutes the
doorbell chimed and she ushered Karen to the comfortable armchair.

"I don't need to sit here," Karen protested.
"Where will you sit?"

"I'm fine." Pamela lowered herself onto the rummage sale chair.

"You're an expectant mother, dear," Nell said. "Let
us pamper you."

Predictably, Karen blushed. Her slight body still
gave only the tiniest hint of her pregnant state, but
she let the roomy chair envelop her and pulled her
needles from her knitting bag. From them hung several inches of knitting crafted from delicate white
yarn in a pattern like fine lace.

For a few minutes, there was silence as people
arranged their yarn just so and examined their projects to remind themselves which direction they were
heading and whether they should be knitting or
purling. But soon needles were dipping and rising as
busy fingers looped strands of yarn and pulled them
tight, and the only sound to be heard was a chorus of
faint clicks.

Pamela had been spending her evenings reading
Time and Time Again instead of knitting, and she was
still working on the same ruby-red sleeve from the
previous week. Pulling it out of her bag now, she re-

membered how Caralee had complimented her on the color, and she felt a sudden pang of sympathy for the young woman. It was true that Caralee hadn't been very sociable, but being sociable didn't always come that naturally to Pamela herself. And the targets Caralee had aimed at on her blog weren't totally undeserving of her scorn.

As if reading her mind, Holly said, "I never really got a chance to talk to Caralee, but she seemed . . . interesting. Such a shame what happened." Without her dimply smile, Holly scarcely looked like herself.

"Troubled, more like." Nell shook her head sadly. "She wasn't adjusting well to being back in a small town."

"She just hadn't relaxed into the pace of things. Of course, I loved it right away—the old houses, and the trees, and all the amazing people . . ." Holly beamed up at Nell.

Pamela had been searching for a way to bring up the coded names Wilfred had helped her and Bettina decipher in Caralee's knitting project. Now she glanced over at Bettina, raising her brows in the subtlest of questioning expressions. Bettina caught her eye and gave a nearly imperceptible nod. The jade pendants at her ears bounced. Pamela was just about to open her mouth, but before she could get a word out, Bettina said, "She'd managed to make enemies though."

"The police have declared Caralee's death an accident," Roland said firmly. "So enemies aren't relevant because the person responsible is some fool who doesn't know how to store furniture properly. There might be grounds for a lawsuit, however."

Nell started in before Roland had finished, her voice overlapping his. "Bettina and Pamela"—she

fixed Bettina with a stern gaze and then focused on
Pamela—"you two are not going to get involved in
this. I know you both think you're the town detec-
tives." Her hands trembled and one of her needles
slipped from her grasp, but she went on. "I never ap-
proved of that, even when there had clearly been a
murder and the police were floundering around.
And this time—let it be. Caralee died in a tragic accident. That's all." She picked up the errant needle,
examined her knitting, and said, "Drat—I dropped a
stitch."

Pamela nodded, but she said, "We're curious
though—"

Roland cut her off. "What makes you think she had
enemies? She never said much of anything, to me anyway."

With a sly smile, Bettina pulled from her knitting
bag the homely product of Caralee's industry, lumpy
and gray, still attached to one of her needles. "Morse
code," she said. "Wilfred figured it out. Caralee was
getting into character, and just like Madame Defarge
she was coding people's names into her knitting."

Pamela took over. "In the story, Madame Defarge
lists the names of aristocrats who are destined for the
guillotine. Evil people who she thinks deserve to
die." She wouldn't tell them about the blog, at least
not yet. Caralee had made it clear enough to the
group in person what she thought of Arborville.

Roland set his pink angora sleeve aside and
tugged the piece of gray knitting from Bettina's lap.
He studied it intently. "I do see patterns," he announced. "It's not just careless knitting." He looked
up. "Clever work on Wilfred's part. So who are these
enemies?"

"One of them is Anthony Wadsworth." Pamela shrugged. "Artistic differences?"

"Then there's Thomas Swinton," Bettina chimed in. "The writer."

"*Time and Time Again.*" Nell nodded. "Harold read it. I can't see why Caralee would object to Thomas Swinton."

"How about Merrick Timmons?" Pamela asked.

"Rachelle Timmons! Trophy wife!" Holly laughed. "They just moved to Arborville last spring. Grandest house in town, at least according to Rachelle. She's a client at the salon. Big tipper!" Flashing her turquoise nails, Holly put her hands over her mouth as if to stifle what she was about to say next. It came out anyway, accompanied by another laugh. "She's hardly older than me. Has to be number two. Or three. Or even four."

"It's the old Foster house," Nell said. "Way up at the top of the Palisades, with a view looking over the Hudson. It was the summer home of a publishing baron, back before the George Washington Bridge was built. People came over by ferry. Harold knows about it from the historical society."

Roland consulted the swath of knitting he'd now pulled over onto his lap. "I see four separate sections here, the lumpy sections," he observed. "I guess that's the Morse code. You named Wadsworth, Swinton, and Timmons. Who's the fourth aristocrat?"

Bettina and Pamela spoke at once. "Kent Varnish."

"I don't know him personally," Nell said, "but he's very involved in the community. "He's the president of Hands Across Arborville, and he's in the Arborville Arborists, and he's head of the church council at St. Willibrod's, a member of the Chamber of

Commerce of course, and who knows what else?" She paused, a bit breathless. "I don't see what anyone could find to object to about Kent Varnish."

"He sounds busy," Bettina commented.

"I think we should stick to our knitting," Nell said, still seeming a bit agitated. "There's no point in dwelling on that poor young woman's death when there are other—" She paused and her eyes strayed toward the entry, where they lingered. The lines between her brows smoothed out and her lips curved into a smile. She went on, "Other more cheerful . . . and what do we have here?"

Two kittens tumbled into the room, two of the ginger females. They were followed, cautiously, by one of the black males, the smallest kitten in the litter. The ginger females had been stalking one another, and the tumbling had been the result of a pounce that went awry. Now one lay on her back, fending off the batting paws and teasing nips of the other, while the black male watched them from the edge of the carpet.

"Oh, aren't these just the most awesome!" Holly had tossed her knitting aside and slid from the footstool to the floor. She looked up at Pamela, her eyes shining with admiration. "I knew you'd had them . . . and now here they are. Just amazing!"

"I can't take total credit," Pamela said. "It was actually Catrina's doing."

Holly held out a palm and the ginger females left off their sparring to investigate. Karen leaned forward in the armchair and held out a timid hand as well.

"What are you going to do with them?" Roland asked, in the same tones one might use to inquire about plans for some curious acquisition.

"I'll keep one," Pamela said. "Catrina needs company."

From the direction of the kitchen there came a squeal, then another one of the black males came tearing around the corner. He slid across the stretch of uncarpeted floor between the entry and the living room and dove under the footstool. He was followed by the other ginger female, the bold one, who had quickly established her rule over her siblings. Happy that she had vanquished him, she joined her sisters in their play.

"Five of them?" Roland said, with obvious distaste.

"Actually," Pamela said, "there are six. There's another black one."

Holly rocked back on her heels. "Will you . . . let people adopt them?"

Bettina's eyes grew wide. She gave Pamela a nod and a satisfied smile and mouthed, "Bingo!"

"Why, yes." Pamela tried not to sound too eager. She had five kittens to find homes for, and people were always more interested in things that weren't too easy to get. "They're not quite ready to leave their mother yet, but when the time comes . . ."

"That would be awesome!" The ginger female who had been the first to sniff Holly's fingers had now climbed onto her thigh and was busily kneading the fabric of her jeans, purring as Holly scratched between her ears.

"They *are* hard to resist." Nell's knitting rested in her lap and she watched as the male who had hidden under the footstool crept warily out, only to retreat when the bold ginger female lunged at him. Pamela imagined the same tender expression on Nell's face as she watched her own children play.

"Are you interested, Nell?" she said.

"Oh, dear"—sadness replaced the tender expression on Nell's face—"Harold and I are too old to start over with a kitten. It would outlive us."

"No!" Holly looked stricken. "You'll live to be a hundred, at least." She reached for Nell's hand.

Nell shrugged. "One has to be realistic. Harold and I have had a wonderful life. And we have a few years left, I'm sure. But a new kitten . . ."

Karen gazed at Nell from the depths of the armchair. "Don't talk like that," she said, sounding ready to cry. Her face was flushed and she was blinking, wiping at one eye with a delicate hand. "What would Knit and Nibble do without Nell?"

At that, Bettina was on her feet. "I think it's time for peach cobbler," she announced. "Any takers?"

Pamela bounced up from the rummage sale chair, and the two friends hurried to the kitchen.

The ground coffee beans waited in the filter atop the carafe, and tea leaves had already been measured into a graceful thrift store teapot with climbing roses meandering over its china surface. Pamela started water boiling in the kettle as Bettina set the dessert plates out side by side.

"I'll carry things," Holly said from the doorway. She caught sight of the cobbler and crossed over to the table. "You are an amazing cook, Pamela," she said. "It's almost too pretty to cut into."

But Bettina plunged the serving spoon into the cobbler, carving out a scoop that included both baked peach slices and pastry topping, golden brown with a glittering sprinkle of baked-on sugar. She gently deposited it on one of the dessert plates. The fragrance of peaches and sugar was almost intoxicating.

"There's a choice of cream or ice cream," Bettina said. "Holly, will you go take orders?"

Pamela turned away from the counter. "There will be cream and sugar on the coffee table, so people can add their own cream if that's what they prefer. But they should let us know if they want ice cream." The kettle began to whistle and Pamela focused on pouring boiling water over the ground coffee in the paper filter. Once that was done, and the bitter aroma of brewing coffee began to compete with the sweet aroma of the cobbler, she filled the kettle and set it boiling again for the tea.

Bettina continued to serve the cobbler, and soon each plate held a piece of the pastry topping, like a ragged-edged free-form biscuit, tucked next to a generous scoop of the tawny fruit, gleaming with its rich syrup.

Holly was back. "Cream for Nell, ice cream for Karen—and me, and Roland wants his plain." She reached for the cut-glass cream pitcher and sugar bowl. "I'll take these out," she said, "and I'll be back to deliver cobbler."

By the time Pamela entered the living room with four cups of coffee on a tray, the kittens had all retreated, perhaps disconcerted by the hustle and bustle of refreshments being served. The plates of cobbler had all been delivered, four with crests of vanilla ice cream forming milky rivulets as it melted onto the still-warm cobbler. Nell and Karen had their tea. Pamela tugged the rummage sale chair nearer to the coffee table and settled down to taste her handiwork.

For a few minutes the only sounds were nonverbal, mostly "mmm" and its variants. Bettina was the first to articulate an actual sentence. "You certainly did justice to those peaches," she said, and there was no disagreement. Pamela was happy to concentrate on her cobbler and coffee, picking up fragments of conversation from here and there. Holly, on her footstool near Nell's feet, had asked Nell about her work at the women's shelter in Haversack and was gazing in admiration as Nell described the Wednesday morning story time she did for the children. Bettina had brought a chair in from the dining room and perched near Karen to discuss babies—though Karen's was not yet born and Bettina's new granddaughter was all the way up in Boston.

Roland set his empty plate on the coffee table with a *thunk* and a jingle of fork against china. "Back to work," he said, pushing back his well-starched shirt cuff to consult his impressive watch. "I have a quota to meet here." He picked up his knitting, guided his right-hand needle through the next loop on his left-hand needle, and twisted a strand of pink angora yarn around his index finger.

Holly was on her feet in an instant, collecting plates and silverware. The only hints of what the plates had contained were dabs of peach syrup and trails of melted ice cream. Bettina gathered the cups and saucers back onto their tray and followed Holly to the kitchen, while Nell followed with the cream pitcher and sugar bowl. Karen started to pull herself out of the deep armchair, but Bettina motioned her back. "Stay off your feet while you can," she said with a wink. "You'll have plenty to do after December." Karen smiled shyly and picked up her knitting.

Nothing remained for Pamela to carry except the napkins. She entered the kitchen to find Bettina standing at the sink. But she wasn't washing dishes.

She was staring fixedly out the window. The cups and saucers and dessert plates and silverware all sat on the table near the remnants of the cobbler, over which Nell was stretching a piece of foil while Holly returned the foil to its drawer.

"Can you see the moon from there?" Pamela asked.

Bettina stayed facing the window but looked back over her shoulder. "I thought I saw car lights in Richard's driveway," she said.

Pamela felt a stirring in her chest like a small creature moving about, a kitten perhaps, but all she said was "Oh."

"Are you all right, dear?" Nell focused her kind gaze on Pamela. Her hands paused and the foil glinted in the bright kitchen light.

"Of course." Pamela continued on her way toward the table and nestled the lacy white bundle of napkins in a pile to go to the laundry.

"I don't think he's back though," Bettina added. "No lights have come on in the house."

"Probably just someone using the driveway to turn around." Pamela wasn't sure whether she felt disappointed or relieved.

"Such a nice man," Nell said. She looked at Holly. "I think you're the only person in our little group who hasn't met him." She looked back at Pamela. "Has he been away?"

"Volunteer work in Maine," Pamela said. "It seems to have stretched on longer than he expected. Not a big deal though. I'm sure he's fine."

Pamela almost never blushed, but she felt her cheeks growing warm. To hide her confusion, she murmured something about making sure they'd collected everything that needed collecting, and hurried back to the living room.

Karen and Roland had remained behind when everyone else pitched in on the cleanup, Karen almost lost in the big armchair and Roland across the room on the far end of the sofa. Both had been knitting when Pamela left, but now only Karen was busy, eyes rapt on the delicate piece of work suspended from her needles—and perhaps daydreaming about the little person who would one day wear the garment she was shaping.

Roland was not knitting. He had set the pink angora sleeve—only half a sleeve really—aside and he was focused on his right foot. He was bent nearly double, leaning forward so that only the top of his head, with its close-cropped salt-and-pepper hair, was visible. With his right hand he seemed to be adjusting something on his faultlessly polished shoe. But as Pamela watched, what she had assumed was a dark shoe took on a life of its own. It scampered away, now looking rather furry, then returned and attempted to scale Roland's calf, struggling for foothold in the tight weave of his pinstripe trousers.

A voice that had to be Roland's, but was scarcely recognizable, said, "You're a gutsy little fellow, aren't you?" And Roland's hand scooped the kitten up and deposited it in his lap. He looked up, noticed Pamela watching him, and cleared his throat. In a voice even deeper than the normal Roland voice, as if to compensate for the cooing tones in which he had addressed the kitten, he said, "He wandered in here. I wasn't sure what to do." He lifted the kitten, which fit easily into his large palm. Pamela recognized it as the tiny male that was the smallest kitten in the litter. "Have you . . . come to take him away?"

"Is he bothering you? I'd hate for you to get cat hair on your nice suit."

"I . . ." Roland cleared his throat again. "It doesn't matter." He frowned, set the kitten down on the sofa, checked his watch, and picked up his knitting. "I should be getting back to work." The kitten snuggled up to Roland's pinstriped thigh and closed its eyes.

Chapter Twelve

Holly and Nell returned from the kitchen. They were laughing, but behind them Bettina looked worried. She quickly glanced toward Pamela, who had resumed her seat on the rummage sale chair and picked up her knitting.

"Are you okay?" she mouthed.

Pamela nodded, momentarily puzzled. Watching Roland with the kitten had distracted her from the reason she'd fled to the living room. Then she remembered. "Fine," she mouthed back, and fingered her cheek to confirm that she was no longer blushing.

Soon everyone was back at work, and a lively conversation sprang up about the best place to look for pumpkins: the farmers market in Newfield, the farm stand along Route 19 in Kringlekamack (where one family still maintained a farm in a town that had once been only farmland), or the pumpkin sale run by the Chamber of Commerce to benefit service dogs—starting the very next weekend.

"The Chamber pumpkins are always very expensive," Bettina said.

"But it's such a good cause." This from Nell.

"Is the farm stand part of a real farm?" Holly asked, seeming amazed.

"It certainly is," Nell said. "And there used to be a real farm right here in Arborville. Out where Roland lives."

Roland popped to attention when his name was mentioned. He hadn't been knitting, just staring into space in a very uncharacteristic way. "That's why people call it 'The Farm,' " he said.

"Well, *duh*!" Holly laughed. "I should have known that, but I have so much to learn about this awesome town."

The conversation returned to pumpkins and became even livelier. Despite that, no consensus was reached about the best place to buy them, though there was general agreement that price should not be the only determining factor.

On the stroke of nine p.m., Roland opened his briefcase. He'd reached the end of a row, and the partly finished sleeve dangled from one needle. He methodically threaded the other needle through the skein of pink angora yarn and stowed sleeve and yarn in the briefcase, clicking down the metal tongue that latched it closed. The commotion disturbed the dozing kitten and it roused itself, leapt off the sofa, and wandered toward the dining room, where a door led into the kitchen and the communal bed in the laundry room beyond.

Bettina tucked her project into her knitting bag and stood up. "I'll get started on those dishes," she said over her shoulder as she headed for the kitchen.

Karen, Holly, and Nell gathered their things and clustered around Pamela in the entry, saying goodnight and congratulating Pamela on the cobbler. But instead of joining them, Roland lingered in the living room.

Pamela waved a final goodnight from the threshold, stepped back into the entry, and closed the door. Roland advanced across the carpet, looking as grave as if he was about to raise a serious issue at a corporate meeting. "A word with you, Pamela, if I might," he said, and cleared his throat.

"Sure." *What could it be?* Pamela asked herself. *Is he about to resign from Knit and Nibble?* A twinge of sympathy made her brow pucker. Perhaps he'd felt out of place the whole time. It was true that Nell could be a bit short with him, and Bettina teased him now and then.

"I'd have to speak to Melanie, of course, and there's Ramona to consider." Pamela nodded, trying to project encouragement—whatever might be forthcoming. He cleared his throat again. Had the change in the weather brought on a cold? Roland had been clearing his throat a lot this evening. He went on. "But subject to their approval, I . . . we . . . could take one of those cats off your hands. That is, if you think I . . . we . . . could provide a home like the home you'd want for them, if you . . . of course you wouldn't want to think they . . . Ramona is a dog, after all, but . . . a home . . ." His syntax began to fray and his voice trailed off.

Pamela bit her lips to stifle a laugh. "You wouldn't be particularly interested in that little black one, would you?" she asked.

Roland's face tightened and his brows drew together. "Is he spoken for?"

"Not yet," Pamela said. She smiled. "Except by you . . . subject of course to Melanie's approval. And Ramona's."

Roland stooped to pick up his briefcase. "I won't keep you any longer then." He squared his shoulders. "I should know by next week. Then, maybe they'll be ready soon?"

Pamela nodded. "Probably a month."

After Roland was on his way, Pamela joined Bettina in the kitchen, allowing the laugh she'd suppressed to bubble up as Bettina regarded her curiously. "Roland wants a kitten," she said when she could talk normally again. The foil-covered cobbler still sat on the table, but the dishes and silverware had been whisked away into the dishwasher. Bettina was drying her hands.

She set the dish towel aside to clap. "I told you letting the kittens come out while everyone was here would be a good plan." She counted on her fingers, "One to Holly, one to Roland, you keep one . . . and I'll take three."

"No, no!" Pamela laughed again. "I can't let you do that. There's plenty of time yet, and Nell might come around, and even Karen—though with a baby on the way she might worry about adding a cat to the mix."

"And Dave is allergic to wool. Maybe that carries over to cats."

"I can always put a note on the bulletin board at the Co-Op, and post on AccessArborville."

Bettina pulled a chair out from the table and sat. "So," she said, "on the topic of Caralee, what did we learn tonight that's useful? We already knew that Merrick Timmons had a trophy wife."

Pamela took the chair across from her. "It definitely fits with the kinds of things Caralee was making fun of on her blog—people not realizing how idiotic they seem. Old guy thinks he's young again because he can afford a young wife. Everybody else thinks he's an old fool."

"But what could Caralee say about the trophy wife issue that wasn't obvious already?" Bettina asked. "Old guy with young wife. *Duh!*"

"And would he have had access to the storage room between six and seven the night Caralee died?"

Bettina shrugged. "We don't know."

"*But*"—Pamela drummed the tabletop with her fingers and Bettina leaned forward expectantly—"I just remembered something Nell said."

"Which is?"

"Kent Varnish is in the Arborists." Pamela drummed faster.

"And?"

"The Arborists were using one of the church meeting rooms that night. Remember? Some of them were standing around outside when the police were interviewing people."

Bettina nodded vigorously, setting the curving tendrils of her red hair to bouncing and making the jade pendants at her ears swing wildly. But suddenly she was still, except for the earrings, which still swayed. "What could Caralee have known about him that was all that bad? From what Nell said, he sounds like a pillar of

the community. He'll probably be out there ped-
dling pumpkins with the Chamber this Saturday."

Pamela slid the foil-covered dish of cobbler to the
center of the table. She lifted the foil. "Plenty left in
here," she said.

Bettina patted her stomach. "I couldn't, really."
She reached for the foil and pulled it back a bit farther. "It was awfully good though. So maybe . . . just a
tiny . . ."

Pamela tugged the foil from Bettina's fingers and
smoothed it back down. "I'm thinking of Harold,"
she said. "Nell said he knows Kent Varnish, much
better than she does. Nell isn't a gossip and even if
she did know something, she wouldn't tell us. But
Harold . . . under the influence of cobbler . . ."

Bettina gazed admiringly at Pamela. She nodded.
"He might talk. And since it's for a good cause, I can
live without a second helping—though if there's any
left . . . after you share it with him . . ."

"Nell will be at the women's shelter tomorrow
morning," Pamela said, "reading stories to the children. I heard her tell Holly. I'll pay a call on Harold
while she's gone."

Pamela felt a soft pressure against her collarbone,
like gentle kneading. She opened her eyes to find a
pair of amber eyes staring into hers. The white eyelet
curtains at the windows glowed as brightly as if the
sun had risen hours ago. "What time is it?" she asked
Catrina, who was perched on her chest. Catrina
sprang to the floor and Pamela rolled over to consult
the clock on the night table.

It was nearly ten a.m. No wonder Catrina had

been curious about her mistress's state. Pamela sat up, yawned, and swung her feet onto the rag rug at the side of her bed. After Knit and Nibble ended, she'd stayed up past midnight reading *Time and Time Again*, which she was starting to think of as *Time and Time Again and Again and Again*. The characters couldn't seem to stay in the same bodies for more than a few chapters, being reborn—again and again—into periods of history noted for unrest and misery.

It was only while she was brushing her teeth that she remembered the morning's errand—a visit to Harold Bascomb with a gift of peach cobbler. If all went well, she'd come away knowing what it was about Kent Varnish that had made Caralee decide he deserved the guillotine. But she'd have to move fast. Nell would only be gone for a few hours. Pamela dressed quickly and followed Catrina down the stairs.

In the kitchen, she set water boiling for coffee, scooped cat food into Catrina's bowl and kitten food into the kittens' bowl, and slipped a slice of whole-grain bread into the toaster. She hurried down the front walk to collect the *Register*. She noted in passing that Richard Larkin's driveway was empty, but she was resolved to concentrate this morning on Kent Varnish.

While the boiling water was dripping through the ground beans in the coffee filter, she buttered her toast and extracted the *Register* from its flimsy plastic sleeve. There was no time to read it though—only time for one cup of coffee and hastily nibbled toast. Then Pamela took from her cupboard a thrift store plate that had borne gifts of Christmas cookies back and forth between her and Bettina for years. She arranged a generous portion of the leftover cobbler on it and wrapped the offering carefully in foil. As she worked, kittens roamed about underfoot.

Hurried though she was, she couldn't resist a tiny detour as she neared the stately brick apartment building at the corner of Orchard Street and Arborville Avenue. She veered off the sidewalk onto the asphalt of the parking lot to peek behind the wooden fence where the building's trash and discards awaited collection day.

But as she stepped up to the opening between the fence and the back of the building, she jumped back in alarm. Mr. Gilly, the building's super, straightened his lean body—he'd been hunched over a garbage bag that had evidently been attacked by some scavenging wild creature—and said, "Didn't mean to scare you!"

"You didn't really," Pamela said. "I mean, you did, but it wasn't your fault." She was grateful she hadn't dropped the cobbler.

"Still jumpy about what happened last week? Somebody dying and all, right next to your house?" He lifted the flap of his shirt pocket and pulled out a pack of cigarettes and a lighter. Pamela recognized this gesture as a sign he wanted to chat.

Pamela was torn. She needed to confer with Harold before Nell got home from story time at the women's shelter. But Mr. Gilly talked to everybody about everything. He seemed eager to talk about Caralee's death, and he'd probably discussed it with countless other people in the week since it happened.

He fished a cigarette out of the pack and turned away to light it, take a long puff, and exhale.

"The police say the young woman's death was an accident," Pamela said.

"Yeah—I saw that article in the *Advocate*." Mr. Gilly took another puff of his cigarette. He studied Pamela's face as if debating whether to proceed, but then he went on. "There's unavoidable accidents," he said, "and then there's avoidable accidents."

"Really?" Pamela tried to make her voice convey both flattery and surprise.

Mr. Gilly nodded sagely. "Ben Skyler gets away with a lot up there." He waved toward the church with the hand that held the cigarette.

"He does?" Now Pamela truly was surprised. Ben had struck her as conscientious.

"Careless," Mr. Gilly nodded again. "Like I said, there's unavoidable accidents and then there's avoidable accidents. If you put a careless man in charge of an overstuffed storage room, you've got an avoidable accident waiting to happen."

Pamela felt herself start to frown but willed her forehead into smoothness. She didn't want to discourage Mr. Gilly's musings. "The Players didn't look after that stuff themselves then?" she said, hoping Mr. Gilly wouldn't think she was contradicting him. If Ben Skyler not only unlocked the storage room but had charge over its contents, new and interesting possibilities came into view.

"He's just as happy to have anybody else do his work for him," Mr. Gilly said. He leaned close to Pamela. "Takes too many jobs on the side, if you ask me." He made a sweeping gesture that took in the parking lot, the apartment building, and the lawn they were standing on. "This all keeps me busy. I'm not looking to do more. But that Ben—he juggles this job, that job, working for that big shot Merrick Timmons, up on top of the Palisades. Nothing gets done right if you try to do too much. That's what I always say." He raised the cigarette to his lips with a flourish.

Pamela saw her opening. "I'd better let you get back to it," she said. With a smile and a wave, she was on her way.

Chapter Thirteen

As she climbed the hill toward Harold and Nell's house, she pondered what she'd just learned. It was possible that Ben Skyler was supposed to keep the storage room neat, and that Caralee's death had been his fault—the result of an avoidable accident. But on reflection Pamela doubted that the church custodian's duties extended to taking care of the theater group's property. As far as she knew, the church let the group use its facilities for no charge, so it was unlikely that custodian services were provided.

Talking to Mr. Gilly hadn't been a waste of time though. He'd linked Ben Skyler with Merrick Timmons. If the only thing Caralee had objected to about Merrick Timmons was that he had installed a trophy wife in a trophy house, it was hard to see why he'd have thought he needed to kill her. People in Arborville hadn't needed a blog post to set their tongues wagging about the new owner of the Palisades mansion and his very young wife. But what if Caralee had known more about him? Things he'd prefer remain secret—at least from the stratum of Arborville society he was trying to impress.

Ben Skyler did odd jobs for Merrick Timmons, and Ben Skyler had a key to the storage room where Caralee met her fate. He could have gone into the storage room anytime at all and arranged the pile of furniture so that as soon as Caralee pulled out a chair the whole thing came crashing down.

Pamela continued up the hill. She now had one interesting tidbit to report to Bettina. And the interview with Harold might well yield another. She glanced down at the foil-covered plate bearing the offering of cobbler, and blinked as the sun reflecting off the foil dazzled her eyes.

No one answered when Pamela rang the doorbell at Harold and Nell's, though Harold's car, a decades-old Volvo, sat in the driveway and the garage door was open. Pamela retraced her steps, descending the stone steps that connected the front porch of the Bascombs' substantial house with the sidewalk below.

"Harold?" she called, venturing up the driveway. Perhaps he was puttering in the garage. She stepped out of the sunlight into the garage's shadowy interior and called again, "Harold? Are you in here?"

There was no response, but as she stepped across the oil-stained cement floor, moving toward the door that led into the Bascombs' mudroom, she heard a thumping sound from somewhere. She paused and held her breath, straining to listen. The thump came again, and then in a slow, rhythmic series. She stepped closer to the wall. The thumping stopped for a minute, but then it started again.

Pamela turned and headed back toward the driveway. As she stepped through the garage door she realized she could hear the thumping more clearly in the open air, and it was coming from the Bascombs' backyard. It was also, she noted, accompanied by a male voice singing a jaunty tune.

She made her way along the side of the garage, skirting the narrow border where Nell's iris grew. As she rounded the back corner, she caught sight of Harold in the far corner of the yard near the compost heap. He was holding an impressive-looking ax. Behind him was a jumble of hefty logs sawed into fireplace-sized lengths. In front of him was a giant log with a small log balanced on top. To the side was a tidy pile of split logs, their cut surfaces a satiny chestnut brown. Harold hefted the ax, raised it over his shoulder, and brought it down on the top of the small log. There was a sharp crack as the small log fractured into two halves, and then the ax thudded against the upturned end of the giant log. Harold's voice rang out in a triumphant peal: "Cut that wood just right!"

He noticed Pamela and leaned the ax against the giant log. "Work songs," he said, panting slightly. "Makes the work go faster." A lock of his thick white hair, damp with sweat, had fallen over his forehead. He pushed it back with a grimy hand.

"You have a nice voice," Pamela said. "I like to hear men sing."

"That's how I won Nell's heart," he said with a grin. "But you didn't climb up that hill to compliment me on my voice. To what do I owe this visit?"

Pamela extended her hands with the foil-covered plate balanced on them. "There was some cobbler left last night after Knit and Nibble finished. I thought you might like a piece."

He raised his eyebrows and the grin grew wider. "Are you sure that's the only reason? Not that I don't welcome a chance to taste your cobbler. Nell said she couldn't resist—and you know how she disapproves of sugar." Pamela's eyes strayed to Nell's expansive vegetable garden. It took up a quarter of the large yard and was neatly laid out in rows of climbing things, low bushy things, and unruly vines bearing green and gold squashes.

Harold accepted Pamela's offering and set it on the giant log. "Was that all Nell said about last night's meeting?" Pamela asked.

"Well"—Harold put his hands on his hips and continued to grin—"there was mention of a piece of knitting, a posthumous message from Caralee Lorimer involving the names of certain prominent Arborville citizens. Nell pooh-poohed that notion of course, or at least she made it very clear to me that I wasn't to tell you any secret things that I knew about Thomas Swinton, Merrick Timmons, Kent Varnish, or Anthony Wadsworth when you came around asking."

Pamela felt her shoulders droop. "Am I really that easy to figure out?" she said.

"Hands Across Arborville." A spark of mischief appeared in Harold's faded blue eyes. The weathered skin around them crinkled. He laughed. "And lots of other places too. Wandering hands, you might say."

"Kent Varnish?"

"He likes the women," Harold said. "And rumor has it"—he winked, leaned closer, and raised a large-knuckled hand to his mouth in a parody of someone imparting a secret—"there's more than one Mrs. Varnish."

Pamela took a step back, narrowly missing a split log. "How could that be?" she asked.

"Not officially, of course," Harold said. "But he's set her up in an apartment over in Haversack. I believe there's a Baby Varnish too."

A horn beeped at Pamela just after she crossed Arborville Avenue and was starting down Orchard Street. She turned to see Bettina's Toyota pulling to the curb. Bettina leaned across and opened the passenger-side door. "Jump in," she said, "but move the tomatoes first."

The passenger seat held an assortment of tomatoes ranging in color from deep brownish red to pale yellow and in shape from bulbous globes the size of a palm to delicate oval miniatures.

Pamela gathered them up, cradling them in one folded arm, and slipped in beside Bettina. "Where did you get them?" she asked. "Mine are all gone."

"Community gardens," Bettina said. "I'm doing an article for the *Advocate* on harvest time. Meredith Rawlings showed me around and I interviewed a couple of people who were up there working. 'Too many tomatoes,' one woman said, as if there could ever be too many tomatoes." The journey to Bettina's house had taken barely a minute. She pulled into her driveway and turned to Pamela. "So," she said, "tell me if your errand with the cobbler paid off."

"I have many things to report." Pamela handed a few tomatoes to Bettina and reached for the door handle.

"A bird in the hand is worth two in the bush," Wilfred exclaimed as they walked into the kitchen and he caught sight of the tomatoes. "I was just about to run to the Co-Op." Bettina handed them to him and he lined them up on the pine table. Pamela added the ones she was carrying to the collection. "With all this bounty," he added, "what would you say to bacon, lettuce, and tomato sandwiches?"

Pamela and Bettina nodded, and Wilfred opened the refrigerator. As he set strips of bacon to frying in his cast-iron skillet, Pamela described her conversation with Mr. Gilly. "So," she concluded, "if Merrick Timmons wanted to get rid of Caralee, he could have hired Ben Skyler to do the dirty work. Ben could have unlocked the storage room and rearranged the pile of furniture anytime at all."

"Assuming," Bettina said, "Ben would have been willing to kill somebody for money."

"Mr. Gilly doesn't think much of him." Pamela shrugged.

The seductive aroma of frying bacon began to rise from the stove. Bettina sighed with appreciation, but she stayed focused on the topic at hand, commenting, "We still don't know what Caralee had on Merrick Timmons that he'd be desperate to protect."

"But now we *do* know what secret Kent Varnish might want to protect," Pamela said. "And I think I'm in love with Harold Bascomb."

Bettina's eyes widened. "Really?"

Pamela laughed. "He's Nell's. And he's a little old for me. But wait till you hear what he told me about one of Arborville's most public-spirited citizens."

As Pamela began to describe what Harold had told her about Kent Varnish's Haversack hideaway and the sweetie he supported there, along with the child he had fathered, Wilfred stepped away from the stove. When she finished, Wilfred began to laugh with delight, but Bettina shook her head sadly.

"That is just shameful," she said. "What would Dolly Varnish think if she knew?" She looked up at Wilfred. "And why are you laughing?"

Wilfred blinked, tightened his lips into a firm line, and swallowed hard. "I was imagining what the St. Willibrod's church council would think if *they* knew, dear wife. You know I'd never approve of . . ." He paused in confusion. Meanwhile, the smell of the frying bacon had taken on a scorched quality. With one long step Wilfred was back at the stove. "Rescued it," he called. "It's just right."

Bettina jumped up. "We'll want to have the sandwiches on toast," she announced, and in a minute she was standing at the counter popping bread into the toaster.

"I'll slice a tomato," Pamela said, selecting a huge deep red one from the collection on the table, "and we'll need lettuce." As she turned to head toward the part of Bettina's spacious kitchen where cooking took place, she noticed Wilfred's hand resting on Bettina's shoulder, rubbing it gently. His other hand wielded the spatula with which he was scooping bacon slices from the skillet.

Exploring the refrigerator, Pamela found a head of lettuce in Bettina's vegetable drawer. She peeled off three large leaves, washed them at the sink, and patted them dry with paper towels. Then she carved the tomato into thick rounds. Soon six slices of toast lay on a cutting board, garnished with mayonnaise. Wilfred arranged four strips of bacon on each and Pamela added a lettuce leaf and a tomato slice, the red flesh glistening with juice.

After they'd eaten and Wilfred had retreated to his basement workshop, Pamela lingered at the pine table. Every bite of the bacon, lettuce, and tomato sandwiches had been devoured and only toast crumbs remained on Bettina's craft-shop plates. "We have to figure out where Kent Varnish was between six and seven the night Caralee died," she said. "We know the Arborists were meeting at the church that night, but what time do they start? Would he have been around between the time Rue left and the Players started to arrive?"

Bettina nodded. "I've seen him in Hyler's at lunchtime," she said. "In fact, Caralee once mentioned that he was a regular—to the point that when he ordered, he just said, 'Bring me the usual.'"

"I'll bet she loved that," Pamela commented. "But let's drop by there tomorrow, strike up a conversation with him—you're good at that. We'll see what we can find out about what time the Arborists show up for their meetings." Pamela stood up. "I'll ring your doorbell at noon," she said, "and be sure to wear your walking shoes. It's only five blocks and there's no reason to drive." Bettina sent her home with a few tomatoes.

At home, Pamela collected her mail from the box on her porch. Surveying the assortment of catalogs (Thanksgiving-inspired covers—already!) reminded her that she hadn't checked Richard Larkin's mailbox for a while, and last week's *Advocate* was doubtless languishing somewhere in his shrubbery. She set the pile of catalogs on one of her porch chairs and retraced her steps to the sidewalk. Then she cut across Richard Larkin's yard, scooping the *Advocate* out from under a holly bush. Nothing was spilling from his mailbox, but inside it she found the twin of a catalog she had just received, offering gift baskets of Vermont cheese.

Sudden relief nudged at her brain, though she'd been trying so hard to deny she was worried. Only one stray catalog. He must have gotten in touch with the post office to extend the hold on his deliveries—otherwise his mailbox would be overflowing by now. So he must be okay, and hadn't been eaten by a bear, and had just decided to stay in Maine a bit longer.

But as she climbed the steps to her own porch, she recalled the last time she'd put a hold on her mail, for a weeklong trip to a textile workshop in Providence. The card hadn't asked for a return date. It had just instructed her that mail delivery would resume after she collected the mail that had been held.

Once inside, she lifted a kitten out of the box that held Richard Larkin's mail and newspapers and added the new items. Wrestling kittens scattered and their ball of yarn rolled across the floor as she stepped into the kitchen to check the kittens' food bowl and the water bowl. A website had advised that kittens starting to eat solid food should be offered many small meals, so she spooned a few more mounds of kitten food into the plastic bowl.

Five emails, accompanied by beeps and chirps, appeared in Pamela's inbox as soon as she awakened her computer. The first was from Penny, the next three were notices from the Arborville Library about upcoming events, and the last, the slowest to arrive, was from her boss at *Fiber Craft.* It was marked with the little paper clip symbol that meant a work assignment was attached. Wanting to savor the enjoyment of reading her daughter's note, Pamela first glanced quickly at the message from her boss. "Too whimsical for our readers? Please advise," it read.

Her curiosity piqued, she opened the attachment. The article was titled "My Life as a Sheep." "Could be fun," she murmured, and turned to the email from Penny.

It was a newsy note. Penny had interviewed a local artist for a history report. She'd added a thrift store jacket to her usual sweater and jeans uniform and gotten many compliments. It was starting to get cold in Massachusetts and the leaves on some of the campus trees were turning red. She was already looking forward to coming home at Thanksgiving. But at the end, she departed from her cheery tone to say, "You never answered when I said I hoped you weren't getting involved in anything having to do with that accident at the church. I do not want to have to worry about my mother!"

A lump made its way into Pamela's throat and she swallowed hard. She hated to lie. But it wasn't fair to burden Penny with the knowledge that she and Bettina were busily trying to identify a killer, because obviously a killer could kill again if he (or she) felt threatened. Perhaps the best thing would just be to not respond for a bit. Something might come to light in the next day or two, and Bettina could pass a tip to Detective Clayborn and Caralee's murderer would be brought to justice and that would be that.

Now for "My Life as a Sheep." But as she began to read, another thought intruded, a positive thought. Penny would know if something had happened to Richard Larkin. Of course. Penny was in touch with

Laine and Sybil, even though she was up in Massachusetts and Laine and Sybil were at NYU in the city. If Laine and Sybil were worried that their father had vanished, they'd say something to Penny. Of course they would. And Penny would say something to her.

She returned to "My Life as a Sheep," but yet another thought intruded. Richard Larkin had once said that when he was in Maine he didn't cook for himself. It was shortly after he had moved from Manhattan to the house next to Pamela's and he was explaining why he wasn't familiar with the need to secure one's garbage from the raccoons. Perhaps, like Kent Varnish, he had a whole other household—but in Maine, not Haversack—and he had extended his stay in Maine because he couldn't bear to pull himself away from his . . . sweetie. Then she reminded herself that Richard Larkin, as a single man, had every right to do just exactly as he pleased.

Pamela returned once more to "My Life as a Sheep," willing herself to concentrate on her work and nothing else. Three more articles to be evaluated arrived while she was still pondering it, and by the time she had made her way through all the articles, it was nearly six p.m.

If she wrote up her comments before going downstairs for dinner, she could devote the evening to *Time and Time Again*. The interview Bettina had scheduled with Thomas Swinton was three days away, and Pamela was still hoping that something in his book would nudge her in a useful direction. Was there a question she could ask him whose answer or failure to answer would enable her and Bettina to cross him off their list of suspects—or solidify his place there?

Two of the articles were definite rejections, one so poorly written that it would take heroic efforts to make it readable and the other too basic to interest the readers of *Fiber Craft*, though Kool-Aid tie-dye was certainly a fun idea. "Depictions of Weaving on Greek Vases of the Archaic Period" was a definite win—complete with spectacular photographs of the vases the author had studied. About "My Life as a Sheep" she wrote, "Describing wool production from the point of view of a sheep is quite original, though admittedly whimsical. I suppose sheep do feel a bit chilly after shearing, and I'm concerned this information might upset some readers. But on the positive side, the author cleverly works in details of interest to anyone who enjoys crafts involving wool. The quality of the writing is excellent, and the author's claim to authority (proprietress of an upstate New York sheep farm) unarguable."

Downstairs, Pamela studied the contents of her refrigerator and realized a visit to the Co-Op was called for—and soon. She'd stop there after the lunch at Hyler's with Bettina. Meanwhile, there was a bit of Co-Op cheddar left, and a few eggs. She'd make a cheese omelet and slice one of the community garden tomatoes Bettina had sent her home with, and she'd garnish the tomato slices with olive oil and basil from the basil plant on the back porch.

An hour later, she settled down with *Time and Time Again*. As she opened to Chapter 37, she discovered that the time-traveling protagonists were revisiting the Revolutionary Era, and a dramatic scene was unfolding in the Mittendorf House. Pamela had been there once, of course, because the Mittendorf House was a county landmark—but her visit had taken place several years ago. Wilfred had said some of the members of the historical society read the book, presumably with no objections to its historical accuracy. And anyway, even if Thomas Swinton had fudged details, what was the point of writing fiction if you couldn't fudge? An author wouldn't kill someone for fear she'd point out that the real Mittendorf House was nothing like what he had described. Would he?

Chapter Fourteen

"Don't need this, sweetheart," the confident voice boomed. "Just bring me the usual." Pamela and Bettina were sitting at the very next table, but the voice would have reached them even in the farthest corner of the room. They turned to see the grimacing server reach for the oversize menu the owner of the voice was flourishing in her direction.

"Kent Varnish," Bettina whispered, though there was no need for discretion. Hyler's at lunchtime was abuzz with conversation. Pamela and Bettina had arrived fifteen minutes earlier. They were surveying the Reuben sandwiches that had just been delivered by the server who was now ministering to Kent Varnish. The sandwiches were grand constructions of grilled rye bread, with melted cheese and bits of deep pink corned beef escaping from between the slices. They reposed on oval plates decorated with pickle spears and little paper cups of slaw.

"Back with your lemonade in a second," the server called to them as she headed toward the counter, menu in hand. Kent Varnish watched her depart and then glanced toward Bettina and Pamela. He was a florid man with dark hair receding from a broad forehead.

Bettina had taken particular care with her toilette that morning. She was wearing a form-fitting jersey dress in vivid shades of red, orange, and fuchsia, the colors so lively that they distracted from the fact that Bettina was none too svelte. A triple strand of coral beads accented the deep V-neck, and coral and gold earrings adorned her ears. But obeying Pamela's command that she wear walking shoes, she'd accessorized the outfit with her red sneakers.

Bettina smiled in response to Kent Varnish's glance, then devoted herself to her sandwich. The lemonade arrived. Soon Pamela and Bettina were lifting forkfuls of sandwich trailing long strands of melted cheese to their mouths, dipping nibbles of slaw from the little paper cups, and savoring crisp bites from the pickle spears. When the sandwiches were nearly gone, the meal turned more leisurely. They began to chat about a new reporting assignment Bettina had for the *Advocate*—Adopt a Pet Week at the county shelter. But all the while, they were keeping an eye on Kent Varnish.

When it looked like he had nearly finished his meal—"the usual" had proven to be a Reuben—Bettina suddenly veered from the plight of abandoned pets to raise her voice and announce, "It's losing leaves so early this year. I think there's something wrong with it but I just don't know what to do."

Kent Varnish looked up from the remains of his sandwich and set down the pickle spear he was holding. He fastened his gaze on Bettina. She smiled.

"I know a bit about trees," he said.

"You do?" Bettina purred. "You're not one of those daredevils who climbs . . . ?" Kent Varnish was well into middle age, and he had the physique of a man who ate Reuben sandwiches for lunch every day, as well as doughnuts for breakfast—and probably didn't counterbalance these meals with salads at dinnertime. No one could have seriously mistaken him for a professional tree-trimmer.

But with complete seriousness, he replied, "Valuable work, but I feel I can be more useful on the ground." He edged his chair closer to Bettina and smiled. "Kent Varnish. Arborville Arborists."

"Oh, my!" Bettina clapped her hands and her fuchsia nails glittered. "Do you think you could . . . ? I'm just on Orchard Street. Across from the church. It's not far."

"Are you in the Dutch Colonial?" Bettina nodded. "That's a black walnut you've got."

"Amazing," Bettina said. "How did you know?"

"The Arborists meet at the church." Kent Varnish edged his chair closer. "Every Wednesday night. I know all about your trees." He let his hand rest on the back of Bettina's chair but his eyes wandered to Pamela's face.

"Wednesday nights?" Bettina frowned, but prettily. "Wasn't it a Wednesday night when that terrible accident happened to that sweet young woman? Were you there then?"

"I was at a church," he said, looking back at Bettina. "But not that church. Can't be in two places at once." Pamela suppressed a laugh. He probably tried though—Arborville and Haversack. But he went on.

"They had an emergency at St. Willibrod's—a flood in the vestry. I'm head of the church council and I had to be there."

He focused on Pamela again. "How about a smile," he said. "Give a smile to get a smile. That's my motto." He displayed his own teeth and added, "Come on. A smile doesn't cost anything."

Pamela summoned up a reluctant version of her social smile, but Kent Varnish had ceased paying attention. A man of age and build similar to his own had slipped into a chair next to him and the two were already head-to-head in deep conversation.

Pamela and Bettina glanced at each other, acknowledging that the meeting with Kent Varnish was over. They returned to their meal, finishing up the last bites of the Reubens and maneuvering their straws to reach the last few drops of lemonade, the drink's tart sweetness now diluted by melting ice.

The lunchtime crush was easing as people settled their checks and headed out the door. Kent Varnish slipped a ten-dollar bill into the server's hand with a lordly gesture and told her to keep the change. Before leaving, he leaned toward Pamela and Bettina's table to offer a cheery good-bye, though his cheer was focused more on Bettina than on Pamela.

"You could have acted a little more friendly," Bettina whispered as Hyler's door closed behind Kent Varnish.

"You're better at that than I am," Pamela said. "And anyway, we found out something useful.

"Cross him off the list?" Bettina raised her brows and tightened her lips into a quizzical knot.

Pamela shrugged. "He had no way of knowing we think he killed Caralee. Nobody except us even be-

lieves her death was anything but an accident. So he
probably really was at St. Willibrod's dealing with a
plumbing crisis. Chatting with two fellow towns-
people isn't like being questioned by the police—
where you'd make up an alibi if you didn't have a
real one."

Bettina nodded. "We can always follow up about
the flood in the vestry if all our other suspects fall
through."

"I sort of hope it does turn out to be him," Pamela
said. "He's so creepy."

Bettina laughed. "You haven't met Thomas Swinton yet."

The server delivered their check and Pamela com-
puted the tip, then reached into her handbag for her
wallet. She counted out a few bills, slipped them and
the check under the salt shaker, and started to rise.

Bettina reached out a cautioning hand. "Let's take
our time," she murmured. "Craig Belknap usually
comes out for a break after the lunch crowd leaves
and I want to have a little chat with him. I'm going to
tell him I'm doing a follow-up article on the 'accident' for the *Advocate*."

"But he—"

"I'm still curious about him," Bettina said. "And
anyway, a follow-up article might be a good idea." She
tilted her head and pursed her lips. "I don't think we
have enough to fill the next issue. There's harvest
time at the community gardens, and the Aardvarks'
homecoming game at the high school . . ."

" 'All the news that fits.' " Pamela quoted the Arborville residents' affectionate description of their
town's weekly.

Bettina surveyed the room. "There he is now." She

nodded toward the booth in the far corner near the swinging doors that led into the kitchen. "Act inconspicuous," she said. "You were asking him questions at the reception after Caralee's funeral and he'll be suspicious if he realizes we're together. If he thinks I'm just trying to fill a few columns in the *Advocate*, he's more likely to open up."

Pamela shifted her chair to the side. She watched discreetly as Bettina made her way across the restaurant, threading between the worn wooden tables and straight-backed wooden chairs toward the booth, with its burgundy Naugahyde upholstery. Craig Belknap was sitting on the bench facing the street, studying Bettina as she advanced toward him. As Pamela had noticed before, it was difficult to pick out anything distinctive about the young man. The soft lines of his face and his light brows gave him an innocent air, though the twist of his mouth hinted at something more complicated. He'd hung a white chef's jacket on a hook at the side of the booth and was wearing a nondescript dark T-shirt.

Pamela studied the passing scene through Hyler's front windows. A leggy young blonde woman with a bouncing ponytail pushed a stroller along the sidewalk. A man in a fluorescent green safety vest waved a utility truck into a parking space across the street. A white-haired woman with a cane headed toward the ATM outside the bank. Only a few tables were still occupied and Hyler's was quiet enough now that Pamela could hear the low murmur of Bettina's conversation with Craig Belknap.

Her thoughts turned to plans for the rest of the day. That morning's email had brought a message from her boss concurring with Pamela's recommendation that *Fiber Craft* publish the article about images of weaving on Greek vases. "The December issue is shaping up to be all about weaving," her boss wrote, "and this will fit in beautifully—so please edit ASAP." But first, she'd stop at the Co-Op. She needed cheese and bread and fruit, and vegetables for salad. And she'd make something for dinner that could come back for a few more meals, something like meatloaf. That was it. She'd bake a meatloaf, and a potato with it for tonight, and then there would be leftovers.

An interesting little drama was playing out on the sidewalk in front of Hyler's. The leggy young blonde woman pushing the stroller had evidently finished whatever errand had taken her north on Arborville Avenue and she was passing the window again, heading the other direction. But her passenger now scorned his stroller and seemed determined to walk, though at a snail's pace. And she seemed pressed for time. So after a few hesitant steps, she scooped him up and tried to settle his squirming body back into the padded comfort of the stroller. He resisted, and his red face and agonized expression made it clear he was determined to remain free.

His screams were so frantic that they reached all the way to where Pamela sat, several tables back from the windows. But something else reached her ears too, from the other direction.

"Ghoulish," the voice said, "and for a lame little paper like the *Advocate*?" It was a male voice, but strained to such a pitch that a listener would have been hard-pressed to know that—except Pamela turned to see Craig Belknap half on his feet and leaning toward

Bettina with an expression as agonized as that of the toddler on the sidewalk.

"I didn't mean to upset you," Bettina answered, in tones as soothing as the voice she used when Woofus needed comforting.

"Like you care?" He leaned farther and tensed his fingers as if ready to pounce.

Bettina edged her way out of the booth. She rose to her feet and began to back away. Looking embarrassed, Craig Belknap sank back down. The server had been watching from behind the counter but now went back to tidying the pile of menus. Bettina continued backing away, but her eyes were still fixed on Craig Belknap.

Thus it was that she didn't notice the chair directly in her path. Suddenly there was a screech as wood scraped against wood, a clattering sound as the chair tipped over, and a yelp and a thump as Bettina landed in a heap on the floor.

Pamela rushed to her side from one direction and Craig Belknap from the other. Their eyes met over the prone figure of Bettina. "You?" Craig said, then, "You put her up to this." He buried his face in his hands and slowly dragged them over his forehead, cheeks, and chin as if attempting to wipe away his anger. When he had finished and dropped them to his side, he seemed calmer.

Ignoring him, Pamela stooped and turned her attention to Bettina. Before she could say anything, Bettina struggled into a sitting position. "I'm okay," she said.

"Are you sure?" Pamela put her arm around Bettina's shoulder. The server had rushed over too, and now offered a hand to pull Bettina to her feet. Craig Belknap righted the overturned chair.

Once on her feet, Bettina flexed her elbows and bent each knee. "Everything's working," she said. "I'm just a little shaken up."

Pamela led her to the booth and eased her onto the seat. The server, her brow furrowed, leaned down. "I could call nine-one-one," she said.

"No, really. Please. I'm fine." Bettina waved the server away. Indeed, she seemed fine. Even the bright red curls brushing her forehead and framing her cheeks were undisturbed.

Pamela remained standing, and so did Craig Belknap, and it was Pamela he addressed. "I wasn't anywhere near the church that night, okay? I told her, and now I'm telling you—*again*, though I thought I made it clear to you at the reception after the funeral. The group wasn't rehearsing my scenes and I had something else to do. I don't know why you both think somebody killed Caralee on purpose and especially why you think that somebody was me."

"The argument I overheard from my front lawn," Pamela said.

"You don't understand at all." He shook his head sadly. "You don't understand what that was about."

"Then tell us where you were Wednesday night. Somebody saw you leaving Hyler's well before your usual quitting time."

"I don't have to talk to you," he said, and ducked back through the swinging doors that led to the kitchen.

"I guess he doesn't," Bettina said with a disgusted shrug. She leaned on the table as she rose slowly to her feet. Pamela watched, concern making her eyes seem larger and darker. She reached out a hand, but

Bettina smiled and took a few tentative steps. "Perfectly fine," she announced. "Shall we head for the Co-Op? Thursday night is baked salmon and Wilfred has been looking forward to it."

Standing on the sidewalk in front of the Co-Op, Pamela scanned the bulletin board on the market's façade. The cards offering kittens to good homes had disappeared—perhaps a good sign, suggesting as it did that the kittens had found good homes, and rather quickly. Hopefully when the time came for her to seek good homes for whatever kittens remained after Knit and Nibble had claimed their choices, kittenless good homes would still remain in Arborville.

Inside the Co-Op, Pamela steered her cart over the worn wooden floor toward produce. Bettina, with a basket slung over her arm, headed down one of the Co-Op's narrow aisles toward the fish counter at the back of the store. Browsing among bundles of leafy greens, pyramids of bright fruit, and bins of dusky potatoes and golden onions, Pamela added a cucumber, three tomatoes, a bag of apples, a baking potato, and an onion to her cart. She picked up a pound of freshly ground beef in the meat section and a wedge of Vermont cheddar at the cheese counter, then she proceeded to the bakery counter, drawn by the aroma of sugary things just out of the oven. Bettina was already there, slipping a white bakery box tied up with string into her basket.

"Apple turnovers," she announced.

Pamela requested a loaf of whole-grain bread, sliced, and soon they had gone through the checkout lane and were once again out on the sidewalk, strolling along Arborville Avenue toward Orchard

Street. They had reached the corner where a small shelter and a bench marked the stop for the bus to Manhattan when a jingling sound emerged from the depths of Bettina's handbag.

"My phone," she exclaimed. "I didn't know it was on." She lifted it from her bag, said hello, and listened for a second. "It's Penny." She handed the phone to Pamela. "And she sounds worried."

Chapter Fifteen

Pamela's heart stirred with a ragged thump and she felt her breath stop. She set one of her canvas grocery bags on the bench and took the phone from Bettina's hands. In a tiny strangled voice, she said, "Penny?"

"I've been calling and calling," Penny said. "And your cell phone too. Where have you been?"

"What's wrong?" Pamela sank onto the bench and Bettina perched beside her, an arm around Pamela's shoulders.

"You never answered my email. And that makes me think you're doing exactly what I was afraid you were doing." Bettina's phone made Penny's voice sound high-pitched and tinny, but her anger was clear.

"Are you okay?" Pamela's heart hadn't stopped thumping.

"Of course I'm okay," Penny said in the cell phone voice. "I'm calling to make sure *you're* okay—that you're not doing anything dangerous. I know you and Bettina think you can figure things out better than the police can."

Pamela took a deep breath. "She's okay," she whispered in an aside to Bettina. "She called because she thinks we think Caralee was murdered."

"We do think that," Bettina whispered back.

"Shhh!" Pamela frowned at Bettina and returned to the phone. "The police are confident Caralee's death was an accident," she said. "So what would we even do?"

Penny was silent for a minute. Then her voice came back. "You're sure, Mom? You're sure I don't have to worry?"

"Absolutely positive," Pamela said firmly. "You don't have to worry." She handed the phone back to Bettina.

"Was that honest?" Bettina asked as they resumed their walk home.

Pamela didn't answer. "You don't have to worry" could mean a lot of different things. It didn't necessarily mean that there was nothing to worry about.

Back at home, Pamela put her groceries away and settled down at her computer for an afternoon of work on the magazine. Hours passed and as the light behind her curtains began to wane, an aggrieved meowing at her office door reminded her that dinnertime was drawing near.

Downstairs, the first order of business was tending to the needs of seven hungry creatures, with scoops of cat food for Catrina and kitten food for her offspring. The kittens waited eagerly for their food, weaving complicated patterns of ginger and black as they milled around Pamela's feet.

Once Catrina and the kittens were hunkered down around their bowls in their accustomed corner, Pamela started work on the meatloaf that would be her own dinner. From the cupboard she took her favorite mixing bowl, the caramel-colored one with the white stripes near the rim, and from another cupboard she took the metal loaf pan with the faint patina of rust that never seemed to hurt anything. The baking potato sat on the counter where she'd placed it when she took it from one of her canvas grocery bags earlier that afternoon.

She had a fresh loaf of whole-grain bread now, so the heels that remained from the previous loaf would become the breadcrumbs for the meatloaf. She set the heels out on the counter, along with the package of ground beef, the Co-Op onion, and an egg. Her mother had always put a dollop of catsup in meatloaf, along with a teaspoon of dried herbs. Pamela had adopted the catsup and herbs as well, but fresh herbs when they were available. And along with the other herbs on her back porch, she currently had a vigorous stand of parsley in a clay pot—so hardy that it had survived the previous winter to reappear with the daffodils in the spring.

She grabbed her cooking scissors, hurried down the hallway to the back door, and stepped outside. The sunset blazed through gaps in the trees that marked the border between Pamela's backyard and that of her neighbor to the southwest. But the shrubbery was already masked in shadow. She stooped toward the pot of parsley and reached under the lacy foliage to snip the stems. Clutching the harvested parsley like a bright green posy and rising to her feet, Pamela dawdled on the porch for a few minutes marveling at the orange-red sky, which shimmered like glowing embers.

But she was distracted from her contemplation of the sunset by a rustling in the hedge between her yard and church next door. The hedge ran along the property line all the way from her front yard to the very back corner of her lot, skirting the church itself, the auditorium, and then the church parking lot. She glanced over to see the tall shrubs that made up the hedge swaying, then a figure emerged out of the shadows. She hadn't turned on the porch light when she came out. She'd been able to find the parsley perfectly well though the day was fading. But perhaps seeing a light would have made the intruder less bold. Now she edged toward the back door, feeling her heart speed up while he—it *was* a he, dressed in jeans, a dark T-shirt, and a baseball cap—strolled across her lawn and vanished behind the garage. He reemerged to stroll back across the lawn and wiggle through the hedge onto the church's property.

The baseball cap, pulled low on his forehead, had obscured much of his face, so all she knew was that a medium-tall man with a medium build had been lurking in the hedge along the side of her house and then had briefly explored her backyard. But, she reflected with a pang and her heart sped up even more, he could have made a thorough inspection of her front yard, her porch—and even peered in her living room windows—before turning his attention to the back.

Pamela reached for the doorknob with shaky fingers. Back in the kitchen, she added the handful of parsley to the arrangement of bowl, loaf pan, potato, and ingredients for the meatloaf. But the food might as well have been made of wax for all the interest in cooking it now provoked. Fear had driven her hunger away, and her throat felt too tight to swallow.

Normally the appearance of a strange man in her yard wouldn't have caused alarm. Few people in Arborville fenced their properties, and rather than walk up one block, around a corner, and down another, people sometimes took shortcuts and nobody cared. But Pamela and Bettina had been none too subtle in their quest to prove that Caralee's death wasn't an accident—particularly in their conversations with Craig Belknap, a medium-tall man with a medium build who could easily pull a baseball cap low on his forehead to become indistinguishable from any other medium-tall man with a medium build.

Pamela opened her front door cautiously and peered out, nerves making her heart tick like a busy kitchen timer. Welcoming lights were on at Bettina's house, and an hour or so spent with friends would quell the unease that had overtaken her. Besides, she wanted to confer with Bettina about this new development. She stepped onto the porch, keys in hand. A few people were hurrying along the sidewalk, probably on their way to rehearsal. Maybe Craig Belknap's scenes were being rehearsed this evening too. That thought made Pamela stop breathing completely. Maybe he'd shown up at the church, recalled that the person who'd been so curious about his whereabouts the night Caralee died lived right there in that big wood-frame house, and decided to take a look around in case he ever needed to silence her once and for all. If he'd killed once, he could kill again.

Making double sure to lock the door behind her and giving the knob an extra twist just to set her mind at rest, she hurried down the steps. She was grateful for the traffic on the sidewalk. Craig Belknap wouldn't attack her with other people around, especially people who knew him from the Arborville Players. She paused at the curb as a car cruised by. It turned to head into the church driveway, and its headlights swept the pleasant house, almost a twin of Pamela's, that flanked the church property on the other side. Pamela darted across the street and in a minute she was ringing Bettina's bell.

"Something's wrong!" Bettina exclaimed before the door was even fully open. She pulled it wide and reached a welcoming hand toward Pamela. She was still wearing the vivid jersey dress she'd worn for lunch at Hyler's, but she'd added a colorful apron styled after the look of a 1950s housewife. From behind her came a mournful whine, and Woofus edged around his mistress's thigh to regard Pamela with apprehensive eyes. With her other hand, Bettina gave Woofus a comforting pat, then she turned her attention to Pamela.

"Come in, come in," she said, "and tell us what happened." The reference to "us" was in fact accurate because Wilfred was just stepping through the arch that separated the dining room from the living room. He wore an apron tied over his bib overalls.

"You're cooking!" Pamela took a step backward. "I didn't mean to interrupt. It's dinnertime"—she stopped in confusion—"of course. I was starting to cook. But then—"

"Come in here and sit down." Bettina put her arm around Pamela's shoulders and guided her toward the dining room and then into the kitchen beyond. Wilfred followed and Woofus brought up the rear. Once they reached the kitchen, the dog retreated to a far corner and watched the proceedings warily.

Seated at Bettina's well-scrubbed pine table with a

glass of white wine in front of her, Pamela began to feel calmer—and a bit silly to have created such a bother. But she tried to explain what had brought her hurrying across the street. "Someone was sneaking around in my yard," she said, "right at sunset, and it could have been Craig Belknap though I couldn't tell for sure because he was wearing a baseball cap, and he'd pulled it way down as if he was trying on purpose to disguise himself. And after today, especially . . . he thinks we both suspect that he arranged that furniture to crush Caralee."

"Well, I would have been scared too," Bettina announced. "And I'm glad you came here instead of staying in that big house alone. We can all sleep here tonight, and Woofus will make sure there are no intruders." She glanced toward where the shaggy creature cowered against the wall. "Won't you, boy!" She stood up. "There's plenty of salmon—and wine—so let's have a nice evening."

Wilfred had been listening from the other side of the kitchen, where he stood at the counter arranging broad slices of salmon in a Pyrex baking pan. He patted the last glistening pink strip into place and gestured at Bettina to stay put. "Too many cooks spoil the broth, dear wife. And anyway the salad is done, and the brown rice is underway, and I'll just pop the salmon in and join you and Pamela for a glass of this nice wine."

"He makes the best sauce when we have salmon," Bettina said. "He's been retired almost a year now and my old faithful menus have been quite transformed."

"Butter, capers, lemon juice, and a little mustard," Wilfred said, a pleased smile lighting up his ruddy face. "Nothing to it and it only takes a few minutes."

*   *   *

An hour later they were sitting around Bettina's dining room table in contented silence. As if the splendid meal hadn't been enough, Bettina had brought out the apple turnovers she'd bought that afternoon at the Co-Op and topped them with vanilla ice cream. Only a few pastry crumbs and dabs of melted ice cream remained on Bettina's sage-green plates, and the hand-woven napkins from the craft shop had been removed from laps and lay in crumpled folds on the table.

Pamela bestirred herself and began to collect the plates and silverware, but Wilfred insisted the cleanup was his job.

"But you cooked," Pamela said.

"Please sit down." Bettina touched Pamela's arm. Pamela obeyed, and the two remained at the table talking about Bettina's plans for the next day— babysitting the Arborville grandchildren—and their Saturday meeting with Thomas Swinton. From the kitchen came the sounds of running water and jingling silverware, and the clatter of plates, pots, and pans being shifted here and there. What a comforting sound, Pamela reflected. She and her husband had shared kitchen duties as well. The image of Richard Larkin came into her mind and she quickly banished it. There was no reason to think about him at all, except in a neighborly way.

Wilfred rejoined them soon, and the conversation turned to the doings of the historical society. "I should get going," Pamela said at last, stirring in her chair.

"No!" Bettina shook her head in alarm and her coral and gold earrings swayed wildly. "You'll stay here tonight, of course. Wilfred Junior's bedroom is

Wilfred's den now, but the bed is made up in Warren's old room."

"But . . . Catrina." A small wrinkle appeared between Pamela's brows and her lips twisted in dismay. "She sleeps with me now. She won't know what happened to me . . . whether there will ever be cat food again. And she's got kittens to nurse." She stood up. "I've got to go back. And I'll be fine. Really."

Pamela didn't mention that she had a second reason for wanting to return home. She was eight chapters from the end of *Time and Time Again* and was determined to finish it by Saturday's lunch with its author—though she hadn't yet hatched any brilliant ideas about what Caralee might have been planning to reveal about Thomas Swinton or his book on her blog.

Bettina stood up too. "I'm coming across the street with you," she said, "to make sure you get back safely." Wilfred started to rise but Bettina motioned him to stay in his chair. "We'll be fine," she added. "We'll take Woofus."

"I will certainly come as far as the porch, dear wife," Wilfred said, leaning on the table as he rose to his feet. "Better safe than sorry."

Woofus came too, as far as the edge of the porch. But as they all stepped out into a night with a hint of late-September chill in the air, a commotion on the sidewalk made the dog jump back skittishly, almost tripping Wilfred.

A small group of people had paused at the end of Wilfred and Bettina's driveway, but the commotion proved to be nothing more than hysterical laughter. Then headlights emerged from the church driveway and a car swung onto Orchard Street, followed by another.

"It's the Players," Bettina said. "Rehearsal must be getting out."

She and Pamela made their way along the path that led from the porch to the driveway. As they started down the driveway, the group—a man and two women—moved farther along the sidewalk. The hysterical laughter had abated, but not the general merriment.

"He *is* a fool," one of the women was saying, "but it's still a cool part. I was lucky to get it. Too bad about Caralee though."

"That accent cracks me up," the man said. "*Sooo veddy, veddy British*—and to think he's really from Bayonne."

"His wife is his biggest booster," the other woman added. Pamela recognized her as the older woman in the colorful long skirt who one of the police officers had interviewed the night Caralee died. "I've been in the Players forever, long enough to be on the list for those ridiculous Christmas letters she sends out. I swear, she must sit down at the computer every night to catalogue what he did that day. I'm surprised she doesn't include the menus for his meals."

"Or what time he took his bath," the man added, and they exploded into laughter again.

"Or what kind of toothpaste he uses," the younger woman cried, her voice shrill with hilarity.

The older woman caught sight of Bettina and Pamela. "I'm sorry we scared your dog," she said.

"Oh, he's just a nervous nelly." Bettina laughed. "How are your rehearsals going . . . without . . . ?" She paused. "What a shock that was! Such a shame."

"We're doing okay." The young man spoke up. "We'll be ready. Lorraine here—aka Madame Defarge—is a quick study." He patted the younger woman on the back.

"I think Craig Belknap is in the play," Bettina said. "That nice young man who cooks at Hyler's?"

"Sydney Carton." The older woman nodded. "Quite a plum role."

"He must be very dedicated," Bettina commented. "Cooking all day and then rehearsal every night."

"Not every night." The older woman switched from a "yes" nod to a "no" head shake. "It depends whose scenes we're working on."

"I thought I saw him earlier," Pamela said.

"Must have been his doppelgänger." The young man laughed. "Tonight we concentrated on the wine shop scenes."

The three Players continued on up the street and Bettina and Pamela looked at each other. "If he wasn't at the rehearsal, does that make it more or less likely that he was in my yard?" Pamela asked. "It wasn't seven yet when I saw that man, and they start at seven."

"I don't know." Bettina shrugged. "But we've got plenty to talk about."

"Bayonne," Pamela murmured.

"I'll be over as soon as I finish babysitting duty tomorrow," Bettina said. "And you be sure to lock your doors and check your windows tonight."

Chapter Sixteen

The next morning, as the kittens milled around their food bowl, tiny ears sleeked back, attacking the chicken-fish blend Pamela had offered them for breakfast, Pamela herself waited for her coffee to drip into its carafe and pondered. Five suspects, she said to herself. First, Craig Belknap—at least Bettina thought he belonged at the top of the list. And one couldn't discount the ferocious argument Pamela had overheard, the lack of an alibi, and now the fact that he might have been casing her yard.

As she removed the drip filter from the carafe and poured a cup of coffee, her thoughts turned to Anthony Wadsworth. There was no doubt about his access to the storage room. Anything Rue said or didn't say to the police about that could easily be discounted as a wife covering for her husband. And now, based on the conversation she and Bettina had overheard the previous night, his motive for wanting Caralee out of the way couldn't be clearer. If Caralee had revealed on her blog that his grand British manner and his claims of triumphs in the London theater world were total fabrications, he'd have been mortified.

She took a sip of coffee and slipped a slice of whole-grain bread into the toaster. Kent Varnish, she reflected, had a motive: the sweetie—and Baby Varnish!—in the secret hideaway in Haversack. He definitely wouldn't have wanted that revealed on Caralee's blog. And he had access to the storage room—the Arborists used one of the church's meeting rooms for their meetings. But there was an alibi, though they had only his word that he missed the meeting the night Caralee died because he was dealing with a flood at St. Willibrod's.

The toast popped up. She put it on a plate, buttered it, and turned her attention to Merrick Timmons. He had access to the storage room—albeit indirectly—in the person of Ben Skyler, who did odd jobs for him and reportedly wasn't the most upstanding individual. What about motive though? Having a big house and a trophy wife wasn't all that shameful—but perhaps there was more to be discovered.

She set the plate of toast on the table, along with the cup of coffee. Thomas Swinton was last on the list. Caralee had included him among the doomed aristocrats, and announced that he'd soon be featured on her blog. But why?

Then she paused and frowned. Maybe there were more than five. Should she add the troubled husband who she'd met at the reception after the funeral? He might have decided that if he couldn't have Caralee, no one else would have her either. And what about the understudy—Lorraine—who'd won the role of Madame Defarge after Caralee was out of the way? What better motive could there be than eliminating your competition?

Pamela had been thinking so hard her coffee had gotten cold. She emptied her cup back into the carafe and set the carafe to warm gently on the stove. Work for the magazine waited on the computer, she was sure, but she was suddenly curious about Merrick Timmons. She'd take a newly heated cup of coffee upstairs and, before doing anything else—except checking email of course—see what the Internet could reveal about him. And since the meeting with Thomas Swinton loomed, and she'd finished *Time and Time Again* the previous night, she'd take a look at Thomas Swinton's website.

Chapter Seventeen

A few minutes later Pamela was clicking on one of the many references that had come up when she keyed "Merrick Timmons Northern New Jersey" into the Google search box. "My, my, my," she murmured as she scanned a year-old article from a weekly distributed in Haversack. The headline read SLUMLORD TIMMONS AGAIN EVADES DEMANDS FOR REPAIRS BY TENANT ADVOCATES.

Other references yielded similar information. The *Register* had even included Merrick Timmons in a three-part series on the affordable housing shortage in Northern New Jersey. He was profiled as the worst of a bad lot—landlords who let their buildings deteriorate but were quick to evict tenants who fell even a month behind on rent. The series had run nearly five years ago, long before Merrick Timmons had moved to Arborville, and Pamela was certain he would just as soon prefer none of his new neighbors realized how he made his living. Arborville's professional class lived well, but the town had an intellectual and artistic bent and a long tradition of social activism. Information about his life as a slumlord would have made terrific material for Caralee's blog but would have been very damaging to a man putting on airs as a person of taste and refinement.

Somewhat disgusted by what she had learned about Merrick Timmons, Pamela keyed Thomas Swinton's name into the Google search box. His website was the first item to come up, suggesting he got a lot of web traffic. Clicking on "ThomasSwinton.com" led her to a page headed by his name, spelled out in an elaborate script. Beneath the heading was a photo of a middle-aged man with a luxuriant and well-groomed white beard sitting in front of an entire wall of books. "Please let me welcome you into my world," read the caption, "and let me share with you the love of history that inspires my fiction."

He had written a lot of books, long books, and so very many that Pamela imagined he must have worked nonstop seven days a week for most of his adult life. She scrolled through page after page of dramatic book covers—his name becoming a larger and larger part of the design as the years went on—accompanied by glowing reviews.

"Impressive," she said to herself at last, "but something about him apparently didn't impress Caralee." She closed the browser and tackled the day's assignment from *Fiber Craft*.

By noon she was ready for a break, the sustenance provided by the breakfast toast and coffee long since exhausted. She'd have some lunch, and since the work her boss had sent wasn't due back until Monday, she'd take a walk and do a bit of housework until Bettina arrived after her babysitting chore.

A meatloaf sandwich would have been welcome, but the meatloaf hadn't gotten made. She'd put the egg and the pound of ground beef back in the refrigerator before dashing across the street the previous evening. The potato, onion, and parsley—now somewhat wilted—still waited on the counter. She'd revisit that menu plan tonight, but meanwhile grilled cheese would have to do.

As she set out her wooden cutting board and unwrapped the wedge of cheddar she'd picked up the day before, she recalled a scene in *Time and Time Again*. It took place in the kitchen of the Mittendorf House, in one of the time travel scenes, and she'd reflected while reading it that in some ways food preparation hadn't changed all that much. In fact, she recalled that on her visit to the Mittendorf House several years ago, the long wooden table in the kitchen had featured an arrangement of realistic-looking food—eggs, potatoes, onions, and meat not all that different from the ingredients she'd laid out for her meatloaf. Of course, in place of an oven, there had been a grand fireplace that took up a whole wall.

Thomas Swinton might be a bit full of himself, but his knowledge of history seemed genuine. She laughed aloud, remembering the phrase the *Advocate* had used in the headline for Bettina's interview with him: "one of Arborville's intellectual treasures." So suppose he was the one who killed Caralee. What could she have latched on to? What would be the worst thing to happen to a writer who was also an intellectual treasure?

Invigorated by her walk, Pamela cleared the tile floors in the kitchen, back hallway, and laundry room of chairs, rag rugs, and cat- and kitten-food bowls, and litter box. She moved the comfortable bed where

Catrina nursed her kittens and where they still slept to the top of the clothes dryer, assuring a few displaced kittens that the move was only temporary. She poured a dollop of pine-scented cleaning liquid into a plastic bucket, fetched her sponge mop from the utility closet, and applied herself to giving all three areas a thorough scrubbing, then a rinse. Upstairs, she flopped on her bed for a rest and lingered there until the doorbell's chime summoned her down the stairs.

Through the lace that curtained the oval window in the front door, she could make out Bettina's vivid coif bobbing this way and that. She opened the door to be greeted by her friend's back. Bettina was energetically scanning the yard. "No strange men that I can see," she announced as she spun around. She grabbed Pamela's hand. "Were you okay last night?" She had come right from her babysitting duties and was wearing dark blue leggings and a matching tunic with bright embroidered borders at hem, cuffs, and neckline.

"Fine." Pamela led her inside.

"I smell pine," Bettina commented as they walked through the entry. She was carrying a white bakery box.

"Cleaning day," Pamela said. "I scrubbed the kitchen floor. The kittens didn't like the smell, or all the activity. I think most of them are still upstairs."

Bettina set the box on the kitchen table and glanced around. "It looks clean," she commented. "What would you say to another apple turnover?" she asked. "A reward for your industry. I bought six yesterday."

"We'll need coffee," Pamela said. She set water on

the stove to boil and poured beans into her coffee grinder.

"I guess we have a motive for Wadsworth," Bettina said as she reached two cups and saucers from the cupboard.

"Too many suspects." Pamela pressed down on the grinder's top and the blades crunched into the beans, blotting out Bettina's response.

"I said," Bettina repeated, "we'll have to talk to him."

"I agree." Pamela transferred the ground beans into the paper filter she'd placed in the plastic cone atop her carafe. "But wait till you hear what the Internet revealed about Merrick Timmons. I don't know why we didn't think of Googling him sooner." She poured the now-boiling water over the ground beans and as the dark, spicy aroma of brewing coffee wafted from the counter, she described the articles about Merrick Timmons's behavior as a landlord.

"Wow!" Bettina looked up from the turnover she had just transferred to one of Pamela's dessert plates. She had already filled the cut-glass cream pitcher and set out the sugar bowl. "And we know how he could have engineered the toppling furniture."

Pamela nodded. "Ben Skyler." She removed the plastic cone and carried the carafe to the table. "But how could Caralee have gotten onto what Merrick Timmons was up to? Internet, obviously, but something would have had to put that seed in her mind— to research him in the first place. I can't believe she set about trying to find compromising information on every single resident of Arborville."

"Hyler's," Bettina said. "Everybody goes there, and when you're a server people hardly notice you—unless you mess up. I waited tables summers when I was in college. I couldn't believe the things people talked about over meals. Not to mention what they'll say on their cell phones now. Anywhere."

"So," Pamela said, "two things to do." She tilted the carafe and filled Bettina's cup. "First, figure out a way to talk to Wadsworth, and what to ask him. We can't just say, 'Did you kill Caralee Lorimer.'" She filled her own cup. "Second, figure out whether Ben Skyler stayed at work later than usual that Wednesday night. He unlocked the storage room early because Rue Wadsworth wanted to work on costumes, then she left a bit after six. He told us he usually goes home at five. But if his plan was to carry out orders from Merrick Timmons and arrange things to crush Caralee, he would have been lurking around when Rue left."

Bettina had already carved off a forkful of turnover, revealing the apple slices flecked with cinnamon within the tawny pastry shell. She nodded. "Rue might be over there now. Opening night is a week from today—at least according to the press release they sent the *Advocate*. She didn't have much of a start with the costumes the last time we talked to her. I imagine it's crunch time." She lifted the forkful of turnover to her mouth. "We'll give Caralee's knitting project back to her. Pretend we think she needs it."

Pamela picked up her fork, and for a few minutes both concentrated on their turnovers and coffee. The natural sweetness of the apples had been supplemented with a goodly amount of sugar, creating a thick apple-y syrup that coated the tender apple slices.

"I'm not sure what to think about Thomas Swinton," she said as she speared all that remained of the turnover, a knob of crust from one of the corners. "I finished the book, and I researched him on the Internet, and nothing has jumped out at me. So . . . motive?" She shrugged. "And there's no obvious way he'd have had access to the storage room either. But we can ask Rue if she saw him hanging around Wednesday evening . . . if she even knows who he is."

"We're not canceling lunch tomorrow." Bettina sounded truly upset. "He's quite the gourmand. I interviewed him at four in the afternoon the last time and he served tea and éclairs."

Rue *had* made progress with the costumes. Two of the wheeled clothes racks sat out on the polished floor of the auditorium. One held a row of long, full-skirted dresses in mournful shades of brown and gray, pale in spots, streaked darker in others, and creased as if they had been dampened and then let dry with no attention from an iron. The other held shapeless men's jackets in the same sad condition. Rue was sitting in a chair near the doorway that led in from the hall, busy with a sewing project.

"Suitable for the downtrodden masses, don't you think?" Rue said, looking up from what she was doing. "No one in the audience will realize those dresses and jackets appeared in *Carousel* last year. Amazing what you can do with a few bottles of dye." The sound that followed the comment must have been meant as a laugh but it sounded more like a yelp. Rue looked worn out, with dark circles like purplish bruises under her eyes. Pamela supposed the stress of supplying costumes for a large cast was taking a toll.

Rue was working on another dress, but very different from the ones on the rack. It was made from a shiny cloth in a pretty shade of blue and was in the process of having a lacy trim added to its neckline. "Lucie Manette," she said, standing and holding the dress up to be admired. "The actress will be here in half an hour for a fitting, so I've got to keep busy." She sat back down and her needle resumed its steady in and out.

"Very nice," said Bettina, "and we won't keep you. But we brought you something . . ." She nodded at Pamela and Pamela tugged Caralee's knitting project from the Co-Op bag she'd tucked it into at Margo's house.

"That?" Rue looked at it curiously. "I gave that to *you.*"

"But since the production is going forward despite Caralee's death, we thought you'd want it back. Caralee put a lot of work into it—and it *is* the right color."

As Bettina was talking, Pamela edged down the hall and peeked inside the storage room. The jumble of furniture, scenery, and props had all been tucked away since the last time she and Bettina paid a call on Rue—and the arrangement seemed as precarious as she imagined it had been the night Caralee was killed. Clearly the theater group owned more—of just about *everything*—than the church storage room could comfortably accommodate. She stepped back through the doorway into the auditorium.

Rue laughed again, or rather the strange yelp issued from her throat. "We won't need it now," she said firmly, then tucked a pleat into the strip of lace she was stitching into place, and stabbed through lace and fabric with her needle. She looked up to frown at Bettina.

"I guess the replacement actress is a knitter then," Bettina said cheerily. "That's a stroke of luck. Do you suppose"—she bent toward Rue—"she'd like to join our group? New members are always welcome."

Pamela grimaced. It was clear that Rue was losing patience with them. She wasn't nearly as chatty as usual. But they hadn't managed to work the conversation around to the topic they'd hoped to discuss— Ben Skyler's whereabouts on the evening Caralee was killed. Pamela surveyed the auditorium's bare floor. "It looks like you got everything put away again," she said. "That must have been quite a job."

"It was," Rue said, in a tone that seemed intended to discourage further discussion.

"Ben Skyler must be a great help to you," Bettina commented. "My husband chats with him—we're right across the street. He's always busy at something. What would the church do without him?"

"The church would do quite well, I'm sure, and he's never done a lick of work for the Players." Rue concentrated on her sewing as she spoke. "*Not in my job description*," she added, in a surly growl apparently meant as a parody of Ben's speech. "Employing him is pure charity, if you ask me. But"—she shrugged— "it's a church. That's what they do."

"You said he's here every day till five," Pamela said. "We were talking about the night Caralee died."

"He wasn't here till five that day," Rue said. "He unlocked the storage room for me at two, then took off. He said he had a job to do for Merrick Timmons. That's what I mean. The church pays him for twice the number of hours he works."

Pamela stepped over to where the dresses for the

downtrodden masses hung and lifted a hanger off
the rack to study one of the garments. "It seems very
authentic," she observed. "Very historical." Then, as
if the thought had been triggered by what she had
just said, she added, "Has Thomas Swinton ever been
involved with the Players? A production like this
would seem right up his alley."

"Who?" Rue looked up from her sewing, her brows
raised in puzzlement.

"Thomas Swinton," Pamela repeated. "The writer."

"I wouldn't know," Rue said briskly. "And now I
really have to get back to work."

Bettina waited until they were out on the sidewalk
to speak. Then she clapped her hands and said, "I'm
not sure what that information about Ben means,
but you were clever—working Thomas Swinton in."

Pamela nodded. "It occurred to me right while we
were talking to Rue. The Players could have been the
connection between Swinton and Caralee. Let's say
he came in as a consultant—assuming Anthony
Wadsworth would admit that anyone else could be
helpful—" They both laughed.

Bettina finished the thought. "In matters of the
theater," she concluded, her voice parodying Wadsworth's British accent. "So Swinton is there at a rehearsal and he says something or does something
that makes Caralee decide he's good fodder for her
blog. And not being the most diplomatic person on
earth—"

Pamela took up the idea. "*She* says something or
does something to let him know she thinks he's a
complete fool."

Bettina nodded. "But Rue wouldn't have told us that."

Pamela nodded back. "She'd be loyal to the group."

"Undoubtedly." By now they had reached Pamela's front walk. "I'll call for you at a quarter to twelve tomorrow for our lunch date with Swinton," she said. "Wear something nice, and we're *not* walking."

Chapter Eighteen

The apple turnover had provided a very substantial afternoon snack, so hunger wasn't the stimulus that turned Pamela's thoughts to dinner. Those thoughts were motivated by the recollection that a pound of ground beef still waited to be transformed into meatloaf. In the kitchen, she set the oven at 350 degrees, fed Catrina and the kittens, scrubbed the baking potato thoroughly and poked it several times with a fork, and set about chopping onions with her chef's knife. As she chopped, she turned away and blinked as the sharp onion burned her eyes.

The parsley she'd harvested the previous evening was wilted but would certainly serve for meatloaf. When the onions were finished, she chopped the parsley, then tore the heels from last week's loaf of whole-grain bread into bits and used the chef's knife to render them into even smaller bits. As she worked, the sky visible through the kitchen window darkened. Handling the parsley brought to mind the adventure of the previous evening—the man (maybe

Craig Belknap!) snooping around her yard—and her
flight across the street to spend the rest of the evening
with Bettina and Wilfred. She'd returned home to
sleep in her own bed, uneventfully, but she wondered
whether she should be nervous now.

Soon the caramel-colored bowl with white stripes
near the rim held the compact oval of ground meat,
garnished with the chopped onions, the bits of whole-
grain bread, and a dusting of green parsley flecks. She
sprinkled a teaspoon of salt over the bowl's contents
and added several grindings of pepper. The catsup
bottle waited nearby, but the next step was to crack
an egg over the whole. With a wooden spoon, she
broke up the yolk, which was the brilliant orange of a
tiny sun on the verge of setting, added a dollop of
catsup, and then mixed and mixed until all the ingredients had been merged into a marbled pinkish
blend studded with pale onion bits. She smoothed it
into the loaf pan and slid it onto the oven rack, with
the potato tucked nearby.

Time and Time Again sat on the mail table waiting to
go back to Bettina. Glad to be knitting again, Pamela
lounged on the sofa with her project. As she'd neared
the end of the first sleeve for the elegant ruby-red
tunic with the cutout shoulders, she'd debated
whether to alter the pattern so she wouldn't be bar-
ing her shoulders when she wore it. Pamela wasn't an
overly modest person, but she *was* sensible. And a
wool garment that didn't protect the wearer's shoulders from the chill didn't seem sensible. But she'd
decided to follow the pattern as it was written and see
how she liked the result. The sleeves could always be

changed later. The model wearing the garment in
the pattern book looked very pleased to be sporting
such a chic design.

Now the second sleeve was nearly done, a British
mystery was unfolding on the screen before her, and
Catrina was snuggled against her thigh. Lulled by the
even rhythm of the needles, Pamela struggled to
keep her eyes open, but her eyelids refused to coop-
erate. She let them have their way. When she opened
her eyes again, the dour male detective in the mystery she had been watching had been replaced by a
cheerful female detective wearing a period costume.
She realized she had slept through the end of a mystery from one series and the beginning of a mystery
from another series. She checked to make sure she
hadn't dropped any stitches when the hands holding
her needles had sagged to her lap, and headed up
the stairs to bed, Catrina leading the way.

That night Pamela's dreaming mind returned to
the Mittendorf House. Again, she roamed around
the stately room where balls had been held—in real
life, as well as in Thomas Swinton's novel. She admired the gold-framed portraits of gentlemen and
gentlewomen with powdered hair. She peeked into a
side room where an elegant desk and imposing chair
could have served the Revolutionary Era master of
the house as he received callers and conducted his
business. Again, she found herself in the kitchen,
with its huge stone fireplace and bundles of dried
herbs.

But this dream, unlike the one that had been dis-
pelled by Catrina's meowing, did not end there.
Pamela ventured out a back door and through a carefully planted kitchen garden, to an outbuilding several
yards from the main house. A woman stirred a pot over

a fire and explained that in the summer cooking was done in the summer kitchen.

Then the dream morphed into a continuation of an earlier night's dream, the one in which she'd been roaming the halls of the Hilton Garden Inn searching for the room where she was scheduled to give a talk. But now she was frantically roaming through the Mittendorf House, opening doors to no avail. *You won't find the things you're searching for,* said an insistent voice in her head, *because they aren't here.* But the search became so frantic that she was grateful when a gentle paw against her cheek roused her.

Stopping only to tug on her robe and slide her feet into her slippers, Pamela hurried across the hall to her office and pushed the button that would bring her computer to life. Things that weren't there—that was the key, but first she'd have to make *sure* they weren't there. When her computer's screen brightened, a quick Internet search told her that the Mittendorf House was open from ten a.m. to four p.m. on Saturdays.

There'd be plenty of time then, before Bettina picked her up for their lunch date with Thomas Swinton. The Mittendorf House was barely ten minutes away, just above the border between Haversack and Riverton. Pamela spent a few minutes checking her email and was relieved to see that there were no messages from Penny. Hopefully Penny had accepted the guarantee Pamela had given her from the bus stop that when it came to her mother's amateur sleuthing, Penny had nothing to worry about.

Catrina had waited patiently in the doorway while Pamela did her computer chores, but she scampered ahead as Pamela headed toward the stairs and then down to the kitchen. The kittens greeted their mother with hungry squeaks and followed her to the communal bed in the laundry room.

Pamela spooned portions of cat and kitten food into fresh bowls and set them in the corner where the cabinets made a right turn. It was only a little past eight. She could dawdle a bit over coffee, toast, and the *Register* before she had to set off for Riverton. So she filled the kettle and set water boiling for coffee, then headed for the front door to retrieve the newspaper.

As she stepped onto the porch, she was startled to see a man strolling down her driveway. He was halfway to the street, so she was looking at his back, but she could see that he was medium tall with a medium build, and he was dressed in jeans, a dark T-shirt, and a baseball cap. She heard herself gasp and stopped right where she was, watching. He looked like the same man who had been roaming around her yard Thursday night, the man who might have been Craig Belknap. Her first impulse was to hurry back inside, but then a voice in her head told her not to be silly. This man was far enough away that she could retreat if necessary, and here was a chance to solve a mystery, albeit a small one compared to the mystery of Caralee's death.

She took a deep breath and stepped toward the porch railing. "Hey!" she called. "Hey you!"

The man turned. The cap was pushed farther back on his head this morning and she could see clearly that he wasn't Craig Belknap. He was quite swarthy, with heavy brows. So who was he?

"Are you looking for something?" she called. "You're in my driveway."

The man backed up a few steps until he was standing on the sidewalk. "Sorry," he called back. "Didn't mean to intrude. I'm just doing a job for the Arborists." He darted around the end of the hedge that separated Pamela's yard from Richard Larkin's.

The *Register* had landed on the strip of grass between the sidewalk and the street that morning, so she had to go farther than usual to claim it. And by the time she had stooped and stood up, newspaper in hand, and glanced into Richard Larkin's yard, there was no sign of the man anywhere.

"Wear something nice," Bettina had said. Toast and coffee had been consumed and newspaper read, and Pamela was standing in front of her closet. She was still feeling a bit rattled about the strange man in the driveway. He wasn't Craig Belknap, but he said he was from the Arborists. Kent Varnish was an important member of the Arborists, and she and Bettina had only recently been talking to Kent Varnish about his whereabouts the night Caralee died. They had tried to mask their curiosity as nothing more than a sociable chat. But maybe he'd seen through them. Then again, it would be awfully silly to send someone around to silence them who then announced right out that he was from the Arborists.

Pamela sighed. She had too many things to think about without adding wardrobe issues to the mix, but she reached for a clean pair of jeans. Conveniently the lightweight sweater, pale amber, that she'd worn for the last Knit and Nibble meeting was the top item on her stack of sweaters. Surely Bettina wouldn't object to that. And the weather was getting too fall-like for sandals, so she slipped on a pair of soft brown loafers. It was almost ten, and it was time to hurry over to the Mittendorf House.

Bettina was very punctual. The doorbell rang at a quarter to twelve, and Pamela stepped outside still wearing the smile that had gradually taken shape on her drive home from Riverton. She had thanked the Mittendorf House docent, walked across the expanse of gravel that provided visitor parking, and turned back to give the noble pink sandstone structure one final admiring glance before steering her car from the lot.

"Well," Bettina said, "you look happy."

"I can't wait to meet Thomas Swinton," Pamela said. "I'm a huge fan, you know."

Bettina stifled a giggle. "I know you're joking, but keep telling yourself that. He loves admiration." Pamela locked the door and they started down the steps. Bettina continued talking. "I'm not sure there's much point in this, except for the food of course. Caralee *did* knit his name into that project of hers, but we don't even have a hint of a horrible thing she could have known about him—not like with those other guys. And we can hardly come out and ask him what dire secrets he's hiding."

"We might not have to be that direct," Pamela said. "I have an idea."

"You do?" Bettina gave Pamela a curious glance. "What is it?"

"You'll see."

They were on the sidewalk now, Bettina stepping along in a delicate pair of bright pink kitten heels and Pamela striding beside her in the comfortable loafers. Bettina's Toyota waited at the end of the driveway. Retracing the path she'd taken that morning when she set out to fetch the paper reminded Pamela of her encounter with the strange man. Her visit to the Mittendorf House had pushed it into a remote corner of her mind.

"That wasn't Craig Belknap in my yard Thursday night," she said as she reached toward the passenger-door handle.

"How do you know?" Bettina paused halfway around the back of her car.

"He was here again this morning. I got a better look at him."

"He was here again?" Bettina's brightly painted lips shaped an alarmed grimace. "Why didn't you tell me right away? We'll have to get Woofus over here— you can't be alone when we know there's a murderer loose in Arborville and a strange man is showing up in your yard every day."

"He didn't come yesterday," Pamela said.

"Maybe you just didn't see him yesterday," Bettina protested in tones as high-pitched as Catrina's squeals when her dinner was delayed.

"He said he'd been sent by the Arborists." Pamela opened the car door. They weren't going to get off to a good start with Thomas Swinton if they were late for lunch.

"The Arborists!" Bettina's voice rose even higher. "Kent Varnish is in the Arborists, and we haven't totally crossed him off our list of suspects." She folded her arms across her chest. "As soon as we get back from lunch I'm bringing Woofus over here to stay with you."

"I have a houseful of kittens," Pamela said. "I'm not sure that would be a good combination."

"We'll talk about it." Bettina frowned and continued on her way around the car. They settled into their seats and headed up Orchard Street.

Thomas Swinton lived along Arborville Avenue, in the opposite direction from the commercial district and nearly at the border with the neighboring town to the south. That stretch of Arborville Avenue featured grand houses, some of the oldest in Arborville, set well back from the street, with studied landscaping and gracious lawns tended by hosts of landscapers.

The house Bettina pulled up to was an imposing structure built of red brick. White columns framed its front porch, which was centered exactly in the middle of the façade, with two windows on each side. The second floor was equally symmetrical, but instead of a door the windows flanked a small overhang that sheltered the porch.

In keeping with the house's symmetry, the walk leading to the porch divided the lawn exactly in half. The house was set so far back from the street that the walk seemed to Pamela at least twice as long as her own, and she slowed her pace so Bettina could catch up in her delicate little shoes. They had barely stepped onto the porch and Bettina hadn't even lifted a hand toward the doorbell when the door popped open. Thomas Swinton must have been watching their approach from the window.

"Ladies, ladies!" he exclaimed. "Come in!" He seized Bettina's hands in both his own and drew her over the threshold, murmuring, "Bettina—so lovely to see you again." Then he released her hands and turned to Pamela. "And this must be your friend." He displayed a set of very white teeth. "May I call you Pamela?" The well-groomed white beard looked just as it had in the website picture, and the thick head of white hair. But she hadn't expected the little white ponytail that jutted over his immaculate shirt collar in back. And she'd thought somehow that he would be taller—though Pamela was tall for a woman and was used to looking down, rather than up, to meet men's eyes.

"Of course," Pamela said, summoning her social smile. Now he seized Pamela's hands, relinquished one, and held the other to draw her into his grand foyer. Bettina followed. Underfoot was a richly patterned rug and rising before them was a staircase with a bannister of dark, well-polished wood.

"My study," he said, gesturing toward a closed door on the right, "but it's in no state to offer you a tour. When one is in the throes of a project . . . well . . . inspiration, you know. So many notes, so much research."

"What *is* your new project?" Bettina asked. "We'd love a preview."

His smile disappeared and his face froze for a minute. He released Pamela's other hand and clutched his chest. For a moment she thought he was ill, but then he said, "I'm digging deep . . . ideas, ideas, flowing freely, but I'm not ready to reveal them." The smile returned and he stepped toward the door on the left, which was open. "Shall we proceed to lunch?"

A long table, an obvious antique that would have been at home in the Mittendorf House, dominated the room. Three places had been set at one end, with burgundy velvet placemats, white linen napkins, and gold-rimmed plates with a stylized flower pattern, along with crystal wineglasses. A silver trivet sat waiting, for something, with a silver pie-server next to it. Thomas Swinton pulled out a chair for Pamela on one side and one for Bettina on the other.

"Lunch will just be a moment," he said, and bustled toward a door at the far end of the room. In a few minutes he was back, bearing a large pie pan in one hand and a large china bowl that matched the plates in the other. "Quiche lorraine," he announced, setting the pie pan on the silver trivet, "and a salad of butter lettuce with a light vinaigrette." He deposited the salad bowl on the table and stood back to admire the effect. "Cooking is so gratifying," he observed, and gave a contented sigh. Then, as if recalling himself from a reverie, he glanced from Pamela to Bettina and back. "Wine, ladies? Or water?"

"Water is fine," Pamela and Bettina answered in unison.

He headed for the door at the far end of the room and returned in a minute with a bottle of white wine and a tall green bottle of mineral water with an elaborate label. He fetched silver wine coasters from the sideboard, settled the bottles in them, and took his own seat.

Soon the crystal glasses had been filled, and the china plates held slices of the lovely golden quiche and mounds of pale green lettuce with a light sheen of olive oil. "Bon appètit," he said, and raised his glass of wine.

They concentrated on their food for a bit, Bettina breaking the silence to compliment him on the quiche. "A staple of my repertoire," he responded with a satisfied smile. "But you came here to talk about my work, and I won't disappoint you." He let his fork rest on the edge of his plate. "History has always been a passion of mine . . . and you can see that in *Time and Time Again* I'm sure." Pamela nodded. "The sweep of it . . . is so . . . sweeping . . ."

"The way you used the Mittendorf House," Pamela said. "I could see that passion. The Revolutionary War—what an incredible thing to live through, and those characters caught up in the drama of it."

"Caught up. That's the very word. So well put." He seized his fork and waved it for emphasis.

"You must have spent a lot of time at the Mittendorf House," Pamela said. "You seem to know every nook and cranny."

Thomas Swinton nodded. "It's all part of the job. Or the passion, really. My passion." He put the fork down and seized his chest again. "For history." He took a swallow of wine.

"It's a favorite place of mine too," Pamela said as Bettina concentrated on her quiche. The quiche was truly a masterpiece, the custard rich with Gruyère and bits of smoke-cured ham. Pamela hated to neglect it, but duty called. She went on with her thought. "I stand in the kitchen with my back to the hearth and gaze through the window, imagining the generations of women who stood there before me."

Thomas Swinton nodded. "A beautiful image." He took another swallow of wine.

"I love the view of the Haversack River from there. So untouched. I can imagine it looked just like that when George Washington was alive." She gave him an encouraging smile. "Don't you?"

"Oh, definitely," he said. "My thoughts exactly. When I was working on *Time and Time Again*, I often stood on the porch of the Mittendorf House and watched the river flow by. It was as if the water, the trees, the very air . . . as if they all were speaking to me."

"And the sheep!" Pamela exclaimed. "They can be very vocal."

Thomas Swinton's eyes widened ever so slightly. But then he flashed his white teeth at Pamela and chuckled. "Yes," he said, "we can't forget the sheep."

Pamela echoed his chuckle. "That ram seems to enjoy his harem."

He was still chuckling. "Quite the fellow." He regarded Pamela with merry eyes and lifted his wineglass. "Yes, indeed. That ram is quite the fellow."

"Their coats have grown back after that shearing demonstration last spring," Pamela said. "I wonder if they're chilly at first without that nice thick fleece— at least until summer comes."

"Good point." Thomas Swinton nodded sagely. "I hadn't thought of that."

Across the table, Bettina raised her eyes from her plate. A tiny frown and slight narrowing of her eyes suggested she was puzzled. Thomas Swinton swiveled his head in her direction and she replaced the puzzlement with a wide-eyed smile. "I fear I've been neglecting you," he said, "so entranced by your friend's interest in my work. When you called, you mentioned a second interview for the *Advocate*. What would you like to know?"

"Has your life changed since *Time and Time Again* came out?" Bettina asked, adding, "I know it's not your first book, but perhaps the most ambitious— and so well received. I hope you're not planning to leave Arborville now that you're so famous."

Thomas Swinton was chewing. He finished, and swallowed, and then let loose with another chuckle.

"I wouldn't think of it. No, absolutely would not think of it."

"I'm sure the residents of Arborville will be happy to hear that." She reached into her handbag, which she'd set on the floor next to her chair, and took out a little notepad and a pen.

Pamela watched and listened for a few minutes as Bettina launched the interview that was the pretext for the visit with Thomas Swinton. Then she squirmed in her chair and patted around her waist as if feeling for hidden pockets. "My phone," she murmured. "Excuse me. It's a call I have to take." She jumped up from the table, trying not to laugh at Bettina's obvious struggle to hide her amazement.

In fact, Pamela generally forgot to take her cell phone with her when she went out, and most people knew she was more likely to pick up her landline. She had no phone with her today, and if she had it wouldn't have been tucked into a pocket of her jeans.

Chapter Nineteen

Out in the foyer again, she headed toward the front door, stomping in her attempt to make her footsteps audible despite the thick carpet. When she reached the door, she opened it and stepped heavily onto the cement floor of the porch. Then she tiptoed back in, leaving the door open and thankful now for the carpet. From the dining room came Thomas Swinton's voice, apparently extolling the superiority of pen and ink (real ink!) over computers when it came to unleashing creativity.

Thomas Swinton had indicated that the door to the right as one entered the foyer led to his study. Pamela reached for the knob and turned it ever so gently, praying for it not to squeak. Across the hall, Thomas Swinton was still talking about ink. The latch clicked free and Pamela nudged the door, holding her breath and willing it not to creak. It swung open a few inches. She nudged again and leaned close to the wider gap.

She was indeed looking into Thomas Swinton's study. The bookshelves were those he had used as a backdrop for the photo on his website, but the room resembled a setup for a photo shoot in an upscale decorating magazine. It featured a massive desk of dark, polished wood, a leather-covered desk chair, and a pair of file cabinets, also dark wood, and a long cabinet that matched the desk. But there was not a scrap of paper in sight—no piles of handwritten notes, no carelessly stacked books with bookmarks sticking out here and there, not even a blank pad of paper or a pen—with or without real ink. Thomas Swinton's study certainly wasn't the disorderly artist's refuge that he had made it out to be when he declined to give his visitors a tour. Pamela backed away from the door and gently pulled it closed.

In the dining room, the salad bowl was now empty and further inroads had been made on the quiche. Only two pieces remained.

"Is everything okay at home?" Bettina asked as Pamela once again took her seat at the table. Pamela knew from the look on Bettina's face—half admiring, half incredulous—that Bettina could barely wait till Thomas Swinton's front door closed behind them and Pamela could explain what on earth she had been up to.

"Fine," Pamela said. "Someone's coming to repair the dishwasher. Later though—no need to rush our visit." She smiled at Thomas Swinton. He had managed to finish an extra piece of quiche and more salad while holding forth to Bettina—and the rest of the wine too, apparently.

"Shall we have dessert then?" he inquired while reaching for the empty wine bottle. "Or would you like another slice of quiche, Pamela? There's plenty left."

"I'm fine," Pamela said, "especially if there's to be dessert."

"I made a chocolate mousse. And we'll have coffee." He started to rise.

Bettina was on her feet in an instant. "Let me help you clear away," she said, and picked up her own plate. Pamela followed her lead, but Thomas Swinton motioned them both to sit down.

"Ladies, ladies," he said. "You're my guests." He stacked the three plates, balanced the quiche pan on the salad bowl, and set off toward the kitchen with full hands.

Bettina watched until the kitchen door closed behind him. She leaned across the table and whispered, "What are you doing? A herd of sheep at the Mittendorf House that get chilly after shearing? Cell phone calls from a dishwasher repair service when you didn't even bring your cell phone?"

"Shhh!" Pamela repressed a smile. "You'll like it," she whispered back as Thomas Swinton emerged from the kitchen bearing a silver tray.

"*Everyone* likes my mousse," he assured them as he set a small crystal bowl filled with swirls of chocolaty pudding on each placemat. "And to go with . . ." He slid a plate of pale oval cookies from the tray to the table.

"Delicious!" Bettina pronounced when they'd all had a chance to sample the dessert.

As they ate the mousse, he described a series of East Coast book signings he'd done, interrupting himself to bring out coffee when he reached New Hampshire.

They were dawdling over the last few sips of coffee and Thomas Swinton was reminiscing about the year he had two books on the best-seller list at once, when the door to the kitchen opened. A meek-looking woman in an apron stepped through and ventured toward the table. Thomas Swinton paused to look in her direction.

"I'm leaving now, sir," she said. "I'll be back in the morning."

"Very good." He nodded.

"I hope your ladies liked my quiche," she added with a shy smile. "And my mousse."

Pamela and Bettina looked at each other, Bettina cocking her head as if wondering whether she'd heard correctly. But Thomas Swinton picked up right where he'd left off, reliving the week when one of his books edged a rival author's book off the top of the *New York Times* Best Seller list.

Bettina controlled herself all the way from Thomas Swinton's front porch to the curb. But after she and Pamela had settled into their seats for the short drive home, she exploded into giggles.

"*My* quiche! *My* mousse!" she exclaimed. "And then his housekeeper lets the cat out of the bag." The giggles subsided and she turned to Pamela. "What were you doing when you went outside?"

"I wasn't outside," Pamela said. "I was looking in his study."

Bettina gave an approving nod. "And?"

"It wasn't too messy to show," Pamela said. "It was too neat. Whatever he's working on now, he's not working on it in there."

"And the herd of sheep at the Mittendorf House? Wilfred never mentioned them."

"That's because they're not there," Pamela said. "And you can't see the Haversack River from the kitchen, or the porch. All you can see is the back of Wine Wonderland. It's too bad the county let that property go to a developer—the view of the Wine Wonderland loading dock really detracts from the historical atmosphere." Bettina pulled away from the curb as Pamela continued talking. "I went to the Mittendorf House this morning," she explained. "I spent an hour walking around—and then I bought a bottle of chardonnay at Wine Wonderland. It's for you and Wilfred, to thank you for taking me in Thursday night."

"I asked him if he knew Caralee and if she'd ever asked him about his work," Bettina said. "Right after you dashed out. He said he only took questions from people who he thought could understand the answers."

"We have a lot to talk about," Pamela said.

When they got back to Orchard Street they settled in the chairs on Pamela's front porch. Bettina slipped off the delicate kitten heels and wiggled her liberated toes. At first they sat in silence, enjoying the alternation of sun and shade on lawns that still glowed the deep green of summer, and the way the afternoon breeze made the trees sigh. Each was turning over in her mind what she'd learned during the lunchtime visit with Thomas Swinton.

Pamela spoke first. "He takes credit for things he didn't really do," she said, "even petty things, like whether he actually cooked that food." Bettina nodded and Pamela went on. "I don't think he really wrote *Time and Time Again.*"

"A ghostwriter?" Bettina whispered. "A writing version of that woman out there in the kitchen making the lunch he pretended he made?"

"The description of the Mittendorf House in *Time and Time Again* corresponds exactly to the real place," Pamela said. "I double-checked this morning."

"But then"—Bettina wrinkled her nose—"wouldn't that mean . . . ?"

"*Somebody* went to a lot of effort making sure the details were accurate. But that somebody wasn't him." Pamela tightened her lips and shook her head decisively. "If Thomas Swinton had been to the Mittendorf House even once, he'd know that there are no sheep—let alone a ram who enjoys his harem—and that all you can see from the porch is Wine Wonderland's loading dock."

"He's written so many books," Bettina said. "Do you think that all this time . . . ?"

"Maybe," Pamela said. "But maybe not. He could have written his own books at first, but then he got tired, or lost the spark. Or the books were so popular it occurred to him that his publisher could sell a new one every year, but writing a new one took five years."

"And as long as the books had his name on them . . ."

Pamela nodded. "In bigger and bigger type." Across the street, Wilfred pulled into the driveway and climbed out of his ancient Mercedes. He opened the passenger-side door, coaxed Woofus out, waved at Pamela and Bettina, and led Woofus into the house. Wilfred was carrying a large white bakery box.

"Woofus likes to run errands with Wilfred," Bettina said. They stared out at the late-September afternoon, both lost in thought.

Pamela spoke first. "That thing Thomas Swinton said when you asked about Caralee—that he only takes questions from people who he thinks can understand the answers. Meaning, I guess, she inquired about something that he didn't want to talk about. Or didn't know anything about."

"I got that impression." Bettina nodded.

"That suggests to me that Caralee made him nervous." Pamela spoke slowly, as if in the process of working out an idea. She was still watching the shadows on the lawn flutter as the breeze sifted through the tree branches.

"She did make people nervous," Bettina agreed. Then she slapped the arms of her chair in excitement. "That's it, you know!"

Pamela turned to her. "I know."

"She scared him. *She* figured out he didn't write *Time and Time Again.* And being Caralee, she told him what she knew—and what a fake she thought he was." Bettina's bright pink lips curved up in a satisfied smile.

"So he has a motive for killing her," Pamela said, watching the shadows on the lawn again. "But if he did it, he had to know about that unsteady pile of furniture and he had to get in there and do his deed while the storage room was open, but after Rue Wadsworth went home to cook and before Caralee showed up." She turned back to Bettina. "And besides, Caralee said the furniture toppled two other times. He'd have had to be creeping around over there on those occasions too."

Bettina sighed. "He might *not* be our guy then—not like Timmons, with Ben Skyler at his beck and call."

"Or Wadsworth," Pamela added, "who could get in there and mess around anytime the room was open—knowing Rue wouldn't turn him in."

"Or Varnish. Maybe enlisting other Arborists to carry out his dirty deeds . . ." Bettina's voice trailed off and she stood up. Moving gingerly in her stocking feet, she stepped to the porch railing and leaned toward the hedge that separated Pamela's property from the church. She twisted her head to the left. "Someone's in your yard again," she whispered. "A man. Sneaking along the hedge."

Pamela stood up too. "Is he wearing a baseball cap?" she asked.

Before Bettina could answer, the man emerged, striding around the corner of the porch. "Good news," he announced with a cheerful grin. "Your catalpa doesn't have verticillium wilt."

"What?" Pamela folded her arms across her chest. "Who are you anyway? And what's verticillium wilt?"

"Twigs Nilson, at your service." The man swept off his baseball cap and bowed. "Or, to be more formal, Timothy L. Nilson, Ph.D., Associate Professor of Botany, Wendelstaff College."

"This morning you said you were from the Arborists."

"I'm doing a job for them," he said. "Botany. Plants. Trees, you know. *Arbor*—Latin for 'tree.' Checking for diseases. You don't want verticillium wilt. Fungal. Leaves turn yellow. Then they shrivel up and fall off. I thought I saw signs of it the other night, but it was getting dark—just wanted to double-check, triple-check to make sure. It can hit a branch here and there, then before you know it, the whole neighborhood's infected."

With a cheery wave, he was off, striding across the lawn toward the street.

"Well!" Pamela and Bettina both spoke at once.

They sank back into their chairs and looked at each other.

"Maybe we take Kent Varnish off the list of suspects?" Pamela said.

"At least now we know he wasn't sending Arborist hit men around to get you off his trail." Bettina paused for a minute, then she went on. "Twigs Nilson was kind of cute. Smart too, I'm sure."

Pamela laughed. "Bettina! You're a married woman."

"I don't mean for *me*. I mean for you. Maybe he'll come back for another look at your catalpa."

As Twigs Nilson proceeded up the street, he passed a small group heading the other direction. Pamela recognized the threesome she and Bettina had spoken to at the end of Bettina's driveway Thursday night—the young woman who had inherited the role of Madame Defarge, the older woman who said she'd been in the Players forever, and the young man. A car was heading down the street as well, and it slowed as it passed Pamela's house and turned into the driveway that led to the church parking lot.

"It looks like they're having an afternoon rehearsal," Bettina observed.

Pamela checked her watch. "Three p.m. already," she said. "Shall I make some coffee? We can bring it back out here—I hate to waste a beautiful September day like this sitting indoors."

"Coffee, yes," Bettina said, "but no goodies. We're going to Wilfred Junior and Maxie's tonight for Wilfred Junior's birthday. That giant white box Wilfred carried into the house was the cake."

Bettina slipped her shoes back on and they stepped into the entry, dodging one of the kittens, a black male. He was playing with the ball of yarn that had proven to be such a popular toy, batting it across the carpet then pouncing on it before it came to rest.

In the kitchen, Bettina welcomed another kitten, a ginger female, onto her lap as Pamela put the kettle on to boil and set about grinding beans for the coffee. "I like this one," Bettina said, "to adopt. She's not the boldest one, is she? I have to consider Woofus."

The coffee grinder whirred briefly. Pamela poured the ground beans into the paper filter and turned away from the counter. "No," she said, "this one is very sweet. I'm keeping the bold one so Catrina will have company. I can't send all her children away."

The end of the sentence was drowned out by the shrill hoot of the kettle. But Pamela had no sooner lifted it from the stove when the hoot was replaced by a sound equally shrill, this time coming from the street. It rose and fell in waves, each peak louder than the one before until—seemingly right in front of Pamela's house—it subsided in a resentful snarl.

Bettina's eyes widened in alarm. She rose, and the startled kitten leapt gracefully to the floor. Pamela set the still-full kettle back on the stove and followed Bettina as she rushed, in stocking feet again, toward the entry. Through the lace that curtained the oval window in the front door, Pamela could make out the black-and-white shape of a police car parked at the curb. It wasn't exactly in front of her house—closer to the church really.

By the time Bettina ran back to the kitchen to slip into her shoes and she and Pamela bounded down the steps and hurried to the sidewalk, the police car was empty. But another siren, screaming from the top of the street, announced that another police car was on its way. It sped the half block from Arborville

Avenue and swung toward the curb, halting within an inch of the other police car's back bumper. Doors on both sides popped open and a police officer jumped out of each, barely pausing before taking off toward the driveway that led to the church parking lot. Pamela recognized one of them as the young woman officer with the sweet heart-shaped face who lately had the assignment of making sure Co-Op patrons didn't park in the space reserved for delivery trucks.

"Oh, my!" Bettina looked up at Pamela. "As Wilfred would say, misfortunes never come single."

Chapter Twenty

"Let me run back and close my front door," Pamela said. "We want to find out what happened, don't we?"

"Of course." Bettina straightened her back and lifted her chin.

Pamela hurried back to her porch and up the steps to close the front door. A minute later she was back on the sidewalk, watching Wilfred dart across the street. "Misfortunes never come single," he panted as he gained the curb. Bettina took his hand.

Pamela led the way, past the front of the church and down the driveway toward the parking lot. But the double doors to the hall that served the auditorium and the meeting rooms were closed, guarded by a stern-looking police officer.

"We're neighbors," Pamela said, trying to seem concerned in a neighborly way, not like someone with—at least in her mind (and Bettina's)—a professional interest in calamities involving the Players. She smiled, but seriously, as befitting what was obviously a serious occasion. "Has something happened?"

The officer tipped his head in the tiniest nod. He didn't look familiar to Pamela. Perhaps he was new on the force. Most of the Arborville police realized they weren't based in a high-crime environment and so didn't have to affect the stoic mannerisms of the police on TV.

"Is everyone . . . in there"—Pamela tipped her head toward the door behind the officer—"okay?"

"This is a crime scene, ma'am," he said. "That's all the information I can give out at this time."

The three of them looked at one another. Pamela shrugged. Bettina and Wilfred shrugged back, and they all turned around and trooped across the parking lot. They reached the sidewalk just as a truck bearing the logo of the local AM station careened into the driveway. It was followed by a huge silver van with the logo of the county sheriff's department on the side. They stood on the sidewalk watching as two figures in white coveralls climbed out of the van. The stern police officer guarding the doors stepped aside to let them enter.

There seemed no point in watching any longer, since the doors were once again firmly closed and the parking lot was deserted except for the one stationary police officer.

"Shall we go home, dear wife?" Wilfred asked, slipping his arm around Bettina's ample waist. Bettina nodded toward Pamela and he aimed his kindly gaze in her direction. "All of us, I mean," Wilfred added. "You too, Pamela. We don't know what happened here"—he waved a hand in the direction of the parking lot—"and you're right next door."

"I'll be fine," Pamela said. "And you've got a birthday party to go to."

* * *

Once back at home, Pamela felt at loose ends. She sat down with her knitting, taking up where she'd left off on the second sleeve of the ruby-red tunic. She also felt very curious, so she turned on the radio. She didn't usually listen to the radio while she knit, preferring to let her mind wander or to watch the television if something good was on. But the truck that had showed up next door, even before the sheriff's van, had been from the local AM station. The station must have gotten word very quickly that something serious had happened, the most obvious thing being another death. They'd want to report the story to their listeners as soon as possible.

She worked for an hour or more, losing herself in the pleasant motions of needles and fingers as the cheery radio voices alternated between news of dubious interest and advertisements for products and services of dubious use. But there was no mention of breaking news in Arborville, NJ. She was sitting on the sofa with her back to the windows that looked out on the street. The windows were closed, but sounds began to filter through—car doors slamming, a revving engine, people calling to each other. The street seemed suddenly alive with activity, as if an event at the church had just ended. In fact it had.

She was on her feet, the trance induced by the steady back and forth of knit and purl swept totally away. The police and the sheriff's van people must have finished their work. The Players had been released to go about their business, though evidently not to resume their rehearsal. Pamela pictured yellow crime-scene tape sealing the doors that the police officer had been guarding. She tossed the partly finished sleeve on the sofa, not even caring that she'd stopped in mid-row. Catrina had just appeared in the arch between the living room and the entry. She looked up as if questioning whether dinner would be forthcoming at the usual time, but Pamela ignored her too—at least for the time being.

She hurried to the door and stepped out onto the porch. A small group of people, including the older woman she'd talked to before, was heading toward Arborville Avenue, just passing the end of the hedge that separated her yard from Richard Larkin's. Pamela hopped down the steps and cut across her lawn, calling, "Hello? Excuse me?" They all turned, most staring at her curiously. But the older woman recognized her and said hi.

"Something happened at your rehearsal," Pamela said.

"Well, *duh.*" It was the young woman who had taken over Caralee's role, and apparently Caralee's scornful personality as well.

"I'm not usually nosy," Pamela said. *Unless you're detecting,* responded a voice in her head. "But I do live right next door," she added, "and . . ."

"You want to know why the police were here, and that crime-scene van," the older woman supplied. Pamela nodded. "Anthony Wadsworth is dead."

Pamela took a step backward, then another. She wasn't totally shocked—she'd already realized something pretty serious had taken place. But Anthony Wadsworth? She and Bettina had pegged him as a possible villain, not a possible victim.

"Did . . ." She paused and the older woman waited, her eyes open extra wide as if she was eager to hear the rest. Pamela obliged. "Did something fall on him?"

"Quite a few things." The woman nodded. The woman who had replaced Caralee hid a smirk.

One of the others chimed in. "The cops asked more questions this time. And they kept us all inside. Something was different, but I don't know what."

Pamela felt slightly guilty. Someone was dead, which was a very sad thing. So why did she feel excited? Perhaps because she liked challenges, she decided as she walked back toward her house. Pondering who killed Caralee had been like tackling a complicated knitting pattern. The end had seemed in sight, with suspects winnowed down to just a few. But now there was a second victim—and that victim was Anthony Wadsworth, who had been one of the suspects. She felt like she had turned the page in a pattern book expecting to find only a few more steps and discovered that in fact the project was scarcely half done—and that the end result would be much more interesting than she had originally imagined.

She climbed her front steps and reached for the doorknob. Inside Catrina greeted her with an annoyed meow, and from the radio came an urgent voice advising that there was still time to save hundreds of dollars in winter heating costs by installing replacement windows *now*. She turned the radio off.

In the kitchen she served Catrina and the kittens their dinners and sliced some of the previous night's meatloaf for herself, eating it with whole-grain toast and a tomato and cucumber salad. Of course Bettina would need to be informed about the news that the victim had been Anthony Wadsworth, but she'd wait till Wilfred's ancient Mercedes was back in the Frasers' driveway. There was no need to disrupt the birthday party.

So Pamela settled back on the sofa with her ruby-red yarn, gratified to discover that no stitches had slipped off her needles when she tossed the project aside. From time to time, she walked to the door and peered through the lace that curtained the oval window, checking for signs that Bettina was back home.

She was startled when the doorbell chimed at about nine p.m. To the doorbell was added a voice, faint but audible, though it came from the porch. "It's me, Bettina," the voice said. "I brought you some cake." Pamela hurried to admit her friend.

Bettina had dressed up for the party. She wore a silky, full-skirted dress in a swirly print that mingled midnight blue and burgundy. Sparkly blue stones adorned her earlobes. She carried a small plate covered with foil. "You must have just gotten home," Pamela said. "I've been watching for you. Wait until you hear what I found out."

"About . . . next door?" Bettina's hazel eyes, wide with anticipation, gazed up at Pamela.

"I'll tell you all about it," Pamela said, leading the way to the kitchen. When they got there, she turned dramatically and said, "Anthony Wadsworth is dead."

"No!" Bettina nearly dropped the foil-covered plate. "Was he . . . ?"

Pamela nodded. "Just like Caralee, except not quite."

She described running outside when she realized the Players had been released to go home. Bettina, listening intently, set the plate securely on the table and began peeling the foil away. Pamela told her how, according to one of the Players, the police had treated Anthony Wadsworth's death differently from Caralee's death.

When the cake was revealed, it proved to be a square from the corner of a sheet cake—frosted with chocolate and with a grooved ripple of chocolate trim edging the base and top on two sides.

"Will you take half?" Pamela asked, studying the generous portion.

"Ohh!" Bettina patted her waistline. "I had two pieces at the party. Please go ahead." She watched as Pamela fetched a fork and napkin and teased off her first chocolaty bite. "This complicates things," she said after a minute or two. "Wadsworth being killed. But how did the police treat it differently?"

Pamela nodded, finished chewing, and swallowed. "They didn't let anybody go outside till they were finished. Maybe you'll find out why when you talk to Detective Clayborn for the *Advocate*. But as far as Wadsworth being dead goes, that probably means he didn't kill Caralee."

"We can cross him off the list," Bettina agreed.

"And Swinton too," Pamela said, "even though he's a complete fraud and would have made great fodder for Caralee's blog." She frowned thoughtfully and took another bite of cake. "Because what threat would Anthony Wadsworth have posed to Thomas Swinton?"

Bettina frowned too. "Yes, the same person most likely killed both Wadsworth and Caralee. So we need a person with a motive that applies to both."

"Probably not Kent Varnish—or Merrick Timmons either then. He could have deputized Ben Skyler to do his dirty work. But with him too—what reason would he have for wanting to get rid of Wadsworth?" Pamela sighed. "I'm afraid the code in that piece of Madame Defarge knitting has led us completely astray and this is all about some whole other something." She carved off a piece of cake from one of the edges that had the chocolate trim.

"Craig Belknap," Bettina said.

"Not so fast." Pamela paused and conveyed the chocolaty morsel to her mouth, then she set down her fork and it clinked against the plate. "We thought we knew why he might have killed Caralee."

Bettina chimed in. "Unrequited love."

"But then why would he kill Wadsworth?"

"Not unrequited love." Bettina laughed. "But he could have resented Wadsworth for something to do with the Players." She studied the cake. "Do you mind . . . just a bit?"

"Help yourself," Pamela said. "You know where the forks are."

Bettina took a fork from the silverware drawer and slipped back into her chair. She eased off a nubbin of the chocolate trim, raised the fork to her mouth, and hummed in appreciation as she swallowed. Then, returning to the topic at hand, she asked, "So did he kill them both?"

"It wouldn't be the same motive," Pamela said. "But it appears to be the same method. That definitely links the two deaths." She sat up straighter, excited by a sudden new idea. "What if Wadsworth killed Caralee and Craig Belknap (in love with Caralee!) found out and decided to kill Wadsworth?"

"Possible." Bettina shrugged. "But it still bothers me that Craig Belknap absolutely refuses to say why he dashed out of Hyler's early on the night Caralee was killed."

"Let's sleep on it," Pamela said, "and you'll talk to Detective Clayborn."

"Not until Monday though." Bettina scooped up another forkful of chocolate trim.

"Be sure to ask him why they kept everybody inside this time."

"Something will be in the *Register* tomorrow," Bettina said. "It's hard to scoop a story when you write for a weekly."

Catrina was still snuggled against the small of Pamela's back when Pamela opened her eyes Sunday morning. Her room was barely light. She lifted her head to bring her bedside clock into view and the glowing numerals told her that it wasn't even six a.m. Normally she would have closed her eyes again and slipped off into a sweet early-morning dream. But a thought had drifted into her mind just as she was falling asleep the previous night, a thought about an important thing she had to remember to do.

Penny! That was it. She sat up, and Catrina surged from beneath the covers and leapt onto the floor. Penny would soon know about this most recent Arborville murder, and it was best she hear the news from her mother first. Pamela swung her feet around and lowered them to the rag rug beside the bed. She couldn't call though. An early call from home on a Sunday morning would seem to announce a disaster. She'd send a quick email—like everyone else her age, Penny looked at her phone first thing. Pamela would just sketch the outlines of the event and say she was fine and would call later. That would be a good plan.

But what were the outlines of the event? She decided to fetch the newspaper first.

Catrina had become accustomed to the morning ritual of her mistress making a quick trip outside before turning her attention to breakfast. But today Pamela stayed outside longer than usual. The sun was barely up and the yard was chilly and gray, but the *Register* already lay at the end of the front walk, a pale oblong in a plastic sleeve. As Pamela made her way down the walk she glanced from left to right, not because she anticipated any threat but because she was curious to see if anyone else was stirring this early on a Sunday morning.

Thus it was that she realized something was different about Richard Larkin's driveway. It had been empty for so long, but overnight a vehicle had appeared. The vehicle was familiar. Pamela recognized it as Richard Larkin's olive-green Jeep Cherokee. He was home. For a moment she felt a bit breathless. Then she inhaled deeply and told herself that she'd wait until he came to claim his mail and welcome him back in a cordial, neighborly way. She continued along the walk toward where the newspaper waited, picked it up, and returned to her house.

Several of the kittens were milling around in the corner where their food usually appeared, their sleek ginger and black bodies intertwining as they jostled one another. Pamela spooned kitten food into one bowl and cat food into another. As Catrina and her brood addressed themselves to their breakfast, Pamela postponed her own in favor of discovering how much the *Register*'s reporter had been able to learn about Anthony Wadsworth's death before the *Register* went to press.

The story was not front-page news, but a few pages in she recognized a familiar sight—the doors that opened off the church parking lot, but with a garnish of bright yellow crime-scene tape. The headline that accompanied the photo read Murder Suspected in Death of Arborville Players' Anthony Wadsworth. Pamela smoothed the page out and leaned closer to focus on the accompanying article.

It described police being summoned when the Player in charge of props for the upcoming production entered the group's storage room to discover an arm protruding from under a pile of furniture. Before the police arrived, several more Players had removed chairs, tables, and a dresser and discovered that the arm was attached to Anthony Wadsworth, who was dead. And apparently police believed he had been murdered.

Pamela reread the article twice to make sure she hadn't overlooked a reference to Caralee's death. The circumstances were so similar—the police were calling Wadsworth's death murder, but had dismissed Caralee's as an accident. Bettina would talk to Detective Clayborn the next day. Surely he'd have a rational explanation. Readers of the *Advocate* deserved no less.

The phone rang as Pamela was halfway up the stairs, on her way to send Penny a quick email while the water heated for coffee. She was equidistant between two phones, but she stopped on the landing, whirled around, and retraced her steps to the kitchen. She picked up, expecting to hear Bettina's voice and ready to agree with her friend that the *Register* article had been singularly uninformative. But the voice on the other end wasn't Bettina's.

Chapter Twenty-one

"Mom?" It was a hesitant whisper.

"Penny!" Pamela lowered herself into the chair she had recently abandoned. The *Register* was still spread out on the table in front of her. "Why are you up? It's Sunday morning."

"I couldn't sleep, Mom. I was worried about you." Penny sounded like the child she'd been until so recently.

"You heard the news then?" Pamela stared at the photo of the doors with the crime-scene tape. "I was going to email you. I didn't want to wake you up on Sunday morning. How did you find out so soon?"

"Lorie Hopkins texted me last night but it was too late to call you," Penny said. "Her mom is in the Players."

"Well, I'm fine," Pamela assured her. "You don't need to worry."

"He was *murdered*, Mom," Penny said as if offering a counterargument, "and I just know you and Bettina are going to decide this has something to do with

Caralee and go running around talking to dangerous people." As if punctuating a dramatic scene, the kettle began to hoot. Pamela jumped up and turned off the burner, remaining on her feet halfway between the table and the stove.

Pamela didn't like to lie. She'd weaseled out of having to lie to Penny about looking into Caralee's death by stressing that the police considered it an accident. She hadn't added that she and Bettina disagreed.

There was silence on both ends for a minute. Then Penny spoke again. "I trust you, Mom," she said in a little voice. "I only have one parent now." Pamela felt her throat tighten. "Promise me you'll stay out of this."

Pamela sighed. "Yes," she said. "I promise." At her feet, Catrina was licking one of her children's fur smooth. "Go back to sleep now. Okay?"

"Okay." Penny sounded more cheerful. She signed off with her usual, "Love you, Mom."

Pamela relit the burner under the kettle and fetched the coffee grinder and beans from the cupboard.

An hour later Pamela stepped out onto her porch again. She carried one of her canvas shopping bags and in her purse was a grocery list. She actually didn't need much of anything, but the bright fall day—and the fact that it was Sunday—almost demanded a walk. To distract herself from the crime scene next door, she was determined to head up the street. A route that took her down the street, and past the driveway that led into the church parking lot, might encourage a detour. And the detour might involve checking on things, like whether the crime-scene tape was still up. And, if the tape wasn't up, whether the double doors from the parking lot had been unlocked as the church prepared for Sunday morning services.

No! she told herself. *Don't even think these thoughts. You promised Penny to mind your own business.*

She descended the steps, made her way down the front walk, and resolutely turned right. A few women strolled toward her, on their way to church, judging by their pretty skirt-and-jacket ensembles. One of them waved at someone and from behind Pamela came a voice offering a cheerful greeting. A few cars cruised by, slowing to make the turn into the church driveway. Pamela resisted the urge to watch and see whether anyone was stationed there to turn them back.

So focused was she on these distractions, and so used to the sight of Richard Larkin's empty driveway, that as she passed his house it took her a moment to realize that something had changed since that morning. The driveway was empty, yes, the way it had been for the past several weeks—but earlier that morning it hadn't been. So he, or someone driving his car, had arrived during the night and then gone away again. She continued on her way as the two topics she was determined not to think about struggled for territory in her brain.

The foray into the Co-Op to pick up the few items—liquid dish soap, kitten food, and mayonnaise—on her meager shopping list took so little time that she tacked a detour onto her walk home. Instead of returning the way she had come, she continued on along Arborville Avenue for a few blocks until she reached the end of the commercial district. Then she crossed the street and cut through a narrow passage between Hyler's and the hair salon to reach Arborville's municipal complex and the town park.

Nell Bascomb was just emerging from the back door of the library as Pamela walked across the parking lot that separated the library from the park. She was carrying a canvas bag that was a twin of Pamela's own—in selling Pamela on the ecological advantages of canvas bags, she had made her a gift of several.

Nell hurried toward Pamela, her faded blue eyes brightened by evident purpose. "You saw the *Register* this morning, I'm sure," she said after she'd acknowledged Pamela's greeting.

Pamela nodded. "I already knew what happened. It would have been hard to ignore the sirens right next door."

"And I suppose you're here because you've figured something out that you think the police can't figure out for themselves." The library and the police department shared the same parking lot. Nell addressed Pamela in the same tone of voice she had undoubtedly used when scolding her children—and which she sometimes used on Harold.

"I . . ." Pamela was so startled she hopped a few feet backward. "I . . . no . . . I hadn't even thought of it. I'm just taking a walk. It's Sunday."

Nell regarded her as if studying a knitting project that had gone awry, eyes intent and brows drawn together over her nose. "I know you, Pamela Paterson," she said. "And I know the kinds of things you get up to. You and Bettina."

"Well, I'm not getting up to this." Pamela tried to look reassuring, and honest. But it *was* true—she'd promised Penny and she intended to keep the promise.

"I want to believe you." Nell grasped Pamela's

hand and gave it a squeeze. "I don't want to be reading about you in the *Register*."

"You won't," Pamela assured her. "Really. You won't."

"I'll see you on Tuesday night then," Nell said, sounding more cheerful. "And I believe we're at Holly's."

"Yes," Pamela said. "Holly's. See you then."

She settled onto the pretty wooden bench that was part of the library garden and watched the goings-on in the park as people flew kites, and dogs and children frolicked on the grass.

She would have to tell Bettina about her promise to Penny—and Nell's concern, Pamela reflected as she turned onto Orchard Street from Arborville Avenue, passing the stately brick apartment building at the corner. But perhaps Bettina would agree that, with Anthony Wadsworth's death declared murder and not an accident, the police could be trusted to do their work. And it was possible that finding the culprit behind this second death would lead to reevaluating Caralee's death as well.

The service at the church had just ended as Pamela approached her house. People were drifting along the sidewalk, heading home on foot, while others made their way toward the driveway that led to the parking lot—answering the question of whether the police had allowed normal parking that morning. Some people lingered on the broad porch near the church's heavy wooden doors, which still stood open, or dallied halfway down the stone steps, immersed in conversation.

In the bustle of people, all dressed in Sunday clothes suitable for a warm fall day, Pamela at first didn't notice Bettina. Then she took a closer look at a group of four women whose outfits made up a veritable rainbow and realized that her friend was the woman in vivid green. Pamela hesitated. She didn't know the other three women and wasn't sure she could summon up enough social chatter to make her presence worthwhile. But as she stood on the sidewalk with her canvas bag, Bettina caught sight of her, waved, and quickly bid her friends goodbye. In a moment she was at Pamela's side.

"Have you joined the congregation?" Pamela asked. Bettina shook her head no and Pamela went on. "Then . . . what . . . ?"

Bettina leaned closer and whispered, "I came over to see if the crime-scene tape was still up, but Marlene Pepper was standing there with her friends and she called out to me. I didn't want to just hurry past, so . . ." She looked around. "The crowd is clearing out. We'll wait a bit, then we can go down there. It's even possible that the doors are open since the church seems to be carrying on as if it's just a normal Sunday morning."

Pamela grimaced and touched her friend's arm. "Bettina," she said hesitantly, "Penny called this morning. She knows all about what happened and she asked me to promise I'd stay out of it."

Bettina's lips—bright red this morning—parted and she made a sound like a hiccup. "Did you agree?" she asked.

"I had to," Pamela said, feeling her forehead crease and her lips twist. "She was so worried. There's a murderer out there and she's afraid something will happen to me if I poke around. And she reminded me that she only has one parent now. Then I ran into Nell in the library parking lot this morning and she gave me a lecture too."

Bettina sighed. "I guess I'll just have to carry on by myself." She turned and scanned the church porch, the steps, and the sidewalk. "The coast is clear." She stepped toward the driveway, then stopped. "You'll meet me at Hyler's for lunch tomorrow though, won't you? I have an appointment to see Clayborn at eleven."

Bettina rang Pamela's doorbell five minutes later to report that the crime-scene tape was still up and the doors were locked. "But Richard's car was in his driveway this morning," she added, brightening. "He was on his porch and he waved at Wilfred. Did you see him?"

"I saw his car," Pamela said. "It's gone now."

"He'll be back." Bettina smiled and squeezed Pamela's hand. "I'm sure."

Bettina had already staked out a table when Pamela arrived at Hyler's Monday morning. The restaurant was filling rapidly as people who staffed the shops, banks, and offices of Arborville's commercial district began to take their lunch breaks.

"Have I got things to tell you!" she cried as Pamela squeezed between two tables to reach Bettina's outpost in the far corner near the large window that looked out on the street.

Pamela reached the table and slid into the empty chair. She frowned and shook her head warningly. "I promised Penny," she whispered.

"But you can *listen*, can't you," Bettina said. "You don't have to say anything."

Pamela didn't answer. Instead, she picked up the oversize menu in front of her and opened it. "The Reuben I had here the last time was awfully good," she observed after studying the menu for a few minutes.

"That sweet little Officer Sanchez is the one who realized he'd been murdered," Bettina said. "Right there at the crime scene. And now the medical examiner has confirmed it." Bettina leaned forward. She was wearing her dangly coral and gold earrings today, with a smart coral-and-blue striped shirt. The earrings quivered. "The Players lifted the furniture off him before the cops arrived and they assumed that's what killed him, like with Caralee. But when the cops got there, Officer Sanchez took a close look and realized somebody had worked him over with a blunt instrument too, and that's what caused the death. Contusions to the scalp and forehead, but he was lying facedown, so the furniture actually only landed on the back of his head."

Pamela couldn't help being interested. And as long as she just *listened*, but didn't say anything, that wouldn't be breaking her promise, would it?

As if she was reading her mind, Bettina said, "You're listening, aren't you?" Pamela dipped her head forward in the slightest nod. At that moment the server appeared at Bettina's elbow. This server was a middle-aged woman, and she'd been at Hyler's since Pamela's earliest years in Arborville. Pamela remembered eating at Hyler's with her husband the day they closed on their house and being served by this same woman.

"Are you ladies ready to order?" she asked.

Bettina twisted her neck to look up at the server,

and her coral and gold earrings swung to and fro. "I'll have the club sandwich," she said, "and a vanilla milkshake."

"And for you?" The server shifted her gaze to Pamela.

"The same." Thinking more about Reubens, Pamela had realized they would always be associated in her mind with Kent Varnish who, even though it now seemed he wasn't a killer, had been a thoroughly unpleasant man.

Pamela was bursting to ask whether Anthony Wadsworth's murder had made the police revisit their conclusion about Caralee's death. But if she seemed too interested in what Bettina had learned from Detective Clayborn, Bettina might talk her into breaking her promise to Penny. As soon as the server recorded their orders and headed back toward the counter, though, Bettina took up where she had left off—in fact, she actually backtracked a bit.

"Contusions," she repeated, "as if he'd been clobbered with something heavy, like a length of pipe. Then whoever it was that killed him piled a bunch of furniture on top of him, so it would look like an accident."

"Caralee," Pamela murmured as if to herself, hoping the word alone would cue an answer to her question.

"I asked Clayborn about that," Bettina said. "He insisted the falling furniture was what killed her, and he still thinks that was an accident. Police are searching for someone with a motive for killing Wadsworth and they think whoever that person is was inspired by Caralee's accidental death to try a copycat thing—get rid of Wadsworth but make it look like another accident." Bettina shook her head. "This Wadsworth death certainly complicates motives," she said gloomily, "but

I'm still really suspicious of Craig Belknap because of the alibi thing—lack of, I mean." She cheered up as the server approached with a large oval plate in each hand, slid the plates in front of Pamela and Bettina, and assured them that she'd be back with milkshakes.

The club sandwiches were triple-deckers, constructed from golden-brown toast dabbed with mayonnaise and interlayered with sliced turkey breast, bacon, lettuce, and tomato. They'd been sliced on the diagonal and each half speared with a toothpick that sported a cellophane frill.

"Here you go," the server announced cheerily as she set the milkshakes, in tall glasses fogged with condensation, on the worn wooden table. Straws protruded at jaunty angles from the bubbly froth that crowned the glasses.

Bettina plucked out a frilled toothpick and set it aside before lifting a hefty sandwich half and opening wide for the first bite. Pamela followed suit, enjoying the crunch of the crisp toast and the play of the salty, savory bacon against the mild turkey breast.

For a time they barely spoke, except to comment on the food, until the sandwiches had been reduced to a few crumbs scattered on the creamy surface of the plates and the last drops of the milkshakes had been slurped from the bottoms of the tall glasses. Bettina was wiping a smear of mayonnaise from her chin when from the back of the restaurant came a curious sound, a whoop like a human voice imitating an air horn. It was only a single whoop, but so loud that conversation ceased at every table and every head turned toward the counter.

The only person visible near the counter was the middle-aged server, and she too was staring in the direction of the sound, which it now seemed had emanated from the kitchen. Before she or anyone else could move, one of the swinging doors that led to the kitchen was flung back and Craig Belknap emerged, wearing a white chef's jacket and a little white cap. His pleasant but nondescript face was flushed pink and he was grinning from ear to ear.

Chapter Twenty-two

"I got it," he shouted and whooped again. "I got the part!" He flourished a cell phone in a triumphant gesture. "They emailed. Just this minute."

The middle-aged server hopped over to him and gave him a hug. Pamela and Bettina looked at each other. Bettina shrugged. Pamela said, "Well, we knew he was an actor. They're always auditioning for things."

A few people who must have been regular patrons jumped up to shake Craig's hand or pat him on the back, but most people picked up where they'd left off—sipping coffee or lifting bites of pie to their lips. Bettina half rose and looked toward the counter to signal that they were ready for their check, but the person who approached their table wasn't the middle-aged server.

It was Craig Belknap.

"Now it can be revealed," he said in a mock-portentous tone. He spread his arms and wiggled his fingers as if about to perform a conjuring trick, his piercing blue eyes lively beneath his light brows. Bettina gave him a skeptical look. He went on. "My

alibi, Ms. Detective, my alibi." Pamela was as mysti-
fied as Bettina, but she said "Oh?" and gave him an
encouraging nod.

He grabbed a chair from a neighboring table and
settled himself between them. His face was still a bit
pink. "I really didn't kill Caralee," he said. "I was in
the city that night on a callback for an off-Broadway
play—and I just found out I got the part."

"Well, congratulations then." Pamela smiled. "So
why couldn't you just tell us that in the first place?"

"Actors are very superstitious. And nothing like
telling everybody in the world that you have a really
good chance of getting a fantastic thing—and then
you don't get it and for the rest of your life people
are asking you whatever happened with that fantastic
thing and you have to say, 'I didn't get it.'" He
looked from Pamela to Bettina and back to Pamela.
"Comprendo?"

Bettina shrugged. "So you'd rather have people
think you were a murderer?"

"It was a *callback*. I passed the audition. Well, me
and about five other people. So then the producers
wanted to see us all again. That's where I was the
Wednesday before last. I felt like I was *so close*"—he
screwed up his face and shaped his hands into fists to
emphasize the words—"and I didn't want to do *anything* to wreck my chances." He relaxed again and
smiled, obviously relishing his triumph. "I did tell
one person though," he said as quietly as if talking to
himself. "I shouldn't have. I told her I didn't see why
they'd want *me*. She got mad."

Pamela nodded. "The argument behind the
hedge?"

Craig sighed. "Yeah. She could be mean . . . or,
well . . . she didn't like it when she thought I was

putting myself down. I couldn't help it. I was rehashing the audition and telling her where I thought I flubbed and maybe the callback was a mistake. There was another guy there named Craig. Maybe they thought they were calling him back."

"We thought you were in love with her," Pamela said. "You bought those flowers for her coffin. And you arranged all that food for the reception."

"She was a good friend," he said. "She really was, most of the time. And she could be fun. The things she used to say about Arborville." He laughed and then stood up. "But I'm still at work, technically." He bowed. "I'll tell Milly you're ready for your check." Then he winked and said, "I didn't kill Caralee"—he leaned closer and whispered—"but I may have killed Anthony Wadsworth."

"What!" Bettina stared at him openmouthed and slapped the table.

"Joke!" he crowed, and danced away.

Bettina had driven to her appointment with Detective Clayborn, so after they paid for their meal they walked single file through the narrow passageway that led from Arborville Avenue to the parking lot shared by the library and police department. Bettina's faithful Toyota Corolla waited there.

"I know what you're going to say," she commented as they approached the car. "I could have walked the five blocks. But I wanted to wear the shoes that went with this outfit"—she lifted a foot shod in a fetching high-heeled bootie, "and these aren't walking shoes."

Pamela extended a foot and regarded her own comfortable loafer.

"Tall and thin people can wear whatever feels good," Bettina said. "I like to dress up a bit. Sometimes you have to suffer to be beautiful."

Soon they were poised at the corner of Arborville
Avenue waiting to make their turn. They'd driven a
few blocks when Pamela spoke. "I'm glad he got the
part he wanted," she said.

"You liked him." Bettina took her eyes off the road
to glance at her friend.

"I never really wanted him to be the murderer.
There was just something honest about him."

"Maybe it was an act," Bettina said with a laugh.
"Then there's Wadsworth."

Pamela dismissed the idea with a laugh of her
own, then she added, "He was just joking. I'm sure."

"Positive?" Bettina asked, turning to glance at
Pamela again.

"Positive," Pamela said firmly.

Bettina turned onto Orchard Street and cruised toward the spot on the block where Pamela's house and
her own faced each other. Then she kept driving.

"We're home," Pamela exclaimed, nudging Bettina's shoulder. "Where are you going?"

"Just checking on something," Bettina said myste-
riously.

She slowed to a crawl in front of the church,
swung the steering wheel to the left, and nosed down
the driveway that led to the church parking lot.
There a lively scene presented itself.

The double doors that had been securely locked,
guarded by the stoic police officer and garnished
with crime-scene tape, now stood open. The parking
lot had taken on a look that was part carnival and
part open-air flea market, complete with music blast-
ing from a portable radio. The portion of asphalt
nearest the doorway was crowded with furniture—tables, chairs, dressers, a sturdy oak headboard. Cheerful
people were hard at work, some sawing or hammering,

others painting. Apparently the task at hand was construction of scenery for the upcoming production.

Giant wooden frames with canvas stretched over them stood upright along the building's brick wall. Most were still blank, but on one a scene of wooden shelves crowded with casks and bottles of various shapes and colors was emerging.

A gray-haired man in jeans and a Rolling Stones T-shirt appeared in the open doorway, a bulging trash bag in each hand. He crossed the asphalt, bouncing in time to the rock beat of the radio, and deposited the bags on a pile of similar bags.

"It looks like they're going ahead with the production," Bettina said. "A lot of retired people are involved in the Players, and they can muster out any day of the week. Good thing too—yesterday this whole place was off limits." She slid into a parking space, pushed her car door open, and started to climb out.

"What are you doing?" Pamela said, reaching for Bettina's arm. "Where are you going?"

"To talk to them, of course." Bettina reclaimed her arm. "How could we ask for a better chance to find out who knows what about Wadsworth's murder?" She was standing on the asphalt now, leaning into the car to talk to Pamela.

Pamela groaned. "I told you I promised Penny I wouldn't get involved," she said wearily.

"But I didn't," Bettina said. "And look—how interesting. That piece of scenery is so convincing I'd think I was about to step right into Madame Defarge's wine shop. Let's go talk to the artist."

"You can go," Pamela said, "but I'm keeping my promise to Penny."

Pamela stayed in the car, but she couldn't avoid over-

hearing people's voices as they shouted over the throb-
bing music. The storage room was evidently undergoing
a major reorganization. The scenery painter was explaining to Bettina that space would never be found for
the *Tale of Two Cities* sets unless some rigorous winnow-
ing out was done.

The man in the Rolling Stones T-shirt darted back
through the double doors and reemerged carrying
two more bulging trash bags. He was followed by another man tugging on a costume rack like the ones
Pamela and Bettina had seen when they talked to
Rue Wadsworth in the auditorium. In fact, it looked
like one of those very racks. It held a row of long,
drab-colored cotton dresses, the garments destined
for the downtrodden masses, as Pamela recalled. The
man tugged it through the doorway and past a cluster of wooden chairs, then paused for a minute,
looked back at it with a frown, and gave it a mighty
jerk.

The rack swayed, the pipe along which the hangers were arranged dipped at one end, and the
dresses slid onto the ground in a confused jumble of
brown and gray. "Oh, blast!" he shouted to no one in
particular. "Why can't this blasted costume rack stay
put together?" With the top pipe detached, the upright supports teetered and soon the entire rack lay
in parts on the asphalt, tangled among the forlorn
dresses.

The man in the Rolling Stones T-shirt sauntered
over and slapped the other man on the back. "Good
work, buddy," he said with a laugh.

Meanwhile, Bettina had finished her conversation
with the scenery painter and was daintily making her
way back to the car in her high-heeled booties. She

stopped, however, when she reached the collapsed costume rack.

"At least they're the costumes for the peasants," she said to the man in the Rolling Stones T-shirt. "A little dirt will make them more realistic."

A few of the women had converged on the mess and were extracting the dresses one by one from the pile, reuniting them with their hangers, and draping them here and there on the chairs and tables. "Busy day," one of them observed to Bettina. "All this work and rehearsal tonight. We persuaded Rue to carry on—valiant woman."

Bettina shuddered. "I'll say so. I don't know what I'd do if I lost my Wilfred."

"Oh, she adored Anthony, no question about that," the other woman said. "She poured her heart and soul into those Christmas letters. But they were both devoted to the theater. He would have wanted the show to go on."

"No sign of Richard yet," Bettina observed, pulling into Pamela's driveway. Pamela made a noncommittal sound and reached for the door handle. "Clayborn said he'd keep me posted on developments in the Wadsworth murder," Bettina added as Pamela stepped from the car. "There's still a few more days before the *Advocate* goes to press. It would be a nice coup for the Arborville Police Department if they could solve the case before this week's issue."

"I hope they do," Pamela said. "And I hope whoever did it confesses to killing Caralee too. Poor Margo—to have her niece's death go unpunished like that. Somebody set that furniture up to collapse again and again until it finally did the job. We tried so hard to figure it out but we had to cross all those people off our list one by one." It had occurred to her that morning that Caralee's ex-husband and the replacement Madame Defarge could be crossed off too. What motive would they have for killing Anthony Wadsworth?

Work awaited Pamela upstairs in her office. An email with ten attachments had been lurking in her Inbox when she checked her email that morning—nine submissions to evaluate and one accepted article to edit. She'd read three of the submissions before walking uptown to meet Bettina at Hyler's, and had decided that "Missionary Influence on Native American Porcupine Quill Embroidery" was a definite yes. Now she removed Catrina from her computer keyboard and settled down for an afternoon of work, hoping that the remaining submissions would be compelling enough to take her mind completely off Caralee, Anthony Wadsworth, and Richard Larkin.

Several hours later, a plaintive meow from the threshold of her office pulled her away from the computer screen. She was suddenly aware that the sky had darkened behind the curtains at her office windows and she had a crick in her neck.

"Okay," she said to Catrina. "Let's go down and have some dinner."

As she and Catrina passed through the entry on the way to the kitchen, Pamela heard noises in the street—Players arriving for their evening rehearsal, no doubt. Certainly a dedicated bunch. Devoted to the theater, as the woman had said of Rue and Anthony Wadsworth that afternoon.

A swirling, furry mass of ginger and black with wispy tails greeted Pamela's feet as she stepped across the kitchen floor on the way to the cupboard where she kept the cat and kitten food. She got the kittens settled with their bowl of kitten food and began to scoop a few spoonfuls of Catrina's food into her bowl. From outside came the sounds of Players hailing one another. It must be fun, she reflected—a lot of work, but fun. Otherwise who'd do it?

She pondered this thought as she served Catrina her meal, and as she stood with one hand on the refrigerator door gazing into its brightly lit interior. There was still a bit of meatloaf left, or she could make an omelet with the new Co-Op cheddar. In the street a horn honked and a voice called out a cheerful greeting. More Players on their way to rehearsal, devoted to the theater.

Pamela slammed the refrigerator closed. In a moment she was standing in the entry reaching for the knob on her front door. Through the lace that curtained the oval window, she could see headlights as a driver slowed to turn into the church driveway. Pamela had waited in the car that afternoon while Bettina circulated among the Players, chatting with them as they busied themselves tidying their storage room and constructing scenery. But she'd seen things, and heard things. Bettina had seen them and heard them too, but she hadn't made the connection. Pamela would explain the connection, and Bettina could take it from there. She leaned close to the lace curtain and stared at Bettina's house across the street. Wilfred's car was gone and no lights were on. They were out somewhere together.

Pamela sighed and almost headed back to the kitchen. But she understood it now, and maybe she wouldn't really be breaking her promise to Penny. If you absolutely knew the answer and you could save the police a lot of effort, that wasn't the same thing as sleuthing. She would just check one detail, and then she'd call Detective Clayborn, and everything would be wrapped up neatly. Like casting off at the end of a long and complicated knitting project.

No Players remained on the sidewalk. Rehearsal must be just getting underway. Pamela hurried down her walk, turned left, and hurried past the church and down the church driveway. The parking lot was brightened by a light on a tall pole at one end, making it clear that the Players had been busy after Pamela and Bettina left. The asphalt lot had been cleared of the miscellaneous furniture and the in-progress scenery. All that remained was a giant pile of bulging black plastic trash bags. Even the destroyed costume rack had been cleared away.

She'd have to go inside.

The double doors were closed, but the one she tried swung open easily. She crept along the hall that led to the auditorium, hearing a hubbub of voices but nothing that sounded yet like actors declaiming lines. Here was the storage room on the left, the door conveniently ajar and an overhead light illuminating all. The furniture arrangement still seemed haphazard, with tables and dressers stacked atop tables and dressers, and chairs tucked randomly here and there. Pamela didn't recognize any of the items that had been arrayed on the asphalt that afternoon. Perhaps they were to be used in the current production and were now onstage or waiting in the wings.

Two costume racks occupied the clear space in front of the furniture, both racks crammed with more garments than they were meant to hold, including the mournful brown and gray dresses destined for the downtrodden masses. Apparently the collapsed rack had not been put back into service. Rather, its contents had been squeezed onto these still-intact racks. But where had the collapsed rack gone? It hadn't been waiting with the trash in the parking lot.

Pamela stepped around the costume racks toward the furniture, scanning the spaces under the tables that made up part of the pile. Then, against the side wall, she spotted what she was looking for—an assortment of pipes, all that was left of the collapsed rack. There were four very long ones and two short ones with wheels. She picked up one of the short ones and the other short one became dislodged, clanging against the long pipes and sliding off the pile. Then two of the long pipes rolled toward her and clanged against each other.

Pamela reached for the other short pipe and ducked behind the nearest costume rack. She examined the two short pipes closely. Whoever had constructed the costume racks had screwed metal fittings shaped like elbows onto the threads at each end of the short pipes. Then he had attached wheels to the elbows.

Pamela examined the wheels, and the threading visible above the junctures where the elbows met the pipe ends. And that's where she found what she'd suspected she'd find. Tangled around one of the wheels were a few strands of grayish hair. She tugged and a hair came loose, a strand about three inches long. She examined that end of the pipe more closely. The silvery sheen of the threads was highlighted by contrast. It was as if a dark fluid had been wiped off the pipe, but some had remained where a few lines of threading were visible at the joint with the elbow.

She was so intent on her task that she didn't realize Rue Wadsworth was watching her until Rue spoke.

Chapter Twenty-three

"I'd ask you what you were doing"—Rue's timid voice hinted at apology—"except I know." Rue looked even more worn than when Pamela and Bettina had spoken with her as she labored over the costume for Lucie Manette, her eyes so large in her delicate face that she almost looked like a cartoon character. "I actually hated him," she said. "He was a pretentious fool and I gave up my own career for him." She sighed. "But first I loved him. He swept me off my feet, so glamorous, so *bohemian*, living with him in a basement apartment while he finished school and washing his shirts in the kitchen sink."

"You wanted to move to California," Pamela said. Standing in her kitchen listening to the Players call to one another she'd remembered overhearing Rue talk to her friend at the reception after Caralee's funeral. A tiny town, Rue had said. And she'd have him all to herself.

"He promised. He said it would be this year." Rue looked so mournful that Pamela almost felt sorry for her. "But then I knew it wouldn't be this year, because he was already planning the Players' schedule for next year, and the year after, and the year after." Pamela nodded. "So I decided to take matters into my own hands," Rue went on, "and scare the Players away. If nobody wanted to try out for his plays, there'd be no more Players. And we could move to California." She gestured toward the pile of furniture and smiled faintly. "An accident waiting to happen."

"Why Caralee?" Pamela asked.

"It could have been anybody . . . anybody at all. It was just supposed to scare people, make them think the Players had been cursed. I was going to invent other disasters too." She drew in a long breath and shuddered. "I didn't mean to kill her. And then it didn't even scare anybody. They all hung around. And he didn't cancel the production, even with somebody dead." She laughed, but it was more like a snort. "Devoted to the theater."

"But you meant to kill your husband," Pamela murmured.

"Damn right!" Rue straightened her shoulders. "And I didn't want to take any chances with furniture not landing where it was supposed to." She smiled. "And now he's gone." Then the smile turned to a frown. "But there they are." She gestured in the direction of the auditorium. "The show must go on. I didn't think we'd need that ugly piece of knitting anymore. But I guess we . . . they . . . will."

Pamela extended the length of pipe she was holding. "Some of his hairs are tangled around this wheel, and his blood is in the threads. That's pretty clear evidence for the police—"

Rue interrupted her, suddenly lively. "I could still go to California!" She shouted it as if it had just occurred to her. "I could go without him. I just need"—

she looked around frantically, then lunged for one of the long pipes lying against the wall—"to get rid of you." She paused and cocked her head. "They're rehearsing now. They've closed the door and they won't hear anything."

Pamela edged backward until she felt a piece of furniture poking her in the back. Rue advanced toward her, waving the four-foot length of pipe. Rue was actually quite strong for such a delicate-looking little thing. She swung the pipe and it crashed against something wooden near Pamela's shoulder. Pamela ducked, but flourished the short pipe she held, hoping to intercept Rue's next swing.

Then from the hall came a male voice. "Hey, Rue," the voice called, "did you find that footstool yet." A minute later Craig Belknap appeared in the doorway. "What's going on?" he asked, his pleasant face looking more amused than alarmed. "Fencing practice?"

"She killed Caralee," Pamela exclaimed. "And then she killed her husband." Rue flailed at Pamela with the piece of pipe again.

"Mrs. W. knocked off Mr. W!" Craig exclaimed with an incredulous laugh.

Momentarily distracted by Craig's mockery, Rue froze. Pamela darted around her, tugged Craig out into the hall, and pulled the storage room door shut. "Dial nine-one-one," she instructed him. "Quick!"

Craig dug his phone out of his back pocket as Pamela held on to the storage room doorknob, straining to keep the door shut fast. But there was no need to strain, or even hold the knob. After a few seconds there came from within the storage room a terrible crash.

"What's taking so long, Craig?" a woman's voice

called from the end of the hall. It was the young
woman who had taken over the role of Madame Defarge. She strode briskly toward Pamela and Craig,
noticed Pamela and said, "Why are you here?"

"There's been a complication," Pamela responded,
turning the knob and giving the door a cautious
nudge. From a distance a faint siren reached their
ears, like a steady whine. Pamela gave the door another nudge and it swung all the way back. The overhead light revealed a sprawl of furniture nearly
covering the whole floor. The costume racks had
been set rolling and were now huddled in the corner
next to the doorway.

Voices in the hall suggested more of the Players
had become curious about the whereabouts of Rue
and Craig. And the siren's rising volume and pitch
suggested it was drawing closer.

Pamela studied the scene before her as Craig stood
at her elbow uttering soft curses. A hand was visible,
emerging from a gap between a toppled dresser and a
table lying on its side. Rue had swung her length of
pipe just as Pamela scurried past her. The pipe must
have connected with something in the furniture pile
and launched an avalanche. Another dresser, precar-
iously balanced, bridged the gap through which
Rue's hand protruded. The siren rose to an almost
deafening scream, then abruptly went silent. In the
silence a tiny voice moaned, "Help."

"She's alive!" Pamela and Craig spoke in unison,
Craig turning and repeating the words to the sizable
group that now stood bunched in the hall.

One of the doors that led to the parking lot flew
open and two officers in uniform dashed through it.
One of them was Officer Sanchez, the woman officer

with the sweet, heart-shaped face and dark hair tidied into a neat twist. "She's still alive," Craig said.
"We need an ambulance."

Suddenly the storage room was crowded with people, hefting chairs, tables, and dressers this way and
that. Pamela took charge of the costume racks, guid-
ing each one through the door and out of the way to
make room for the furniture that was rapidly being
removed from Rue Wadsworth. Within a few minutes, an assortment of chairs had been relocated to
the hall and a table with a dresser on top of it had
taken the place of the costume racks in the front corner of the storage room. The new Madame Defarge
was sitting on the floor by Rue, who had been helped
to a sitting position and was leaning against the
dresser that had nearly crushed her.

"They tried to kill me," Rue announced, directing
her comment to Officer Sanchez. "They did this"—
she gestured feebly at the disordered room—"on
purpose to kill me."

"Not quite," Pamela said. She had tossed the in-
criminating piece of pipe onto the pile with the oth
ers as she hurried to escape from Rue. Now she
stooped toward the pile and retrieved it. "Rue
Wadsworth killed her husband," she explained. "This
piece of pipe from one of her costume racks was the
blunt instrument that caused his contusions. His
blood is still on it, in the threads. And a few of his
hairs are tangled around this wheel."

Officer Sanchez took the pipe from Pamela's hand.
"Is this true?" she asked Rue. Her voice was sharp, and
Pamela was happy to see that she could be stern when
the occasion called for it.

"No," Rue said. "They tried to kill me."

"She also arranged for the furniture collapse that killed Caralee Lorimer," Pamela said. "Caralee's death wasn't an accident."

A siren whooped from the parking lot, then trailed off into a growl. Officer Sanchez shifted her gaze to the other officer, who was standing at attention near a brass floor lamp that had escaped being toppled. "Get an evidence bag," she said. "A big one."

Rue lifted her arm, reaching toward a nearby chair, but cried out in pain halfway through the motion. The arm slipped back to her lap, and she cradled it with the other and groaned. "Something's broken," she said. "I'm sure."

The other officer returned, trailed by two EMTs and carrying a flat bag made of heavy yellow plastic. Officer Sanchez deposited the piece of pipe in the bag and zipped it up while the EMTs knelt by Rue. Pamela backed out into the hall where she stood off to the side while Craig described to the assembled Players how his errand in quest of Rue and the footstool had interrupted an attempted assault.

One of the EMTs darted from the storage room, disappeared through the double doors, and returned pushing a stretcher on crisscrossed metal legs. Pamela's last sight of Rue Wadsworth, except for the photographs that subsequently illustrated the report of her arrest in the *Register*, was of a tiny large-eyed creature fastened to a stretcher with wide straps and being wheeled to a waiting ambulance.

"We'll follow you guys to the hospital," Officer Sanchez called as the EMT, who was the driver, climbed into the ambulance. "Don't do anything with her till we get there." She turned to Pamela and asked if she wanted to press charges against Rue for attempted assault, but Pamela said no. Rue would be adequately punished, she was sure.

As Rue had surmised, the Players—being devoted to the theater—seemed determined to carry on with their rehearsal. Craig rummaged among the disorderly jumble of furniture, pulled out a footstool, and the whole crowd trooped back to the auditorium.

There was still no sign that the Frasers had returned as Pamela made her way along the sidewalk to her own house.

After such excitement, she wasn't the least bit hungry, but it was nearly eight o'clock. Cooking a meal—even a simple one—would calm her down, she knew. Carrying out the familiar motions in her familiar kitchen would make the drama next door seem only a brief interruption in a normally placid, *very* placid, life. She'd make a cheese omelet, then she'd call Penny to let her know that there was genuinely nothing to worry about now.

But she paused midway through counting out three eggs. The mother of Penny's friend Lorie Hopkins was in the Players. Lorie would know very soon that Rue Wadsworth had been revealed that evening as the killer of both her own husband and Caralee Lorimer, and that Rue had then tried to kill Pamela Paterson. She'd better call Penny right now.

As she lifted the phone, she heard heavy feet on the porch. Catrina, who had been dozing on one of the kitchen chairs, snapped to attention, her ears tilted in the direction of the sound. Pamela returned the phone to its resting place and ventured toward the entry. She hadn't turned the porch light on when she got home, hoping to be undisturbed—at least until Bettina and Wilfred came home.

As she stepped into the entry, the doorbell chimed.

Could it be Detective Clayborn? He probably would have questions, and he'd certainly want to deliver a little homily about leaving police work to the police. Yes, she decided, it was probably Detective Clayborn. Nothing dangerous, certainly, since no murderers were any longer at large in Arborville.

It was so dark outside that only a vague human outline was visible through the lace that curtained the oval window. She opened the door expecting to greet Detective Clayborn, with his melancholy eyes gazing at her from his homely face. But instead, she had to tilt her head back to greet Richard Larkin.

"I . . . it's you," she stuttered. "You're okay. I thought . . ." She paused and made a conscious effort to breathe. "I mean," she said, "you didn't come back when you said you would."

Something in his face changed, a tiny muscle tightening—or loosening, perhaps. His expression when she opened the door had been expectant. Now she wasn't sure how to describe it. But he was studying her.

"I didn't mean to worry you," he said suddenly. "I didn't think you'd—"

"Oh, no! I wasn't. It was just that . . ." She backed away from the door.

"May I?" he asked, and waited until she nodded to step in. "I'm sorry it's so late. I've been catching up at the office. I slept there last night. And I wanted to check in with my daughters."

So that explained the car that appeared and then disappeared again. Richard stood uncertainly at the edge of the carpet for a minute. "You want your mail," Pamela said. "Of course. That's why you're here." She backed up farther and waved toward the cardboard box under the mail table.

He bent to pick it up and a kitten leapt out, one of the ginger ones. Richard laughed. "You have kittens." He watched it scamper across the carpet.

"They're Catrina's," Pamela said. "The black stray I adopted. She had six of them last month."

"This little guy looks familiar," he said. "Like a miniature version of a big tom that roams around the neighborhood." He seemed more relaxed now that the kitten had provided a topic of conversation.

Pamela corrected him. "It's a she. And I have two more ginger females and three black males. Most of them are looking for homes."

He watched the ginger kitten, laughing again as it rolled onto its back, the merriment softening his strong features. He stooped again and scooped the cardboard box up with his large hands. "I could use a cat," he said.

"Really?" Pamela smiled and clasped her hands.

"Really." Richard was at the door now, but he paused on the threshold.

"How was it," Pamela found herself asking, "in Maine?"

Richard seemed momentarily startled, as if he hadn't expected she'd want to chat. "Good," he said after a minute. "It feels weird to be back—back to designing buildings for rich people after a stint with Recycle, Renew. Up there, the people I work with are happy as long as their windows keep out the draft— even if they don't all match."

"The kittens will be ready in about a month," Pamela said.

"I'll . . ." He studied the floor for a minute. "I'll be in touch then. About the kitten."

"Some are already reserved," Pamela added, "but you can have your pick of the ones that aren't."

Richard nodded, but still lingered on the threshold, eyes focused on the floor. "I know Penny's away at school," he said at last, "but Laine and Sybil are coming out Saturday for a welcome home barbecue. If the weather holds up, that is. I have some photos from Maine to show them—a regular travelogue." He raised his eyes to Pamela's face. "Maybe you'd like to see them too?"

"I . . ." Now Pamela studied the floor. The ginger kitten darted into view and Richard laughed. Pamela watched as the laugh transformed his features again. "I would," she said after a minute. "I'd like to come. I'll bake something."

She returned to the kitchen to call Penny.

Chapter Twenty-four

"You can read all about it in the *Advocate* this week," Bettina announced. "Including my interview with our very own Pamela Paterson."

Pamela lowered her eyes modestly to her lap, where a skein of ruby-red yarn and the tunic's second sleeve, nearly finished, rested. She and Bettina were sitting side by side on Holly's streamlined ochre sofa. It was so long that there was room for Roland and Karen too.

"What you did was very reckless," Nell said from a love seat covered in an abstract floral print, bright orange and chartreuse. Her kind face looked more worried than angry. "And don't think I don't know about how you bribed Harold for information by offering him some of your peach cobbler. The evidence, in the form of a dirty plate and some crumpled foil, was lying right there on the kitchen counter when I got home from the women's shelter. I suspect you'd like the plate back and I have it right here in my bag."

Pamela studied her knitting.

"Well *I* think what she did was *amazing*." Holly was perched on a chair with an angular chrome frame and a dark green leather seat and back. It and its twin faced the sofa, with the coffee table—a free-form slab of granite on spindly legs—in between. The room's walls were a shadowy gray, and an eye-catching sunburst clock dominated one wall. "I am so impressed."

"And all's well that ends well, as Wilfred might say," Bettina observed.

Nell clucked disapprovingly and launched a new stitch with a vigorous thrust of a knitting needle.

"She saved the police a lot of effort," Roland commented, looking up from a new section of the pink sweater, perhaps the back. "Now they can get back to doing what they do best—as little as possible."

"The *Register* interviewed you too," Karen said, leaning around Roland so she could see Pamela. "You were in that article this morning."

Pamela nodded. "A reporter showed up last night, about nine, Marcy Brewer. She's very energetic. Detective Clayborn was just leaving."

"Rue Wadsworth certainly doesn't look like a murderer," Karen said. "At least judging from the photo in the *Register*."

"I didn't realize it for a long time," Pamela said, "but then it came to me that she had all the access anyone could want to that storage room. She could arrange and rearrange that pile of furniture to her heart's content."

Bettina spoke up from her end of the sofa. "And she confessed to everything, the murder of Caralee and of her husband. I talked to Clayborn today."

"She must have been so unhappy . . . to do such desperate things." Karen shook her head sadly. Despite her pregnancy just becoming evident, her fragile blondness still made her look like a child.

Nell lowered her knitting into her lap and regarded the group with her faded blue eyes. "I'm not sure what punishment the justice system can offer beyond what she must already be suffering," she said.

"Nonsense!" Roland looked up, startled. "She committed a crime—two crimes really—and she has to pay her debt to society."

"I'm not saying she should be let go," Nell protested. "I'm just . . . we can't . . . life is more complicated than our laws would make it out to be."

"Mushy thinking!" Roland tossed his knitting aside. "Why have laws if they don't mean anything?"

Nell half rose. "Of course they *mean* something—"

Roland half rose too, and glowered at Nell. "Well then, what do they mean?"

Pamela felt a hand on her arm and turned to see Bettina grimacing. She patted Bettina's hand and leaned forward. "Nell . . . Roland . . . please—"

But Holly had leapt from her chair. "It's just eight p.m.," she cried, "and *wait* until you all see what we're having for refreshments!" She looked around. "Any helpers?"

"Yes!" Bettina pushed herself up from the sofa, grabbed Nell's arm, and pulled her along as they followed Holly from the room.

When Roland tossed his knitting aside it had landed in Karen's lap. Now she picked up the sleeve, which hung from two needles with an ominous gap between them. "I think you may have dropped a few stitches," she said, nudging one of the needles into an unattached loop.

But Roland didn't hear her. He cleared his throat and sat still for a minute. Then he turned to Pamela.

"I've spoken to Melanie"—his voice was as formal as if he was launching a business proposal—"about adopting the cat." He paused. "That is, if you're still willing," he added hastily. "Melanie doesn't think introducing such a small creature to Ramona would create a problem."

"I wish we could adopt one," Karen piped up in her meek voice, still holding Roland's knitting. "They're so cute, except with the baby coming, and Dave's wool allergy, I'm afraid we'd end up giving it back. But Holly wants one, I know. She can't wait to bring a kitten home."

Pamela had rested her knitting in her lap when Roland began talking. Now she touched the fingers of her left hand one by one. Index finger: Roland, one kitten. Middle finger: Holly, one kitten. Ring finger: Bettina, one kitten. Pinkie: Richard Larkin: one kitten. And—she touched her thumb: She'd keep the bold ginger female. That left only one kitten to find a home for. She smiled to herself. Things were looking up. And the delicious smell of caramelized sugar was drifting in from the next room.

Bettina appeared in the wide opening between Holly's living room and her dining room. "Holly has created a masterpiece," she announced.

Pamela, Roland, and Karen entered Holly's dining room. In the center of her pale wood table with its Scandinavian-inspired lines sat a round platter containing a dome-shaped object covered in meringue coaxed into points and baked to a tawny gold.

"It's Baked Alaska," Holly explained proudly as a chorus of ooohs and aaahs echoed around her. "It's from this amazing 1950s cookbook I found at a garage sale." She displayed a worn cookbook featuring a smiling 1950s housewife on the cover, complete with pearls, an apron, and a bright lipsticky smile.

An elegant chrome coffeepot waited off to the side on Holly's table, with a matching cream and sugar set and a squat pottery teapot. Heavy plastic cups, saucers, and plates in assorted pastels were marshaled nearby, along with a stack of fancy paper napkins. "EBay," Holly commented as Pamela examined a cup. "It's called Melmac. Awesome. I can't believe someone wanted to get rid of it."

"Will your husband come out to share this treat?" Nell asked.

"He's at the salon," Holly said. "We have a few late nights there."

She picked up a long knife and carved out a wedge-shaped serving of the Baked Alaska. When it had been transferred to one of the Melmac plates, its construction became clear: an inner core of pale ice cream, a thick layer of chocolate cake, and then the meringue—and the whole baked just long enough to brown the meringue but not melt the ice cream.

In the living room, the dramatic coffee table proved large enough to accommodate six plates and six cups and saucers. For a few minutes, no one spoke, enjoying the chill of the still-frozen ice cream, the rich chocolate sponge of the cake, and the cloud-like meringue with the sweet tease of slightly burned sugar.

"Everything old is new again," Nell commented as she lowered her fork to her empty plate. "Baked Alaska was all the fashion when Harold and I first set up house. This tastes just like I remember."

Bettina licked a last dab of ice cream from her fork.

"I'm certainly glad it's coming back," she said. "I could eat it every night." She poured coffee from the elegant chrome coffeepot, stirred in cream and sugar, and leaned back on the sofa.

Nell set her teacup back on its plastic saucer. "We're back to six people," she observed.

"No need to recruit another," Roland said. "Six people is plenty."

"Six people is a good number," Bettina agreed, glancing from face to face. "But I know there are many more knitters in Arborville. Marlene Pepper was telling me she's just taken it up again. And the senior center hosts a crafts program. Some of those ladies are knitters."

"Would anyone even want to join?" Karen shivered. "After what happened to Caralee."

"That had nothing to do with the knitting club." Roland's tone was that of a lawyer chastising a lapse in logic. "However, I agree with Karen." He went on, not noticing Karen's look of surprise, his lean face serious. "I don't believe we'd get any takers. Few people make decisions based on what's rational."

"Pooh!" Nell puffed in disgust. "I give people more credit than that. No one's going to believe they're endangering their life by joining Knit and Nibble."

Karen set her cup down with a worried look. "But I"—she glanced around—"now I'm feeling a little bit nervous."

Roland snorted. "If you're going to think like that, then we're all tempting fate."

Karen's eyes widened in alarm. Her hand strayed to the slight thickening at her waist. Nell reached over from the love seat, patted Karen's arm, and directed a scowl in Roland's direction.

"Let's all have more Baked Alaska!" Holly cried, jumping up from the chrome and leather chair. "There's lots. Who's for seconds? And Nell"—she smiled her dimply smile—"would you like to take a piece to Harold?"

"Oh, no you don't." Nell returned the smile and the skin around her eyes crinkled. "I'm not sure what you have in mind, but he's very susceptible to bribery."

"No bribery," Holly said, laughing. "I'll leave solving murders to Pamela."

KNIT

Sachets: For Humans . . . and Cats

These sachets are little knitted bags about three inches by six inches. You can fill them with dried flowers or herbs, like lavender (or catnip!), from your own garden, or with potpourri purchased in shops or online. You can also slip bars of fancy soap into them. Sachets of either sort can be used to give the contents of dresser drawers and linen closets a nice scent. Or, if you give bags containing soap as gifts, the recipient can take the soap out and use it.

It's fun to choose colors of yarn that echo the contents of your sachets, like lavender for lavender (*duh!*) or rosy pink for dried rose petals. If you fill your bags with fancy soap, you can match the bags to the color of the soap. And of course, the front and the back of the bag don't have to be the same color.

If you're not a knitter, watching a video is a great way to master the basics of knitting. Just search the Internet for "How to knit" and you'll have your choice of tutorials that show the process clearly, including how to cast on. This project can be made using the most basic knitting stitch, the garter stitch. For this stitch you knit every row, not worrying about "purl." But the sachets look pretty worked in the stockinette stitch, the stitch you see, for example, in a typical sweater. To create the stockinette stitch, you knit one row, then purl going back the other direction, then knit, then purl, knit, purl, back and forth. Again, it's easier to understand "purl" by watching a video, but essentially when you purl you're creating the backside of "knit." To knit, you insert the right-hand needle front to back through the loop of yarn on the left-hand needle. To purl, you insert the needle back to front.

To make one sachet you will need only about 35 yards of yarn, so this project is a great way to use odds and ends of yarn left over from other projects. A typical skein of medium-weight acrylic yarn from the hobby store contains 170 yards. These directions are based on using medium-weight yarn and medium-gauge needles, size 8, 9, or 10, but obviously the bags don't need to be any exact size. If you're using very fine yarn, you can easily judge how many stitches to cast on to make the bag three inches wide, or as wide or narrow as you want it to be.

You will be knitting a front and a back and sewing them together on three sides. To make a front (or a back), cast on 12 stitches. Use the simple slip-knot cast-on process or the more complicated "long tail" process. Either works fine. Leave a tail of a few inches. If you cut the yarn off right at the beginning of your first row, the knot can loosen and stitches will unravel. The tail will be hidden inside later. Keep knitting until your piece of knitting is about six inches long. Make your last row a "knit" row rather than a "purl" row and then cast off. The instructions for casting off are usually part of a "How to knit" video or you can search "How to cast off." Leave a tail of about 24 inches after you cast off the last stitch. You will use this tail to sew your bag together. Cast on another 12 stitches and repeat the same process to make the back (or the front) of your bag, but you don't need to leave a long tail when you cast off. Just a few inches is fine.

Now it's time to sew your front and back together. Arrange the two pieces with the right sides—the obvious stockinette sides—facing each other, in the same way that you put right sides of fabric together when you sew a seam. Make sure the short edges where you cast off are at the same end. This end will be the open top of the bag. Use a yarn needle—a large needle with a large eye and a blunt end. Thread the needle with the long tail and stitch the front and back together all the way around three sides starting with a long side. To make a neat seam, use an over-cast stitch and catch only the outer loops along each side. When you've finished the third side, you should be back at the bag's open top, meeting up with an-other tail. Unthread the needle and tie the remaining yarn to the other tail in a tight knot. Trim these tails to a few inches and use the yarn needle to hide them, stitching small stitches in and out along the seam for an inch or so and then clipping the shorter tails that are left. You will still have two tails hanging at the bottom of the bag. They will be hidden when you turn the bag right side out, but you can trim them to an inch or so if you like.

After you've turned the bag right side out, fill it with your dried flowers, herbs, potpourri, or a bar of fancy soap. Gather the neck of the bag together, loop ribbon around it and tie a bow.

If you're giving the sachets as gifts, you can attach tiny name tags or cards with messages. Use a pretty font from your word-processing program to print the name tags or cards.

For pictures of many finished sachets, including a catnip sachet, visit the Knit & Nibble Mysteries page at PeggyEhrhart.com.

NIBBLE

Pamela's Peach Cobbler

This is best if you make it when peaches are really in season, a narrow window in some parts of the country. It can also be made with many other kinds of fruit, like blueberries or other berries, or apples. It's also a great thing to do with rhubarb, if you are a devotee. But you will need much more sugar with rhubarb, about ¾ cup more.

Ingredients for peach cobbler:

4 cups peaches, peeled and sliced
5 tbs. sugar, divided
2 or 3 tbs. rum or bourbon (optional)
1½ cups flour
3 tsp. baking powder
½ tsp. salt
½ cup plus 2 tbs. melted butter, divided
⅓ to ½ cup heavy cream
9-by-12-inch baking dish (exact size isn't crucial)

Butter your baking dish, fill it with the peaches, and sprinkle 1 tbs. of sugar over them. Use more sugar if you wish, but the cobbler dough is also sweet. Sprinkle on the rum or bourbon if you are using it.

For the dough, sift together the flour, baking powder, and salt. Using a spoon, not a mixer, blend in ½ cup of the melted butter and 3 tbs. sugar. Add heavy cream, a bit at a time. You want a soft dough but you don't want it to be runny.

Drop the dough in patches on top of the fruit using a spoon or your fingers. Pat it down to smooth it, but it's not necessary to cover every spot and it's okay for the dough to be thicker or thinner in places. Chill the cobbler in the refrigerator for at least half an hour.

Heat the oven to 425 degrees. Take the cobbler from the refrigerator, brush the top with the remaining melted butter (you might need to remelt it), and sprinkle on the remaining 1 tbs. of sugar. Bake the cobbler for half an hour or more. You want the top to look puffy and be lightly browned.

Serve it warm (but not hot) or at room temperature, with vanilla ice cream or heavy cream.

For a picture of the finished cobbler, visit the Knit & Nibble Mysteries page at PeggyEhrhart.com.

Grab These Cozy Mysteries
from
Kensington Books

Forget Me Knot Mary Marks	978-0-7582-9205-6	$7.99US/$8.99CAN
Death of a Chocoholic Lee Hollis	978-0-7582-9449-4	$7.99US/$8.99CAN
Green Living Can Be Deadly Staci McLaughlin	978-0-7582-7502-8	$7.99US/$8.99CAN
Death of an Irish Diva Mollie Cox Bryan	978-0-7582-6633-0	$7.99US/$8.99CAN
Board Stiff Annelise Ryan	978-0-7582-7276-8	$7.99US/$8.99CAN
A Biscuit, A Casket Liz Mugavero	978-0-7582-8480-8	$7.99US/$8.99CAN
Boiled Over Barbara Ross	978-0-7582-8687-1	$7.99US/$8.99CAN
Scene of the Climb Kate Dyer-Seeley	978-0-7582-9531-6	$7.99US/$8.99CAN
Deadly Decor Karen Rose Smith	978-0-7582-8486-0	$7.99US/$8.99CAN
To Kill a Matzo Ball Delia Rosen	978-0-7582-8201-9	$7.99US/$8.99CAN

Available Wherever Books Are Sold!

All available as e-books, too!

Visit our website at **www.kensingtonbooks.com**